I0609755

The Northlore Series
Volume Two
Mythos

www.nordlandpublishing.com

Copyright

ISBN Print: 978-82-8331-025-2
ISBN E-book 978-82-8331-026-9

Cover motif Evelinn Enoksen
Cover design Ashraf E. Shalaby
Illustrations by Monica Hansebakken

First Published 2016

www.nordlandpublishing.com

Dedication

To all those who kept the faith . . .

Contents

Introduction..1
The Saga of Egill Olafson..3
The Mountain-Farer 14
Váli 16
I am of Jötunheim 30
Odin's Saga 31
Dark Period..42
The Gospel of Odin 43
On the Tree 66
Burnt Einar 68
The Song of Spells I 79
Hungry is the Wolf 80
Creator Deceiver Destroyer 95
Into The Storm 96
Sapling 122
How 'Bout Them Apples..123
The Song of Spells II 140
All that Glitters 141
Valkyrie..164
Past Bound...166
Loki 174
Freya's Graces 175
Balder..191
Old Gold's Last Stand..192
Trickster's Grace 197
They're Coming..199
Thor's Exclamations 209
Saga...210
The Song of Spells III 218
Death Amongst Us...219
Yggdrasil 234
Closing Time 235
Contributors 253

Introduction

Mythos is the second volume of the Northlore series, and much like in book one, *Folklore,* the various contributors were inspired by old tales. Not trolls, selkies and huldr this time, but by the gods and demi-gods of the Norse pantheon themselves.

The Aesir, as they were known, contain a number of familiar, and perhaps not quite so familiar names. And while some have drifted into comfortable obscurity, the names of others are still marked by the English speaking world on a daily basis, even if they are not aware.

Odin, Thor, Tyr and Frigg, are commemorated in the names of our weekdays. Tyr for Tuesday, Odin for Wednesday, and you can probably guess the rest.

The Norse gods were a rambunctious, quarrelsome and often very human ideal of godhood and were a fitting theology for a people that spawned the Vikings.

Tales of the gods' exploits were told wide and far, and continue to be retold today in one form or another.

But the world has changed greatly in the last thousand years since the Aesir's fall from grace, and not necessarily for the better. Population increase, famine, disease, and war on an impersonal mega-scale are all symptoms of our modern age.

Yet the pagan gods of the far north have not abandoned us, as they still walk the earth. From the trenches of the Somme, to the plains of Russia, we get glimpses into the lives of these ancient beings as they navigate their way through history, sometimes touching us at a personal level, at other times using us for their own ends, while some prefer to pass the ages in obscurity, amusing themselves, or just losing themselves, until the end time comes.

Gods don't die unless they want to. And one thing is for sure, Loki is not about to give up on his plans for Ragnarok. Nor is Thor likely to sit idly by and watch the ultimate battle between good and evil take place without picking a side.

But in the meantime, they keep busy where they can, sometimes doing good, sometimes mischief. But they are always closer than you think.

The stories and poems in this anthology visit the Norse gods at different times and places, covering almost fourteen hundred years, culminating in the present day. The stories are presented chronologically, and represent a fraction of the influence and affect that the deities have on our world.

So, if you have ever wondered where the Norse gods went, or what they were doing, then read on, for these are *their* stories.

MJ Kobernus, Oslo, 2016

The Saga of Egill Olafson

I: Skald

It was during the sixteenth year of Jarl Håkon Sigurðsson's reign over Norway that my master had to face the events I relate in this saga. Egill Olafson was his name, feeder of ravens, for he was brave on the battlefield and quick to let his sword speak. Many years have since passed and most in this story have joined their ancestors in Valhalla, but I still remember it all.

The night came early, with its coat of blowing winds; winter was upon us. Everyone had gathered in the hall at Sandefjord, for a skald was there, bringing with him news of the war between the Jarl of Norway and the king of the Danes. My master sat before the fireplace, a horn of ale in his hand, listening with his kinsmen to the skald's deep voice singing the deeds of gods and mortals. Once the songs were done, master Egill went to his neighbor, Hálfdan Gunnarrson, who was famous for his travels all over the known world.

Then to him he said:

> "This night I dreamt,
> That my last breath came,
> But over my head,
> I could see her face,
> She was at my side,
> Smiling at me."

Egill added: "Hálfdan Gunnarrson, I wish to unite our families. Would you give me the hand of Freyja Hálfdanardóttir?"

Halfdan's eye flashed with anger, but he answered with a civil tongue.

"Egill Olafson, helm-bearer! You are a friend and

3

thus I cannot lie. You will not have her, for the Norns have another fate in store for my daughter. She is only to be married with someone decked with fame and gold, and as brave as you might be, I see neither!"

Master Egill had no time to answer to this, the skald was speaking again:

"A prince has come to our jarl's hall,
From the land of Rus he seeks our help.
Holmgård the great has fallen,
Into his enemies' hands it now stands,
The prince came here in hope,
That our strength might overwhelm them.
Unknown lands lie ahead,
To Hel this might be the way,
But fame and gold await there
A hero's hand to seize them!"

Then Hálfdan Gunnarrson turned again towards master Egill: "Go there, and fight for glory. If you prove yourself worthy of my daughter, then perhaps the fates will decree in your favour."

II: Völva

My master returned to his farm. He sent for the völva who lived in the forest. A small, yet terrifying woman, she was enveloped in a blue mantle embroidered with gems and golden thread. In her hand was a long staff, ornamented with crow feathers, and at her side was a leather bag for her talismans; the bones and runes she needed for her wisdom. As soon as she arrived at the farm, everyone fell quiet, looking at her with respect and fear. Völvas are enchantresses, and their words are inspired by the gods. She threw wooden runes on the floor, kneeling to read them in the dim light.

4

"A sea-dragon you'll take,
To follow the northern winds.
From whale-path to misty lands.
Into the mouth of the water-serpent you'll go,
Towards Fate you will travel.
Screams of axes you'll hear,
Feed the eagles you will,
But beware the sleep of swords!

Forty-two feet I see,
But my dream only forty eyes reveal,
To the dawn you'll sail,
To the Tsar's nest,
The fury of the North
In there you'll bring,
And maybe there, glory you'll find
If the Norns have it in mind!"

The völva had spoken, and her word commanded respect. The message was clear: my master must gather a crew and set sail to the east, to the land of Rus.

III: Snekkja
The following day, master Egill gathered his men. The building of the snekkja began. It was designed for speed with a shallow draft hull, which allowed navigation on both fjords and rivers. The boat also had to be light, so the crew could land it on beaches and portage it when required. Its double-ended, symmetrical bow and stern would allow the crew to reverse direction quickly in case of a need to flee, without having to turn the vessel around. Finally, a great woolen sail on a light mast would help give speed, or give the men rest on longer journeys.

The best craftsmen of Sandefjord came to work on

the boat. Some hewed wood, others planed the great planks. Women weaved the sail on a great loom, laying in Odin's triangle in crimson in the middle of the white cloth. Young Bjorn, with his golden hands, was in charge of curving runes and sculpting a dragonhead for the bow.

Two months were necessary to build the *Ormin*, as the ship was named. During that time, master Egill recruited the men that would come with him in his travels. Adventurous minds willing to brave the cold sea and the winter winds: Vikingr.

The völva had spoken of forty-two feet but only forty eyes, so my master hired old Hrolf, who was blind by birth. The thralls told tales of him, saying he needed no eyes to see what was hidden in the mist or under the water. For master Egill, he would be horn-blower for the *Ormin*.

Then finally came the day when the last nail was hammered, and the majestic dragonship put to the water. As soon as the vessel lay at anchor, three ravens came to perch high on the mast rigging. A good omen for our quest, as ravens are messengers from Odin. Everything was ready, and we had the blessing of the gods. It was time to go.

IV: Danes at sea
The cold winds blew from the land of the Ice Giants. It brought with them the whispers of the gods, telling us to hurry. Master Egill was ready to fight the elements, to cross the sea to the foggy coasts of the lands of the Finns, those eaters of men, where was said lay the entrance of the Rus land. This was the unknown, for only rumors had come to Sandefjord about those savage places east of our world.

Ambition had my master. He was eager for fame and

glory, for gold and pride. The Norns would guide him through the fog, and if the gods willed, he would discover what he sought, and then return Sandefjord to take Freyja Hálfdanardóttir's hand.

The men pulled on the oars and we raised sail and let the wind work for us, guiding the *Ormin*.

We kept our silence, listening to every sound the sea might carry to our ears, for we were crossing the watery fields where ravagers pillaged all ships. And then, as they were in every mind, they came, the despised sails of Harald Bluetooth, king of the Danes. Small points at the beginning, they grew fast, for their oarsmen were far more numerous than those of my master.

The race began, and master Egill had no need to urge his crew for each man on the *Ormin* knew only too well what fate the Danes reserved for those unfortunate enough to be caught. We pushed, and pushed again on the oars, and the sail was stretched by the strong wind. The dragonship cut the sea, slicing the waves, carrying the wooden fangs of its figurehead straight towards the strait between the villge of Køpmannæhafn and the small fort of Malmhaug.

But still the Danes were getting closer. Thus my master began to sing, and the crew joined him, for all the hearts were willing to live longer, not that they were afraid of death, but only because they wanted to continue their glorious quest.

> Row, men! Row to the Sun!
> For he's here, behind you,
> Ready, his mouth wide open,
> To seize your boat and swallow it all!
> His name? what's his name?
> You know it, for he's Loki's son,
> Jörmungandr!

Row, men, row a bit more!
For Mjöllnir's voice rises,
Steady, ready to hit,
Midgårdsormen's skull!

Row, men! Row to the Sun!

V: Maelstrom

As the Danes seemed about to catch the *Ormin*, they suddenly changed their heading, turning back with great screams as if they had seen Fenrir before them. Intrigued by this strange move, master Egill ran to the figurehead. It was not a Dane's habit to let his prey escape while they were *fara í víking*, in a raid.

"Maelstrom," Egill screamed, his voice shattered by the howling winds.

The sea is a harsh mistress, and all men hope Rán will not come to seize them, that they won't drown in her embrace. A great maelstrom lay before them, a whirlpool in the middle of the sea, dragging the *Ormin* to it without effort.

The men pulled at the oars, trying to escape the deadly embrace of the sea goddess. The fury of the wind was threatening the mast, and the sail flapped madly.

I prayed then, I am not ashamed to admit. Perhaps it was Thor or Odin who heard my entreaties, for as suddenly as it began, the sea calmed. The men were tired and needed rest, but everyone was relieved to have escaped from both the Danes and the maelstrom.

VI: Rapids

Land was soon sighted. The domain of the Finns, a strange part of the world where shamans and spirits wandered, a place more savage than even Norway. Master Egill watched the stars, trying to orientate himself, looking to find the mouth of the great river that would drive us to Holmgård.

Here it was at last, lost in the fog, and flat, nothing like the fjords of our fathers. The entrance of the Neva River, which would drive the *Ormin* to Lake Lagoda. It would then flow out of the lake through the Volkhov River and the Lake Ilmen. Holmgård would follow. The men rowed, light-hearted, following the banks of the Neva.

A few villages had been built along the river, tempting prey for Master Egill's thirst. The crew welcomed the news with acclamations, and we went our way, pillaging and ransoming the small coastal establishments, taking the opportunity to exercise ourselves for the great battle that would come on the Novgorod fields.

But these distractions weren't the most notable event on our journey. One morning, after a night raid on a fishing village, the tired crew were shocked to hear a characteristic roaring; rapids lay before us, and we would have to row even harder despite lack of sleep and the pain in our muscles. We threw ourselves to the task, rowing hard. Rocks below the water made the way perilous, threatening to wound our dragonship.

Luck was on our side, as no men were lost and damage to the *Ormin* light. Yet the men were exhausted. We had to rest, repairing our ship would come later.

VII: Holmgård
We hauled the ship ashore for repairs. It took several days, during which the crew worked without rest. Once finished, Master Egill decided not to launch. A portage was safer, he said. With ropes and wooden rollers, we moved our dragonship.

When water's not the way,
On the earth the dragon crawls,
So pull on the ropes, men,
Make him be again,
The proud and agile
Sea-worm he once was!

The men sang and pulled hard, and with effort, the rapids were finally at our back. We did not have to sail much further now, as Holmgård, the great city of the Rus, lay before us, its mighty walls still bearing the outrages suffered when the citadel was taken.

The prince's camp was there, besieging the city he once possessed. His tent was in the very center, guarded by tall men dressed in metal. Master Egill entered the tent, bringing his greeting to the prince, offering him our swords and lives for gold and glory.

The prince's plan was to attack the city on the next day at the first hour. The *Ormin* was due to traverse the river, on which the city was built. A low chain blocked the entrance, pulled across from one bank to the other, preventing unwanted ships from entering. Time it was now to pray to the gods, for the next day would find us far too busy.

The camp was asleep and the moon high in the sky when an old man walked in. He passed before the guards as if they could not see him. But I could, and he approached Egill. He wore a floppy brimmed hat, low over his face. One eye was covered by a patch, the other was lit of a grim fire. Bending down, he whispered in my master's ear. Who was it? What did this stranger murmur to my sleeping master? A raven cawed as he left and vanished into the dark. When Master Egill awoke up in the morning, he had no recollection of the strange old man, but he had a plan to lead us past the chain.

VIII: Battle for Novgorod

The day finally came, bringing with it white fog and whispering winds. Master Egill had been charged by the prince to set sail early with the *Ormin*, and to come out of the mist like deadly spirits to strike hard the enemy. And so we did, silent shadows invading the great city of the Rus.

> Father of battle, to sacrifice we run,
> Into the dance of swords we'll about to enter,
> The blood rain will satisfy our thirst,
> And by the end of the day,
> Either covered in fame we'll be,
> Or dine into the Asagrim's Halls!

The chain was there, great links of resilient metal, blocking the entrance to mighty Holmgård. My master's idea was to row hard and gather speed, and as the bow touched the the chain, abandon the oars and run to the stern. The weight would make the bow lift out of the water and pass over the chain. Then the men would only have to go towards the bow to let the obstacle behind, praying the gods that the keel wouldn't break.

> Hail to Runni vagna!
> That made our ship
> Light but strong!
> Hail to the Wanderer,
> For in the city we now are!

Master Egill's plan worked well, and the Norns didn't shear the string of our lives. We entered the city and fought, with sword and shield, hitting hard the enemy, making our way through enemy flesh towards the Holmgård gates.

Master Egill, after an epic fight with the guards, managed to open the massive doors of the city. The prince's men were now flowing into every street, like the plague over a body, overwhelming all resistance in a bloody wave. The enemy's twilight had come, and nothing seemed able to prevent it. Ravens would feast that day, and the next too, for many lives were taken.

IX: Back home
Völva and runes never lie. Victory was ours, and Master Egill's sword was decisive. The prince was back on his throne, and granted my master much booty.

One thing only was still to do. A stone should be raised, eternal proof of my master's courage. Magnus was skilled at engraving runes, so he was given the honour, raising a large stone near the bank of the river:

Here happened the greatest deeds,
And the sword's blood fed the earth.
Egill Olafson, the raven-feeder,
In the battle for Holmgård the great,
Stroke strong and and broke the lines
Of far more numerous enemies.

My master's name would now survive for all time, and be remembered over the ages. Egill gave his orders, and the men sat to the oars, ready to row. They knew that nothing could happen to them, for the gods themselves were with us, Thor and the one-eyed mighty Odin protected them on their journey to glory.

Soon the old Hrolf would blow the horn in the misty Sandefjord, and Master Egill would at last have Freyja Hálfdanardóttir's hand.

This is the saga of my master Egill Olafson, which took place during the sixteenth year of Jarl Håkon Sigurðsson's reign over Norway.

The Mountain-Farer

Ärligvarelse's walking stick was the size of a hundred
year old sequoia.
He had to use it when he walked because his back was
too crooked and weak now; without it, he would fall
over.

As it was, he used the stick as he made his way
through the mountains.

He was traveling to his home (the name escapes him
at the moment, but he remembers how to get there). It
had been a long, long time since he was home. There
were faster, more direct, seemingly less perilous ways
to get there,

but he felt safer taking the mountains.

In his younger days Ärligvarelse and his brothers,
sisters, and cousins could go wherever they pleased.
But with the passing of time, and the passing of his
brothers, sisters, and cousins, the world had become a
different place. Where there had once

been open fields, beautiful woodlands, (*—Ah wait, he
remembers now! His home was called
Bortomträden!—*) lovely streams and rivers, now
stood towns and villages.

Whereas Ärligvarelse's kind were gentle, welcoming
folk, people were not. People greeted them with fear,
with hatred, with loathing.

Yes, the mountains are a safer, more pleasant route,
Ärligvarelse thought.

He wasn't sure what he would find at home, or even if his home was still there.

On some level Ärligvarelse knew he was the last of his kind. He had known for some time now, though he had never actually considered this to be the case, nor had he spent much time thinking about it.

He imagined that the last several hundred years were merely a bad dream, and once back in Bortomträden all would be just as it had been in his youth. He would see Lasivettä, the great waterfall; children would be playing on the grass-covered hills, mothers yelling after them to be careful, and fathers sowing crops.

Yes, it will be nice to be home again.

Váli

It's a dilemma when you are born, become fully grown in a day, and then kill a god, thus fulfilling your purpose for existing. Being a god has advantages, but it can definitely have its drawbacks.

After I killed Höðr, I stayed in Asgard for a while, but that got old fast—I sensed a lot of antipathy from the other gods. They felt bad for Höðr, and thought Odin's revenge cruel. I agreed fully, even though I did the killing. But it was one of those ethical dilemmas the mortals like to wring their hands over. The murder of a relative must be avenged. No one in Asgard wanted to do it, so Odin conceived me just for that purpose. How, then, could I be deemed culpable? Still, the others blamed me for the deed. I grew weary of their coldness.

Now that the defining task of my life was done, what was left? I departed Asgard, descended bifrost to Middle Earth, and headed across the frozen northern territories to find Ruthr, the woman who gave me birth. I would seek her wisdom.

It was fascinating to be amongst mortals. They live simpler lives than the gods, but I would say their lives are more engaging. They feel the passing of time, which is an exciting intoxicant if you have not experienced it. I felt it flow like a river, present everywhere, eddies and currents washing over me, its cool onrush bathing my soul. Of course, it did not affect me as it affected mortals. All the same, I sensed it and it brought a pleasant urgency to life, not the deadening sensation of timelessness I had grown used to in Asgard.

I liked the smells too. There are no smells in Asgard. Pine trees, rivers, the sea, dung, apple blossoms and linden trees, flowers, the breath of beasts, human bodies, a woman's hair—all were like music to me. And the music itself! I boarded at inns and listened to the harpers and lutenists play in the halls. I was so spellbound that people laughed.

"Are you from the forest, boy?" they teased. "Never heard a poet before?"

Of course I'd heard them. I had heard Bragi, the god of poetry, perform. But never had I heard the raw energy of earth and flesh in his words and never the immediacy of improvisation. The wild freshness of what their bards sang invigorated me.

As I continued my journey, the cavalcade of delights continued. I heard music and poetry, ate, drank mead, and at night the women who plied their trade in the taverns lured me to their beds. I lost my virginity more gloriously than most humans ever would, since my ability in the matter—like my ability to fight—was fully developed and generously given.

I journeyed across Gotland, through the country of the Danes, to the lands ruled by the Goths, until I arrived on the wide, flat steppe where the Rus dwell. Winter had come with snow and cold when I arrived at my mother's village.

She came to meet me in a sleigh drawn by hreinin, the great horned reindeer of the north. I knelt in the snow as she stopped. She commanded me to stand.

"You are my son, not a mortal who worships me," she said.

I arose. My mother's light brown hair flowed from beneath the furred hood she wore. Her piercing green eyes revealed her divinity. Her beauty excelled the beauty of all woman I had beheld in any of the realms.

"Come. I'll take you to my palace."

Only then did I notice the animals. Ten or so white foxes flowed around her sleigh. Further off, wolves sat on their haunches, gazing in adoration at her. In the tree line were bears. Who knew what other creatures lay afoot?

"To keep mortals away," she explained. "Come."

I climbed in beside her. She threw a fur over my lap, flicked the reins, and the hreinin pulled us in a circle. Soon we were flying along a road through the ancient forest. The wolves loped ahead; the foxes scurried close to the sleigh. I imagined the bears must be near, though I couldn't see them. We rode in silence.

As the sun sank, we came to her palace, a complex of wooden stave buildings. The main hall towered above the other structures. I liked what I saw. It was simple, devoid of ostentation, reflecting the power of earth, resting beneath the sky, firm and solid on a bed of lustrous white snow.

She handed me over to her servants. They provided me with bathing water and fresh garments. Beautiful women washed me, groomed my hair, clipped my nails, and escorted me to the dining hall.

Again, I beheld simplicity—the elegance of Middle Earth. I kissed Mother and sat beside her. The serving women brought food and we began to eat.

"You grace me with your presence, my son," she said.

"There is grace in your eyes, Mother. For me, I am as graceless as any man on earth or the upper realms."

I explained my anguish and why I had come to her. After I finished, she took a sip of wine.

"Those in Asgard do not have the story right. Were you told Odin deceived me?"

"I was told he came to you in disguise, afflicted you with a disease, and then came in the form of a healer. Some told me"—here I stopped, realizing I had gone too far reciting what I had heard.

"Told you he raped me?" she said, smiling. "Don't

apologize. Many tell that tale. It is not true—all fabrication, I assure you. Odin came to a poor kingdom and made promises to a king who had a beautiful daughter. It was the sort of arrangement you read about in many stories involving gods and mortals. If I would bear a child, Odin would make my father a powerful ruler and I would become a goddess. I thought my virginity worth that—quite a good deal; divinity for one night. Don't you think so?"

I blushed, though I certainly admired her straightforwardness. "Certainly it was a good deal for me," I said.

"Well, yes and no," Mother replied. "You were born. But now you are lost. Pleasure and pain both lie in your path."

"It would seem so. I came here because I thought you might help me decide what course to take in life."

"I'll do my best, Váli. But you'll have to give me time to contemplate."

"Certainly. And what role do you fulfill here, Mother? Do the people worship you?"

"Since I became a goddess by getting laid," she laughed, "I decided to reign here as a goddess of love and fertility. Since I haven't seen Odin from the days he came to me and fathered you, I find lovers amongst the mortals. The women pray for children, and I impart my blessing to their husbands. The men are happy, though I allow none to tell how my blessing is bestowed. The women might not be so enthusiastic if they knew."

"I wish I could find my way. I can only think of living amongst the mortals. I don't know what place I could have with the Aesir."

"Perhaps that's because you're focusing on the wrong thing. You concentrate entirely on your past. You had a miraculous birth. You were given a mission and you fulfilled it. Isn't there something you're leaving out?"

I puzzled a moment and then saw what she was getting at.

"You mean the prophecy that I would survive Ragnarök? That doesn't seem like a future to me. The world will be destroyed. Everyone I know will be dead. I'll be the only one left."

"If you'll survive, it means you can't be harmed by the giants or the great wolf. If that's so, it seems Ragnarök need never come. You could stave it off, perhaps."

"How could I do that?"

"Confront Fenris. He will begin the battle. The Frost Giants will never go to war without him. Unless he swallows the sun, they will never overcome the armies of Asgard. If you should prevent the wolf from going forth, you could postpone the day, perhaps forever. Then you could think about what direction your life might take."

"We can't stop fate."

"Loki did. I despise him, of course, but he did find a way to kill someone who was never meant to die. Perhaps it's possible to infinitely stall the inevitable."

I pondered. Mother ate quietly and let me think. Finally, it made sense. And at least it gave me a purpose. I nodded and we went on with our meal. She asked about Asgard. She had travelled there once.

"Freya wasn't particularly happy to see me, as you can imagine, so I didn't stay long. It was beautiful, but a little boring after a time. I prefer Midgard."

"I can understand that. Mother, if I wanted to pursue your suggestion, where do I start?"

"Find the Wolf. He can be seen in lands of the north, where the Nenet live. They fear his presence. Every year, they say, he comes further south—not a good sign, Váli."

The remainder of our meal was pleasant. Mother told me more about herself. The local people maintained a shrine to her. She had brought prosperity to the area. The cattle, crops, and the families of the local inhabitants produced an abundance.

That night, my mother assigned a young girl to keep company with me.

"She will be for your desire and to keep you warm. In the winter, things can get cold, even in the home of a goddess."

The young woman, beautiful beyond the telling of it, satisfied my needs and the two of us warmed the bed well. Eventually, I married her.

Lyudmila brought me another wonder that, as a god, I had not known. She brought the blessing of simple companionship. Mother intended Lyudmila to meet my needs, just like the professional women in the inns had done, and the first couple of times we were together she fulfilled that role. But talking to her gave me another new joy. Bright, intelligent, witty, her words enthralled me. Soon I began asking her to spend time with me. Whether we talked or not, I enjoyed her presence. Like all the women who served mother, Lyudmila radiated beauty; but the more I spoke with her and the more time I spent with her, the more I saw the person she was. I glimpsed her soul, the part of ourselves that is hidden. Everything we did together formed a peculiar delight. I moved with her to a house on the compound. The hours we spent together there delighted me. Mother warned me about falling in love with the girl.

"She's only a mortal. And she's a commoner."

"You were a mortal once."

"I was, it's true. But I don't have the power to bestow immortality. Only Odin can do that. The girl will grow old and you will always be young. She will die and you will go on living. These things will bring sorrow to your heart."

"Perhaps I could ask Father Odin if he will grant me that boon of making her a goddess."

"I wouldn't count on it."

Mother's warning hit home. I had not seen Odin since he gave me instructions on how to kill Höðr. But if I did something to endear myself to him, maybe he would grant my prayer out of appreciation and thankfulness.

When the fogs of springtime came, Lyudmila and I headed north. The roads were muddy with the thaw, but even as warmer weather came, snow squalls would arise and cold northern air would freeze the ground, so our progress was slow. At night, we huddled in a yurt. We lit no fire. Beasts—mostly white foxes—would come in and keep us warm, covering us with their bodies. In the silence of ancient forests we would make love or simply lie in one another's arms. After two weeks of exhausting travel, we reached the land of the Nenet.

They are wary of foreigners, and with good reason. Slavers had raided their territory in times past. Of course, they are ferocious and brave and know the land of their ancestors. For this reason, they are formidable and one ventures into their land at risk. Lyudmila and I soon became aware that we were being watched. Tribal people live closer to nature and are more sensitive to the divine because of this. They saw the animals that escorted us and simply observed. Finally, a group of their warriors approached, though they kept their weapons sheathed. One of them spoke the

Russian language and he asked our business. Lyudmila spoke to him and translated as I told him my purpose. He was shocked and passed the information on to his people. I called upon Bragi to help me with my speech. Of all the gods in Asgard, only Bragi showed sympathy and friendliness toward me, so I was not surprised when I could suddenly speak and understand the Nenet tongue. I could tell from the amazed look in Lyudmila's eyes that she had been granted the same boon by the god's generosity. When we began to speak to them in their language, the Nenet knew this came as a divine intervention.

I told them I had come to confront the wolf and that I was a son of Odin. The Nenet do not worship Odin by name, though I'm sure they do so in their own way, as they bow down before sacred pillars. How like the veneration of Yggdrasil? When they received us into their homes, I learned from their elders and some of the hunters in their tribe who ventured further north about the habits of the Great Wolf.

He traveled, they said, in a shroud of fog. When he appeared, the creatures of the forest fled or hid; birds did not send out their cries. Silence surrounded the Wolf. After this initial description, I asked his size. They said he towered to the sky. The distance between his eyes was the length of a tall man's body. He was too large to confront. No weapon could stop his advance. He was impossible to kill.

I went to bed that night with Lyudmila at my side. In the quiet of the cabin, lit only by the faint glow of coals from the central fire pit, I pondered what to do. If I assaulted the beast with my sword, I would be like a stinging bee—an annoyance at best. And the Wolf could crush me with a swipe of his paw, as a man swats a gnat. I could not die, perhaps, but I could be mutilated—not a nice state in which to live eternally. This would be a desperate battle.

Even as I considered this, Freya leant her grace to me. I awoke next to Lyudmila's warmth knowing exactly what I would do.

As we broke our fast that morning, I asked some of the Nenet elders to name the most poisonous plant that grew in the vast forests. They were immediate in their answer: a mushroom called the Mistress of Death. The taste of it would kill; only touching it brought on severe sickness, blindness, or insanity.

"It is said the Mistress of Death could poison even a god," one of them told me.

That was exactly what I wanted to hear.

After the meeting, Lyudmila and I heated water and, alone in the yurt, stripped and washed. She asked, as she squeezed warm water from a cloth on my back, why I wished to know about the mushrooms.

"Freya gave me a prophecy," I answered. "I was thinking how futile trying to kill the Wolf would be. I thought if I attacked it with my sword I would be like a bee stinging a full-grown man. Then it occurred to me: the sting of a wasp or a bee is quite painful. Many stings can kill a man or a woman. If I envenom my sword, perhaps I can disable the Wolf—maybe even kill it."

She said nothing. I glanced at her. Mother could not grant her immortality; but Lyudmila should have been a goddess.

"Prophesy teaches us that the Wolf cannot be killed. It is written he will eat the sun at Ragnarök, so he will have to be alive when the last darkness comes. What is said in the sacred lore cannot be false."

She washed me in silence. Prophecy could not be false. But we often do not comprehend the whole.

Someone from the land of the Greeks once told me that an ancient king in their land received a prophecy that he would cross a river and destroy a great kingdom. He attacked a rival nation thinking the prophecy promised him victory, only to find that kingdom he destroyed was his own. Prophecy had dark spots at times. When Lyudmila finished, she began to wash herself. Watching her bathe would incite my lust, so I dressed and went outside. The sun shone brightly. I saw more green in the land. Winter never gives up easily, but eventually Skaði's cold yields. The warmth of the sun shining on the frozen land brings fog. Fog brought the Wolf.

The Mistress of Death grows in abundance when the first warmth of spring is upon the land. The wise women of the Nenet gave me a pair of thick gloves and tough leather bag. We gathered all morning. I brought the substantial cache of the deadly plants back to the yurt.

I had Lyudmila leave, put the mushrooms in a metal pot and heated them over the fire. The plants oozed their deadly poison. When I had extracted perhaps a pint of fluid, I put on gloves and removed the shrivelled mushrooms. Then I boiled the death-bringing liquid. The Nenet gave me a small stone jar with a large enough mouth to insert the tip of my sword. I filled it with death. Then I buried the pot and the sticky detritus of the mushrooms.

That night, as we went to bed, Lyudmila asked me what I meant to do.

"The Wolf cannot be killed. It is an immortal being. But perhaps it can be sickened and disabled. Ragnarök must come, as the prophecy says. But when it will come is not stated. If the Wolf is on the move, that is not a good sign. Perhaps I can disable him and the Twilight of the Gods will be postponed. I'll poison him. It will sicken him for millennia."

She nodded. I could tell she was trying not to weep. I held her and we slept. In the morning, she gave me the pleasure of her body. I dressed and, escorted by two Nenet hunters, set out toward the place where the Wolf had last been seen.

Fog rose. The Nenet came to the place where their laws said they could not go on. They said a line of stones would lead to the wolf's lair. If I followed the stones, I would find him. Fog would come, they said, and I must not stray from the line of stones or I would lose my way.

I started on my journey. The stones stood like lonely sentinels, pointing the direction. Soon, a thick, grey blanket of fog descended. I walked on, barely able to see the next stone ahead, the cold and wet anointing my face. The fog brought silence, nothing stirred. It was as if the land was holding its breath. I had my sword in hand and, hanging from my belt, the stone jar.

I could smell the Wolf long before I saw him. Undoubtedly, he smelled me, tiny as I was. My senses sharpened. I strained to see him through the fog. Two yellow slits peered at me through the grey of fog—vast eyes, larger than any I had ever seen. I knew he could be upon me with one leap. I removed the lid from the stone jar and dipped the end of my sword into it.

The Wolf sprang, going high into the air, meaning to crush me with his paws. I darted to the shelter of one of the standing stones and, when his left paw came down, drove my sword into the tough, black tissue.

He howled, drawing back his foot, rearing in pain. Then he fell. The ground shook. The Wolf whined. I ran through the fog toward the eyes.

I quickly dipped the sword in the venom once more

and ran towards the Wolf, marvelling at the vast body. The paw pad I had pierced bled. The Wolf lifted it, meaning, I think, to lick it but too disoriented and too wary of my presence to raise it to his mouth. Its other foot rested on the ground. I let my sword fall on the pad of his right paw, this time slashing. The wound would not be as painful as the first, but it would disable the wolf more and deliver more of the venom to his blood.

Once more, a roar split the air, like thunder. By now the Wolf's instincts had taken over. He leapt up and lunged. His vast, stinking mouth came close. The wind of his passage almost knocked me over, put I fought against it, and slashed at his nose.

I cut him pretty badly.

The Wolf roared and reared, lifting his front legs off the ground, bellowing out a howl that made my ears ring. I righted myself and dove for the shelter of a standing stone. He came down with a crash that shook the ground and the stone fell.

I managed to get my leg away from it, but it collapsed on my foot. I cried out in pain and wondered if the Fates intended to cut my thread.

But the Wolf had fallen too, coming down on its wounded paws. The poison had begun to have its effect. I thought the creature would take advantage of my immobility and devour me, but by now lethargy had settled over its massive form. The bites of certain spiders can kill a full-grown man or woman. I may have been as small to the Wolf as a wasp is to a human, but my sting held a powerful venom. The Wolf lay panting. It did not have the strength to kill me.

My foot had not been broken, but the weight of the stone had pushed it down into the soft earth and bruised it. I dug with my hands and managed to get it free. Waves of pain radiated from it. I cried out as I stood and knew I needed to move quickly before it became so inflamed I could not walk. I picked up my sword, limped over to the towering body of the Wolf, and slashed an opening in its side. A cascade of blood spurted from it wound, though it was a small cut to the wolf. I emptied the contents of the stone vessel into the open cut. The wolf trembled, though by now its strength had gone and it could not resist.

Still, I dared not push my luck. After I had poured out the poison, I thrust the jar into the furrow of flesh I had made and walked away as quickly as I could. A low growl came from its chest. Its mouth slavered a stream of drool I had to wade through. Dragging my right foot, I limped along, following the line of stones, making my way through the fog, hoping the pain in my foot did not disable me. The standing stones grew smaller. By the time I broke out of the fog and saw the Nenet hunters, I could barely stand.

They lowered me to the ground. One of them felt my wounded foot (it was so sensitive I screamed when he touched it). He and his companion cut the leather away, which caused the pain to diminish. By then, a group of people arrived, Lyudmila amongst them. She cried out to see me hurt but I told her the matter was not serious. The Nenet placed me on a litter pulled by a musk ox, covered me with a blanket, and took me back to Lyudmila and our yurt.

A wise woman spread ointment on my foot. The swelling went down and the pain diminished. Lyudmila washed me. I had the Nenet build a fire and placed my sword blade in it to make certain every trace of the deadly poison was gone. By evening I felt better and could walk again, though my foot was still tender. I went outside and relieved myself. A river of stars flowed through the black sky and a slice of moon hung above the horizon. Red, green, and silver lights danced above the horizon. In the distance wolves howled. The Nenet told me this was a good sign. When the Wolf stalked, animals abandoned the steppe for miles around.

It was not dead though. I believe that it must have had enough strength to crawl back to its lair. I wanted to talk to the Nenet and get their assessment of the matter, but weariness claimed me. Lyudmila undressed me and helped me into bed, then snuggled down beside me.

By morning, the pain in my foot was mostly gone. The Nenet brought a pair of felt boots. I polished my sword and broke fast with the hunters who had led me to the Wolf. I rewarded them with gold. The morning, bright and sunny, cheered me. A good breakfast, the fellowship of capable, intelligent people, Lyudmila's presence, and the return of my stamina after the exhausting fight with the wolf—all of these things cheered me. Later in the day, a group of hunters came to say the fog had lifted near the standing stones. They had seen no sign of Fenris. The Wolf was gone.

I am of Jötunheim

I am of Jötunheim

We who were once blood brothers
Mistrust has torn us asunder
Animosity has torn us asunder

My swift son, my womb-son
Taken as my rival's steed

My fierce son, my wild son
Taken and bound to stone
A sword through his jaws

My coiling son, my long son
Exiled to the sea, awaiting fate
Deadly sport for fishermen

My only daughter, beloved daughter
Exiled from me to rule the shades

My twin sons, my youngest sons
One made to tear apart his brother
And my own child's entrails
They have used to bind me

Oh yes, I am of Jötunheim
And all I ask is a good seat
From which to watch Asgard burn

Odin's Saga

I hung on a windy tree nine long nights,
wounded with a spear, dedicated to Odin,
myself to myself, on that tree where no man knows
where run its roots.

Rúnatáls-þáttr-Óðins, Stanza 138

The old, one-eyed man watched from the edge of the clearing. He did not want to get too close lest they recognise him. Not afraid for himself, but he could not disturb the events that were unfolding. Surrounded by forest, he merged deeper into the shadows, keeping his gaze on the grassy plain where hundreds were gathered before a great tree. Helmed soldiers in chainmail, wielding long seaxes, pushed men and women to their knees, all facing the one in the robes; the priest of the White Christ.

The old man had to admit he was impressed with the priest's imperious confidence. He rubbed his empty eye socket, then spat on the ground. It was tempting, but he held back from a curse. He was not there to cause trouble. It had been decided. Observe, that was all. A Frankish soldier glanced in his direction and the old man froze. *He would not be seen. He was smoke and darkness.* The soldier looked away.

The priest raised his hand, palm outward. "May the Lord bless and keep you from harm," he said, addressing the crowd of men and women that comprised his unwilling congregation. The man's voice carried well. It was deep and resonant, the voice of a man used to being heard and believed, used to being obeyed; a dangerous man. He spoke Latin, the language used in the temples of the White Christ, but the majority assembled in the forest clearing were

31

simple peasants, tillers of fields and keepers of livestock, they would not know his meaning. It was not lost on the old man though. No tongue spoken was a mystery to him.

The priest's clothes were soiled from travel and ragged in places. The old man approved of that. He liked a priest to be more of the next world than this. It did not sit well with him when the spiritual guides of men dressed like kings and princes, and were more powerful than both.

The priest continued. "We are doing God's work. His will directs your hands. Take up your axes and prepare to strike down the idolatry of these poor, misguided pagans."

The old man snorted in derision at that. God's work? Says who? Well, they were not short of conviction that was for sure. Common sense maybe. Common decency too. The priest looked towards him, as if sensing the contempt and the old man pulled his hat lower, covering one side of his face as he moved deeper into the murk. He did not like what was about to happen, but he would not stop it.

This grove was a sacred place where men had worshipped from the time before time. He had been here often and had never hidden his identity. But those days were coming to an end. The priest of the White Christ and the heavily armed men sent by the Frankish king would help see to that. The old man looked in sorrow at the great Ash growing at the center of the clearing. It was ancient, towering over the other trees in the forest. This priest of the new god had come to preside over its destruction and with it mark the end of days for the old ones.

The tree was whispered to be *the* Ash; Yggdrasil. The old man knew the truth of it. Few living knew better.

His own blood had nourished its roots. But the followers of the White Christ cared nothing for the holy places of others. They were scouring the northern lands, burning the hofs and temples, persecuting those who believed in the old ways. And now they were here, in the heart of Germania, about to desecrate the great tree itself, or so they believed. And isn't that what matters most, belief?

At a nod from the priest, the woodcutters stepped forward. It took near a dozen men to ring the tree. They positioned themselves carefully, examining the rough bark with experienced eyes. The priest held up a scroll of parchment. This time he spoke in a language kin enough that the men and women there would know his words.

"By order of Carl Magnus, king of the Franks, defender of the church and ruler of these lands, I declare that this tree is an abomination and must be destroyed. Begin."

And with that, he brought his hand down in a chopping gesture, and the woodcutters swung their axes. The echoing thock of iron hitting living wood resounded throughout the glade. A great cry arose from the men and women under guard, and several were slain as they leapt up, attempting to stop the work. The old man nodded gravely, acknowledging their bravery. To die in defence of their belief was noble, even if it was so clearly pointless. They would be rewarded in the next life.

Again and again the men struck at the tree, the priest urging them on. As the hours passed and the men tired, the priest carried water to them, fetched from a nearby spring. He ordered the soldiers to do the same, which they did not like, but they obeyed. The priest had a feverish look in his eyes and to deny him would have invited his wrath.

Time passed, but it seemed that no matter how hard the woodsmen worked, the tree would not succumb. The old man knew that to be an illusion. Even a mountain could be worn into a pebble. You just needed time. Time was everything.

It was long into the night when the woodsmen saw the first signs that the tree would fall. A shiver rippled through the great trunk, as if understanding it was doomed. The woodcutters exclaimed to each other and worked with renewed vigour. And as the moon, waxing full in argent splendour came into view overhead, flooding the clearing with silver light, a great shout came from the men, soon followed by a tremendous cracking; the tree was splitting. A frenzy of chopping followed and in only moments, the White Ash began to tilt, then fall.

It hit the ground with a shuddering crash so great that the old man stumbled as the earth heaved. Several people did fall, including those unlucky souls in the tree's path. They would not be getting up again. A ragged cheer arose from the woodcutters and soldiers while the priest danced in a frenzy. The old man examined the faces of those forced to bear witness. Some smiled weakly, desperate to show enthusiasm. Others bore their emotions stoically, not wanting to give their enemies the satisfaction of seeing their grief.

But the priest was ecstatic. He took a burning torch and held it aloft, screaming a prayer of thanks to his Great God Almighty. The old man did not want to hear anymore and he had surely seen enough. He had done his duty, what was expected. There was just one more task to perform, dangerous or not.

Walking slowly he emerged from the trees. He kept his head down, making straight for the center of the clearing. He passed the ring of guards and neared the priest. He did not pause, but now he was so close, the old man was surprised at how young the priest appeared. He was barely a man, only a slight fuzz of beard on his boyish chin.

But young as he was, the priest did not lack conviction. He strode quickly to the fallen tree, pulled back his arm, then threw the torch with a grunt of effort. It tumbled end over end as it sailed through the air before landing in the branches of the fallen Ash.

For a moment, nothing happened, then gradually, flames appeared. The fire grew, leaping and dancing, crackling fiercely. A great column of smoke rose, blanketing the stars, obscuring the moon, but the clearing did not dim, the flames illuminating all. The old man shivered in spite of the heat and muttered to himself.

"Fierce is the steam and the life feeding flame
as fire leaps high to heaven itself."

The tree burned fast, the smoke thick and cloying. The old man coughed, covering his mouth with an arm, but he walked on, forcing his way deep into the tangle of branches that had once stood so proud.

The priest watched him, eyes narrowing. Then he turned away, hurrying to one side of the clearing to speak with a veteran soldier. There was nothing he could do about that, so the old man ignored them, continuing to push himself into the tangle of the fallen tree, searching until he saw what he needed. Bending, he pulled a branch free and quickly stripped the slender limb. The branch was long, curved. The old man caressed the wood and it straightened. When he was done, he held a stout staff as tall as himself. He leaned on it, testing its strength. There would be few things stronger, he mused. Satisfied with his token from the burning pyre, he made his way to the edge of the clearing, entering the dark forest of the Teutonweld by one of the many paths.

Just at that moment, the young priest shouted, pointing. The soldier gave orders. Suddenly men were running. They drew their short swords as they skirted the flaming tree, shielding their faces as best they could.

With a last look, the old man turned his back to them, and the fallen tree. As it burned, the noise became physical; a pulsing roar felt as much as heard. The heat was so intense that most were driven from the clearing, seeking shelter behind the lesser trees that ringed the open space. The old man strode deep into the calming darkness of the cool forest. Behind him, the flames reached skyward, higher than the mast of the biggest dragonship.

The old man continued, leaving behind the shouts of soldiers and the roaring flames and smoke. Soon enough he was completely alone in the near pitch black under the heavy canopy. The air was chill, and he pulled his cloak about himself, his breath steaming the night air. The raucous cry of a raven, swiftly answered by another filled the darkness. There was a flutter of wings, then two shadows descended, coming to rest on the old man's shoulders, one on either side. One of the great, black birds chittered in his ear, its caw soft, almost melodic.

"I think I remember," the old man said with a sad smile. It was a joke, a pun on the names of his ravens. He shushed the birds, then continued on the dark path, not minding where it went. He was already lost.

Act II: Odin's Apostle

For three days the old man walked. He passed through small hamlets and isolated farmsteads, taking his rest where he could, granted such hospitality as was possible. It made his heart glad to see how the poor would give a stranger so much. Occasionally small groups of Frankish soldiers would ride past, forcing him to hide. On the fourth night of his wandering, he came to a small hut deep within the forest. It was well kept, with a garden of herbs and vegetables nearby and a running brook providing fresh water. A wisp of smoke through the thatched roof told him there was an occupant, and he shouted ahead.

"Hail, hearth owners. A stranger comes. Will you give him welcome?"

At the sound of his voice, the rough wooden door to the hut swung open, and an impossibly large man emerged. He wore a shirt of grey wool, a wide brown leather belt with a heavy iron buckle around his waist. The patterned weave of his leggings showed him to be a Saxon. He crossed his massive arms in front of his wide chest and eyed the wanderer with frank appraisal.

"Hail, stranger. Where do you go?"

At this the old man simply shrugged. He pulled back his wide brimmed hat, showing his face. At once the huge Saxon's eyes widened and a faint smile played on his lips.

"You are welcome to guest at our hearth, old one. Please, come." He gestured to the open doorway and the darkness within. The old man nodded and made his way inside. He stooped to enter, then turned and watched as his host almost doubled over to pass through.

"You are mighty," the old man said. "A warrior?"

Inside the hut, the middle area of the floor had been

dug out half a man's height, creating a pit. It was lined with stones and covered with deer hides. The old man settled down, sitting on the edge, feet resting on the floor of the pit, warmed by the hearth that burned there. He looked around, then nodded with approval. Clever. The pit provided seating and made the low roof less of a problem. And with the deer hides, it was comfortable enough. The Saxon followed.

"Aye, once I was. Now I tend the charcoal ovens for the iron makers."

The old man nodded, and as his vision adjusted to the muted light he took in the details of the man's life. On one side there was a raised platform with the skin of a bear covering it. Over the fire pit, a tripod held a black-iron pot with a thin stew bubbling within. A scabbarded sword hung on the wall, and by the door an axe was propped up, as if ready for use. There was also a small wooden sword, like a child's toy. So, the warrior had a family.

"My wife and boy are out collecting mushrooms in the forest. When she returns, we can eat. You are welcome to join us, *Wanderer*."

The old man heard the stress the one time warrior put on his name. Aye, he had travelled much in his many lives. And he had a long road ahead of him still. What lay at the end of that journey he didn't know. Even Mimir's gift did not let him see that far.

As the huge Saxon seated himself, he seemed more like a normal man in stature. Even so, the old man was impressed. Though the light was dim, he could make out criss-cross scars on the warrior's arms that spoke of many battles. He closed his eye and let his mind explore the past. He could see his host, towering over lesser men as they fought with shield and sword.

"You were a leader of men, in your time. You fought

the Franks and the Wends."

The Saxon did not seem surprised that he knew this. Further proof that the old man's identity was known.

"Aye, I was once a proud man. A leader, as you say. Now I have a simple life, with a wife and a hearth and am happier for it. A man should be home to care for his family."

The old man considered his words while the Saxon busied himself, dipping two horns into a small barrel. "Here," the big man said, passing the drinking horn. "It's watered mead. Too weak to get you drunk, but it'll stave off thirst just as well."

"You have my thanks. And my blessing."

The Saxon smiled broadly at that. Both sipped their drinks, lapsing into silence. The old man closed his eye again. This time he could see further. In his vision the Saxon was tied to a wooden stake, hands bound behind his back. He was older, but his beard was gone, his hair shorn. A crowd of men stood around him dressed much like the Saxon. But there were others, men in robes; and one in black. At their direction, the men began to place wood around the feet of the huge man. When he was buried up to his knees, a priest stepped forward, the burning torch in his hand dipping to the wood. Clearly the wood had been doused in oil or fat as it quickly caught the flame. The Saxon's eyes opened wide with shock as the pain hit him, but he did not scream. Instead, he looked skyward and in his deep voice yelled, "Odin, receive my sacrifice!"

This angered the priests, and one of them grabbed a spear from a guard and thrust it into the Saxon's belly. Odin opened his eye. He looked with pride upon the man that had gone to his death believing in him.

The White Christ was strong, and he would stay that way for a long time. But not forever. The old Gods would survive. He would make sure of it, the vision had shown him the way.

"I have a job for you Saxon. What is your name?"

"I am Sigberht."

Sigberht, meaning Bright Victory. Yes, a fit name for this task. Odin's eye glittered as his hand reached out to touch the Saxon's face. "You will be my messenger, Sigberht. On you, I will gamble my future. All our futures. You will be *my* rock."

The Saxon did not blink. He gazed into the old man's good eye, drawn closer, spellbound by mysteries he could not understand. The old man closed his eye and his face transformed. He drew in his breath and for a moment he seemed young, a handsome youth, face smooth and soft. Then his eyes opened wide, the empty socket empty no longer. Both eyes were black, a deep abyss with an absence of light more profound than darkness. When he spoke, his voice boomed, shaking the Saxon, the old man's words felt in every chord of his being.

"Three will be chosen. Three will walk in the world. Always three." His gnarled hand gripped the Saxon's face, the thumb tangled in the beard under his chin. He held the man fast, and the Saxon's eyes bored into Odin's infinitely black, unseeing orbs. "Before you die, you must an apostle bind. In three times three hundred years, we will return. And if the three be true, then the tree will be reborn."

There was a noise from outside. Laughter and a snatch of song. The door was pulled aside, flooding the hut with light. Odin released the Saxon, who blinked, momentarily confused, before smiling up at his wife and son.

"We have a guest for dinner. Did you find mushrooms?"

Sigberht's wife was comely, with long tresses braided in the style of her people. She held a basket across her arm, which she placed on the sleeping pallet. The boy was much like his father and promised to be a great man himself, one day. He hopped down into the sunken floor and stared at the stranger unabashedly.

"Aye, we did," the woman said. "You are welcome here, grandfather. Did my oaf of a husband see to your comfort?"

"He did my daughter. Your husband did right by me. I believe all three of you will do right."

Outside the thud of horse hooves were getting louder. Riders, at least five. Soldiers.

"What is your name?"

"Gyfa."

"A gift indeed. You and your son, join us here, please. There is something I will say to you both and there is little time."

A horse neighed gently, and a coarse tongue swore in the curious manner of the Franks. The light around the rough door was blocked, then a pounding fist hammered.

Odin spoke quickly, not letting either the woman or child from his gimlet gaze. But Sigberht reached out and took hold of his sword. The fate of the gods was in *his* hands now.

Dark Period

Odin's eye popped
from its bloody socket.
He dropped to his knees
to capture the anguish,
distil its essence
crystallized in a new orb
not for sight, but vision.

He completed the sentence,
closed the book then buried
its knowledge to sprout
fresh ideas on the barren field.

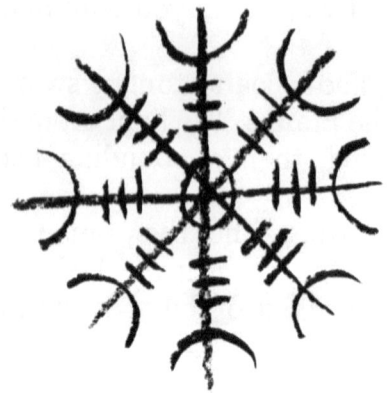

The Gospel of Odin

> Go forth, speak my name in secret,
> let not the law of man constrain you.
> By threes you will teach the sacred runes
> Through which I will be revealed.
>
> From the Gospel of Odin 3:22

For most of his forty years, Sigberht had never thought of himself as a pious man. He had made the odd sacrifice, and the gods knew he had fed enough ravens on the battlefield to keep the choosers of the slain busy, but he was not one for thinking about the afterlife. Sure, he told the occasional story of the gods around the hearth, in particular Thor's many adventures, but that was about it. Mostly, he liked to fight, he liked to hunt, and he liked to be with his woman. Like everyone, he believed that as a righteous man he would go to Valhalla, as his father had.

Yet this new command worried him. If he followed it through, what would happen to him when he died?

He had been travelling now for almost ten years, carrying Odin's message to those men and women who still believed. It had not always been easy, and many times he had thought to abandon his mission, yet something always brought him back. He was tired now, and hoped that his journey was almost over.

As he passed through a village, his long strides scattered clucking chickens left and right. His experienced eye noted that the thatched huts were in good repair, and there was not much smell. It was evidently a prosperous village.

He got curious looks from men and women he passed, as well as outright fear and hostility. His clothes marked him out as a Saxon. The Frankish peasants were right to fear him. But why did his stomach keep turning over? The sight of the stone tower in the distance might have something to do with it.

He approached the great iron-bound oak door, set into a high, stone wall. A dozen good men on that wall could keep hundreds at bay.

Sigberht was taller and stronger than most men. His hair was shot through with grey, yet he was still a man to be reckoned with. As a warrior, he had faced death a hundred times in the shield wall. Yet never before had he felt such a wrenching in his gut. Why did his heart hammer so?

A rope hung by the door and he tugged it tentatively. Somewhere a bell jangled. Faster than he expected, a tiny hatch opened in the oak portal and a pair of eyes under a thatch of straw-coloured hair regarded him.

"Yes, what is it?"

Sigberht could see nothing more of the man on the other side of the door. His brow wrinkled as he considered what he should say.

"I was sent."

"Sent?" came the reply.'

"Yes."

"By whom were you sent?" The voice was patient, kindly.

Sigberht hesitated. He knew what he had to say, but it stuck in his craw. The word would leave a bitter taste in his mouth, but this was his path, his calling.

"God."

If Sigberht had expected anything, it was not that the great wooden door would swing open, and a small man would leap through, brown robes flapping and tonsured head gleaming like a polished egg.

"God? God?"

Sigberht nodded. "Aye, twas God what sent me. I had a vision."

The monk—the word came to Sigberht from somewhere—looked up at him with wide eyes. "You really had a vision? Oh my. Abbot Wulfstan will want to hear of this."

The smaller man pulled Sigberht through the door, leading him like a child by the hand. Sigberht almost stumbled as he paused to survey the inner courtyard where more monks were busy doing tasks that, while familiar to the warrior, nonetheless seemed incongruous. One of the brown robed men was shoeing a horse, while another plucked a pair of geese that hung from a wooden beam. He carefully collected the feathers, sorting them into two sacks. On the other side of the quad, two monks rolled a barrel carefully across the flagstones. Sigberht fondly hoped that it contained beer. Still more men busied themselves in the daily work of the monastery. Then faintly, as if far distant, he could faintly hear men chanting. A shiver ran through him. The monks were casting a spell.

The young doorkeeper pulled Sigberht after him along corridors of stone. Soon enough they arrived at another iron-bound oak door. The monk knocked, and waited with head bowed. When it opened, the man that stood on the other side looked much like him, only older. The same pale hair, the same gleaming patch of skin on his head. Sigberht suspected they shaved it deliberately. Why they did that he could not fathom.

"What is it, Aethelraed? Who is this man?"

Aethelraed looked up, his eyes shining. "Father, he claims to have had a vision. Tell him." He tried to push Sigberht forward but the mountain of muscle did not move.

The Abbot looked up expectantly at the rough form of the giant before him. "Well?"

Sigberht drew a deep breath, his chest expanding visibly. In his deep bass voice, the words came easier this time. "It is true. I had a vision. From God."

The abbot regarded him for a moment. Then turned and went back into his room. He beckoned for Sigberht to follow. When Aethelraed also entered, the Abbot shook his head. "Don't you have gate duty?"

The younger monk's face reddened, but he nodded, pulling the door behind him.

"Come, my son, sit. I would hear your tale."

Sigberht looked about for something to sit on. The small bench looked entirely too spindly for someone of his size, yet he gently lowered himself onto it. After a few alarming creaks, it was apparent that it was stronger than it looked. Sigberht relaxed.

The Abbot sat in a much more decorative chair, with carved back and arms. What appeared to be a rendering of a man, nailed to a cross, formed the back piece of the chair. The White Christ. *The enemy.*

The older man saw Sigberht's gaze. "Christ supports us all, in one way or another."

Sigberht nodded, suppressing a smile. The nailed god. How he could support anything when he was pinned to a cross was something he did not understand.

"Now," the Abbot began. "Tell me about your vision."

Sigberht pursed his lips, then let out a sigh. "I was hunting. In the forest. I was about to loose an arrow on a doe when I heard a voice."

The Abbot nodded. He leaned forward, eyes never leaving the Saxon's.

"Then what happened?"

"I looked around, but there was no one there. I could've sworn I heard someone say my name. So, I took aim at the doe. A sweet young thing that would've kept my family fed for a week. Then I heard it again. The same voice. This time, it did not just say my name, it gave me a charge."

The Abbot's eyes were shining, and his mouth hung open. One hand gripped the heavy arm of his chair, while the other went to the simple wooden cross around his neck.

"The voice told me not to be afraid. It said I was chosen. That I had to come to a place of learning and walk the path of the scholar. It said I had to learn the art of," Sigberht struggled to remember the unfamiliar word, "writing."

At this, the Abbot's eyes opened wide. "But you are pagan, are you not?"

Sigberht nodded, "Aye."

The Abbot leaned back in his chair, eyes looking to the ceiling. "The Lord moves in mysterious ways."

Sigberht glanced up, but saw nothing more mysterious than spider webs in the joists.

"I told the others in my village. They were angry and cast me out," he lied, the words falling like honey. "I've been walking for weeks, trying to understand. When I saw this great house of God, I suddenly understood. I was sent here . . . to you."

The Abbot stood, and rushed to stand before the Saxon. "Yes," he breathed. He seized Sigberht's hand, clutching it to him. "Yes, you were sent, my son. A strange gift, but we are not to question the ways of the Lord."

He dropped Sigberht's hand, and held his own above the Saxon's head. Words spilled from him, words that Sigberht could not understand. He feared it was a curse, and lurched to his feet.

The Abbot continued regardless, ". . . et semper, et in saecula saeculorum. Amen."

"What are you doing," Sigberht gasped.

The Abbot looked up. "You do not speak the holy tongue?"

At Sigberht's shake of his head the abbot tutted. "We shall have to remedy that. But first, let's take care of your more immediate needs. A bath, then food. Cleanliness is next to Godliness, after all."

Sigberht had never heard that the gods cared if you were clean or not, but the mention of food brought a smile to his face. "Yeah, food. I could eat a horse."

"That won't do. That won't do at all. We need our horses to plough the fields. But we have gruel. We find that spiritual men should not be concerned with things of the flesh. And that includes the belly."

As if on cue, Sigberht's stomach rumbled.

Sigberht had bathed in cold water before, but never in what he suspected was a horses' trough. When he was done, he was given a rough woollen robe to wear. It was too small for his massive frame and did not sweep the ground as it did for the other men in the monastery, ending halfway up his ankles. And the sleeves were too short, his massive, scarred forearms showing.

Aethelraed laughed. "You look ridiculous. We shall have to see about getting a robe made that suits your needs a little more . . . modestly."

Sigberht was not amused, but the promise of food quelled any retort. Aethelraed led him to a large room, decked out with long benches and eating boards. It was like a chieftain's hall, except there were no shields hanging from the walls, nor straw on the floor. There was, however, a large chair, sitting on a raised dais at one end, with two lesser chairs beside it. They stood behind their own eating bench. No doubt the Abbot liked to look down on his men, Sigberht thought. Not so different after all.

"This is the refectory," Aethelraed said. "The monastery began as a coenobitic order, but now there are several solitaries amongst us. However, we come together at mealtimes. Of course, we observe the silence, while a chosen reads from the scriptures."

Sigberht let the words wash over him, their meaning lost. The little monk was like an excited child, but Sigberht found himself willing to tolerate Aethelraed's enthusiasm. At least, for a while. But right now his stomach was ready to revolt and the big man with it. "When do we eat?" he grumbled.

At that moment a bell chimed, and the hall quickly filled with silent monks. No, not quite silent, Sigberht observed. The men talked with their hands. They gestured, and made subtle shapes that clearly had meaning.

Aethelraed pushed him towards a bench, and the two sat. Other monks came in carrying platters with bread, cheese and other foods. Immediately, Sigberht reached out to snatch a loaf.

There was a gasp from the assembled monks at the table, and every eye in the hall turned to stare. Sigberht reddened and slowly replaced the bread.

The Abbot entered then, flanked by two other monks. They sat at the head table. A portly monk began reading from a great book, his voice sonorous. Sigberht did not know what was said, but he found the rhythm calming.

At an unspoken signal, the monks began to help themselves, while others came and ladled out a thin gruel into wooden bowls.

The meal continued in silence, and yet conversation was held by many men, their hands making intricate gestures, combined with raised eyebrows, slight nods, or shakes of their head and other body language.

Sigberht ate, happy enough with the food. It was plain, but it filled his belly. Life in a monastery was clearly not so bad, he thought.

"Gods damn!" The wooden rod came down on the back of Sigberht's hand for the hundredth time.

"Nihil sub sole, you dolt! Sole! Not soli."

Sigberht grunted, then grit his teeth as the cane came down again.

"And that's for taking the Lord's name in vain."

It had been almost four months since he had arrived at the monastery's gate. In that time, he had been beaten, humiliated, half-starved and had his hair and beard cut, even getting a tonsure. By a truly heroic act of will, he had not killed a single man, although he had come close on a couple of occasions. Odin would be more amused than impressed, he was sure. His place in Valhalla would not be secured in battle against a deadly foe armed with sword and axe, but rather against an old man with a cane.

Not everything was terrible though. Aethelraed had proven to be an amusing friend, spinning tales of faraway places and peoples. He claimed that he learned about them in books. This piqued Sigberht's interest mightily, making him work harder than ever.

Sigberht focussed on the tiny black markings on the parchment, their meaning not quite as mysterious as they had once been, and continued reading. With Odin's help, he would not feel his tutor's wrath again that day!

As the months passed, Sigberht learned to

appreciate that not everything the Christians did was odious or crazy, but always he kept to the true path. With his days filled with prayer, instruction in reading and writing, and finally the most esoteric of arts, illustration, he felt that he was getting closer to achieving the goal Odin had set before him.

"This is the scriptorium," Abbot Wulfstan said. Sigberht had been denied access to this part of the monastery until now and he looked about with avid interest. The scriptorium was a tall chamber, with four stone columns holding up the arched roof. It was surprisingly bright. Six large windows, set high in the walls, allowed light to flood the floor. The windows faced east, to ensure the most sun possible. Sigberht was amazed to see the windows contained real glass. In spite of himself, he was impressed.

A half dozen monks were bent over their lecterns, quills scratching. One was carefully applying blue ink to a depiction that Sigberht now knew represented the White Christ's mother, Mary.

The Abbot looked at him sternly. "You will abide here, and do everything brother Dunstall tells you. He is the precentor."

Sigberht nodded. He had been told, in no uncertain terms, that he was on probation. It was a great honour to be allowed to work in the scriptorium, and his being chosen had caused some resentment amongst the monks.

Wulfstan spoke briefly with Dunstall, then left. Sigberht walked over to an empty lectern and began to sit.

"What do you think you are doing?" Dunstall said, his voice like gravel.

Sigberht sighed. As always, it would not be so easy. "Sorry, brother. What would you have of me?"

"You can start by making ink. We always need ink. Never have enough. And no talking!"

Sigberht nodded and went to the corner where a table sat. On it stood a basket filled with oak-apples, little round nuts that grew on oak trees. These had come from the Levant and at great expense. Sigberht did not doubt it, but he did not have the first clue what the Levant was, or where. He began to crush the stone hard nuts in the mortar, his muscled arms well suited to the task. Dunstall watched him and nodded in encouragement.

"Good, that is the way. When you have a fine powder we will add the salmortis and then the gum arabic."

More weeks passed, and Sigberht learned the secrets of ink production, and how to store, preserve and finally, use it. He was given a simple text to copy out as his first trial with quill and ink.

After a morning of studious toil, he showed his work to Dunstall.

"Did you do this?" The older monk asked, clearly surprised.

"Aye, brother. This was the task set for me."

"It is exquisite. How can you possibly have so skilled a hand, in so short a time?"

Sigberht merely shrugged. Dunstall took the square of parchment and left. When he returned, he looked at the huge Saxon with a measured glance. Then his eyes crinkled as he smiled. "The Lord moves in mysterious ways."

That night, at dinner the hall was quiet, as usual. But Sigberht detected more than one clandestine conversation about him. He could see the sign for 'oaf' and 'miracle.' Seemingly, brother Dunstall did not mind talking when he wanted.

The weeks passed, and Sigberht worked hard to

learn the art of writing. He became as skilled as the best of the monks, and before long he was asked to teach others. He enjoyed the attention and the respect it earned him, but that was not his mission.

At night, when all were sleeping, he would make his way to the scriptorium, and by the light of the moon and a few stolen candles, he would work, writing the words that came to him, decorating the borders of the pristine vellum with sinuous animals, locked in an eternal embrace. On one page he drew a great tree, its roots growing deep, its branches reaching the heavens. But always he wrote the words. Words of power, words of wisdom. The words of the High One.

He was almost finished, his mission almost complete. A month after he had started the Gospel of Odin, there was a wave of curiosity and excitement amongst the monks, as the Abbot had a visitor from Rome. A great carriage dominated the courtyard. The four horses that pulled it were housed in the stables, with the monastery's own horses having to make do in the fields. A contingent of guards were given leave to use a house in the nearby village, while the Roman guested in the monastery.

At dinner that night, there was a new face in the hall. A man dressed in finery that would not have been out of place on a prince or king, his fingers bedecked with jewels. Around his neck was a large gold cross, but fashioned curiously. It was pointed at the bottom, shaped almost like a dagger. The Roman sat with the Abbot at the main table, his manners imperious.

For the first time, Aethelraed was chosen to read during the meal. He began nervously, but soon found his stride. Sigberht's command of Latin was good enough to know the meaning now, and even though he did not agree with the statements, he could appreciate the grace and poetry of the words. A strange feeling filled him. Pride for his young friend standing at the lectern.

The stranger at the Abbot's table looked around the hall, his pinched face not hiding his distaste of the food. Finally, he came to Sigberht and he held the Saxon's gaze, before looking away. Sigberht could not be sure, but he thought there was an instant when the man recognised him.

After the meal concluded, Sigberht made his way to compline, the seventh and final service of the day. He stopped in the great courtyard as he heard the tell-tale slap of leather on stone. A moment later and Aethelraed caught up with him.

"Did you see the Cardinal?" he said, breathlessly.

"That popinjay was a Cardinal?"

Aethelraed nodded. "From the Vatican. The Vatican! Can you imagine?"

Sigberht shook his head. "Not really. What's he doing here?"

Aethelraed looked around, as if he were about to reveal a secret. "He's here to determine if you are what everyone is saying. You know . . ."

A sudden stab of fear struck at Sigberht's heart. How could they possibly know? "What is everyone saying about me?"

"That you were chosen."

"Oh." He almost laughed. With a slap of Aethelraed's back that almost sent his friend sprawling, he replied. "I *was* chosen."

After compline, Sigberht walked back to his cell. More than once he caught looks of admiration, as well as some sly glances that were clearly jealous, indeed, almost malicious. Men are men, he thought. No matter if these monks thought themselves holy.

Sigberht lay awake on his cot, eye closed, listening to the changing sounds of the monastery. Snores emerged from many of the small cells. His thoughts turned to the Roman, a frown creating furrows in his face. Did the man from the Vatican have a magic that could undo him? He looked out the small window. The moon was rising. It was almost full. Tonight he would finish the Gospel.

He got up, and left his cell as quietly as he could, making his way to the scriptorium. It was empty, as was to be expected. He filled a horn with ink, then took a knife and some quills, sitting himself at the lectern closest to the window. As luck would have it, the moon was low, and there were no clouds, so he could see well enough. He pulled the vellum that he had stolen weeks before from beneath his robe, staring in wonder at what he had made. Then he sharpened the quill, dipped it into the ink, and continued writing, setting down the words that had been his mission.

For many hours Sigberht toiled, carefully crafting words inspired by the gods, perhaps even by Saga and Bragi. Soon enough he was done. There, before him lay the testament of the High One.

He packed up his things and returned to his cell just in time to be 'roused' for vigils, the first of the morning prayers. He hid the Gospel behind the bed, then hurried out, yawning, looking for all the world as if he had just awoken.

Aethelraed joined him as he walked the cloister towards the oratory. He smiled up at Sigberht, his eyes shining.

"G'morning." He grinned. "And how is Saint Sigberht?"

A nearby monk spluttered, suppressing a laugh. Sigberht cuffed Aethelraed amiably across the back of the head.

"Enough of that," he said. "I'm no different than any of you lot."

As they neared the oratory, the Cardinal stood waiting. Sigberht bent to pass through the doorway, but the man caught his arm.

"I would have words with you, brother," the man said, in Latin.

His accent was strange but Sigberht understood. He nodded, then followed the man dressed in silk into the herb garden.

"This vision you had. You claim it was from God."

Sigberht shrugged, carefully composing his answer. He was not used to speaking the Church tongue. "I don't know that I ever said that. I just said that I was sent here to learn the arts of the scribe."

"And learn them you have, I understand." The Cardinal pulled a parchment from inside his sleeve, unrolling it. It was the sample Sigberht had made for Dunstall in the previous month. He waved it at like an accusation.

"This is remarkable. I have to wonder how it is possible that a man like you—" he looked Sigberht over, his contempt barely masked—"could have done it. And so soon in your teaching. It is, shall I say, rather incredible?"

Sigberht did not answer. He bent down and plucked a sprig of rosemary, rubbing it between his fingers, smelling its scent.

"All men are equal in God's eyes," he said finally. "What does it matter if I, or some other man was chosen to do His work?"

"But you were pagan. A believer in false gods! An idolater!"

"And now I am a monk. It is not for man to question

the Lord of Hosts."

"No. But it *is* my job to question you. I wonder if you still have a pagan heart? Maybe you are the wolf in sheep's clothes."

This was a sentiment the Cardinal could accept. He eyed the Saxon suspiciously, then walked away.

The following day, Aethelraed found Sigberht plucking the higher apples in the orchard. A large basket, brimming full, beside him. The younger man was almost bouncing in his excitement.

"Did you hear?" the little monk said.

"Hear what?"

"I am to leave!"

"What? Why?" Sigberht replied, astonished.

"Word has come that Irish monks have found a great island in the northern sea. I am one of the three from this chapter that have been chosen to carry the word of God to that remote place and establish a new monastery."

Sigberht was impressed. He had heard of the cold isle, but knew of none that had been there. He frowned.

Aethelraed noticed his expression. "Don't worry, you big oaf. I'll be fine. God will be my shield."

Sigberht almost laughed at the thought of the little English monk with a shield. He would probably drop it on his foot and crush his toes.

"Well, much as I hate to admit it, I am going to miss you," he said.

Aethelraed beamed. "You could come too. If you speak with the Abbot, I'm sure he would not refuse. After all, if we are to build a monastery we are going to need someone with more brawn than brains!"

Sigberht considered for a moment. It was one of the last places in Midgard that the White Christ had not yet infected. Of course, that was largely because there were very few who lived there. But if he could join the mission, he could spread the true religion, let it put down new roots before it was too late. Sigberht wondered if the Norns were pulling his thread towards that far distant place. It made sense. He would take Odin's Gospel there himself.

"Yes, why not? I will speak with the Abbot."

The day passed as they all did, in work and prayer. But at the first opportunity, Sigberht went to the Abbot's chamber. He knocked gently at the door. It was opened not by Abbot Wulfstan, but by the Cardinal.

He looked up at the Saxon, his face carefully neutral. With a slight gesture, he commanded the big man to enter.

It was clear that he was using the Abbot's chamber for his own. There was a great chest by the bed filled with luxurious clothes as well as several large, leather covered books.

"It is good that you came, Saxon," the Cardinal began. "I had meant to call you here shortly."

He indicated the tiny stool that Sigberht had used the last time he had been in the room. He sat, delicately. The stool creaked less, testimony to the weight he had lost since he had joined the monastery.

"I have some questions. I want to understand you better."

Sigberht nodded, but he was confused as to what the pinch faced Cardinal could mean.

"You say you were pagan, but that you saw the light of God. And it was His will that brought you here."

Sigberht shrugged his massive shoulders. "Aye."

The Cardinal leaned in close, his dark eyes focussing on Sigberht's blue. "But what if was not God who commanded you. What if it was the Devil? What if you were brought to this holy place as a serpent to the lamb?"

Sigberht chuckled, a deep rumbling. "And how am I, just a man, to know these things? I heard what I heard. I did as I was commanded. What else is there?"

The Cardinal sneered. "Exactly. How are you to know anything? You are just a simple man. It is up to those more knowledgeable than you to judge your actions. And your heart."

The Cardinal touched the cross around his neck, one finger caressing the sharp point at the bottom. "I think you are not what you say. Yes, you are a Saxon. But you have not been reborn in Christ. I believe you to be the agent of Satan. And I will prove it."

He strode across the chamber, to another door and pulled it open. Four armed and armoured men entered. From their bearing, Sigberht knew they were trained and experienced. He tensed, waiting for the attack.

It did not come. Instead, the men surrounded him. When he stood he towered over them, but with four heavily armed men, he did not have a chance. Whatever they wanted, he would have to go along with it.

"We are going for a walk, Sigberht the Saxon," the Cardinal said.

It had been months since Sigberht had been outside the monastery's walls. The Cardinal and the soldiers marched him through the courtyard, past the Cardinal's carriage, and out the great door. Aethelraed opened it for them, his eyes wide. He did not speak, nor would he meet Sigberht's gaze.

Many other monks stood about gawking. One or two faces wore looks of satisfaction, while others gaped in confusion. No one tried to intervene. As they were passing through the gate, Abbot Wulfstan appeared. He hurried after them, in an ungainly flapping of arms.

"What is the meaning of this, Cardinal Vincenzo? Where are you going with brother Sigberht and who are these soldiers?"

The Cardinal turned and eyed the Abbot for a moment. "We are just going for a walk, my dear Wulfstan. There is nothing to concern yourself over. And if *brother* Sigberht is what he says, he has nothing to worry about either."

And with that, he passed through the gate. One of the soldiers prodded Sigberht forward, and they started to march towards the village. Sigberht could clearly hear Wulfstan ordering Aethelraed to find the infirmarian, the monastery's healer, then the portal slammed behind them.

As they walked, the Cardinal talked amiably, almost as if they were friends.

"I have travelled a lot, you know. I have seen the court of the Holy Roman Emperor. I have seen the great cathedral in Constantinople, what your people call Miklagarðr. I have been called to many great cities in many countries. But sometimes, I get sent to small villages in tiny backwaters, just such as this."

As they entered the village square, Sigberht became aware that a crowd of men and women were standing in a circle around a wooden stake, stacked with wood. A roughly dressed peasant stacked another armful of dry branches at its base. But what caught his attention were the two men gripping the arms of a once handsome young man. And even though his lip was swollen and bloody, and his eyes blackened by bruises, Sigberht knew him and he moaned in dismay. His son.

The Cardinal saw his reaction, and a brief smile

played over his thin lips. "This young fellow has been caught speaking blasphemy. He has been telling stories of pagan gods and goddesses. And even worse, he was caught in possession of sorcerous symbols." At that, Vincenzo produced a silver pendant, shaped like a stunted cross; Thor's hammer.

"He has been condemned to die. I have already judged the matter. But imagine my surprise, when I visited the monastery to speak with the Abbott and I saw *you* sitting at the monks' board. The resemblance is uncanny, is it not? You could almost be family. Perhaps, father and son?"

The Cardinal smiled broadly. "God is merciful, even to unbelievers, Sigberht. Heresy must be rooted out, of that there is no question. But perhaps not every branch of a tree needs pruning. If you confess your treachery, I will spare the boy."

For the first time in his long life, Sigberht felt overwhelming fear. Not for himself, but for his only child. He clenched his fists, his huge muscles straining, but he kept control. To act foolishly would be to ensure both their deaths. He turned to Vincenzo.

"What is it that you want, Roman? You want me to beg?"

"No, Sigberht. Just tell me the truth. The truth will set you free."

Sigberht held the smaller man's gaze. "What is truth?"

At this the Cardinal gasped. "Your own words condemn you! Is that not the very same thing that Pontius Pilate said to our Lord?"

Sigberht chuckled. "Yes, it was. And then he went out and addressed the Jews, telling them that he found no guilt. Is that not also true?"

The Cardinal scowled. "Yes, you have the right. But

your knowledge of scripture is not evidence of your piety, but rather, proof of your deceit. Even the Devil may quote scripture, were it to serve his end."

Sigberht shrugged. "A man is what he does, not what he says. Wouldn't you agree?"

The Cardinal considered that statement for a moment, his eyes narrowed. "Yes," he said slowly. "Yes. I would agree."

"And have I not prayed at every bell? Did I not work hard to create books glorifying the Lord of Hosts?"

"Ita vero," he said. "You speak rightly. The Abbot has nothing but praise for you. But he is a simple man. He looks for miracles and he found one in you. But I see something else. I see a man who is cunning, intelligent and who carries a secret. Is this not also truth?"

Sigberht did not reply. The Cardinal turned, and gestured. The two men holding Sigberht's son began to push him towards the stake. Sigberht closed his eyes, his face anguished.

"Let him go! Let him leave the village, and I will tell you the truth."

The Cardinal smiled. "Very well." He pointed to the men holding Sigberht's son. "Release him."

The villagers let the young man go, and he staggered, but kept his feet. He straightened, standing tall, then looked to Sigberht. He gave a simple nod in recognition then slowly made his way from the village, one foot dragging. When he was out of sight, Sigberht sighed.

"I am Odin's man. He came to me and gave me a charge. The White Christ is strong, and he will rule for an age. But a time will come when he will fall and the gods of my ancestors' will return. It is my task to carry that knowledge and share it with those who follow the old ways."

Vincenzo chuckled. "It is as I suspected. When I saw

the boy, and I saw you, I knew. You have failed in your duty, Saxon."

Sigberht laughed. "No, little man. You have failed. You have no other choice but to kill me now. Let the people here see how a real man dies. I will martyr myself for my god. Would you do the same for yours?"

In spite of his words, Sigberht was crushed. A man does not fear death. But he had a charge from the High One. The gospel was sure to be found in his cell. With that destroyed, his mission would truly be a failure. There was only one final way to serve his master. He addressed the crowd.

"You who are present this day, will witness the death of a true believer. Hear my words, and remember. This day, I die for you."

"Enough," Vincenzo said savagely.

One of the soldiers hit Sigberht across the head with the pommel of his sword, and the Saxon fell to his knees.

"Take him. His own words have condemned him."

Dazed, Sigberht was dragged to the stake and forced to stand. The soldiers joked as they bound his hands to the rough wood.

"Getting nippy," one said.

"Might be a good idea to light a fire then," said the other. They both laughed. Sigberht laughed too, much to the astonishment of the soldiers.

Another stepped forward and poured oil onto the kindling. The Cardinal stared at him, a leer twisting his face. A soldier passed him a lit torch. In his other hand, he clutched his cross.

Just then the villagers surged forward, pushed from behind. A party of monks burst through, Wulfstan at their head. Sigberht looked up at the commotion. He smiled. At the rear was Aethelraed. The Abbot marched up to the Cardinal.

"What do you think you are doing? Release him, at once!"

Cardinal Vincenzo shook his head, pointing the flaming torch in accusation at Sigberht. "This foul creature is a minion of the Devil. He is in league with Satan. By his own admission, he has declared himself a servant of Odin."

Wulfstan's face went white and he turned to face the Saxon. "Is this true, Sigberht. Did you deceive us?"

Sigberht met his gaze. "Aye, it's true. I had need of your monastery."

The Abbot's hand went to his mouth, the other grabbing the wooden cross around his neck. He muttered a prayer, eyes heavenward. The Cardinal turned and casually tossed the torch onto the kindling at the edge of the pyre. It caught immediately, going up with a whoosh. A wave of heat washed over Sigberht, and he turned his face to the side. This turned into intolerable pain, as the flames climbed higher.

Sigberht grit his teeth. He sought out his friend in the crowd, locking eyes with Aethelraed. As the flames reached Sigberht, blackening his robe and then his skin, he gasped, but kept his eyes on the young monk.

He shouted, "Should any hold me dear, remember my words. The Spear Lord will return. Remember!"

The flames grew higher. The cardinal struck out at a soldier. "Why does he not scream? The fire is not hot enough!"

The Cardinal came closer, but could not approach, the heat forcing him back. He turned and grabbed a spear from a soldier, then thrust it into Sigberht's side. Sigberht felt the blade pierce him, but by then that pain was lost in a lake of agony.

Aethelraed looked away. But as the villagers began

to mutter, some falling to their knees before the spectacle, he turned back, eyes wet with tears, but on his face a look of fierce pride for his friend. His hand went inside his sleeve, and he pulled something free, holding it aloft. All eyes were on the pagan and the Cardinal. But Sigberht watched only his friend, who clutched a rolled up bundle of vellum pages in his hand. The Gospel of Odin! For a moment, Sigberht feared Aethelraed would toss it onto the fire, but he hid it in his sleeve, then, with a last nod, he turned and left the village. That moment Sigberht knew. Aethelraed would carry it to Iceland; his mission would not fail.

Finally, Sigberht could not keep his pain inside, and he looked to the sky and bellowed, "Odin, receive my sacrifice!"

The Cardinal thrust once again with the spear, its point finding Sigberht's belly. But the rope holding Sigberht to the stake had burned through and though his skin was black and blistered, his hands were free. With a great roar, Sigberht pulled the spear free and turned it. The smoke was thick, the pain beyond bearing. He could not see his enemy. But there, in the darkness, a flash of gold. With the last of his strength, Sigberht the Saxon threw his spear.

On the Tree

Nine Poems from the Broken Tongue

I.
Today
the meaning of ropes
and bark
lessons of being
bound
in one place long
enough to feel
sap
running
from branch to bole to
root.

II.
Listen
to wind
in the leaves
and make
sense
of squirrels
as they
chatter
from branch
to branch

III.
What you feel
in your wrists
won't count
as misery
not yet, because
you are still
too young
and your hair
tangles
in the nests of birds.

IV.
This is the night
of lightning and rain
then thunder
and shivering wind.

V.
In the morning
you hear
cries in a new
wind blowing
from the sea
blowing
your name
from your body
with a sigh.

VI.
Your voice
is a whisper
then a song.
How can
this be when
your lips
crack brown
as the dead
leaves
on a branch
ready to fall?

VIII.
Now at last
you are
nothing
neither
lascivious
nor chaste
nor honor
bound
to give your
hands away.

VII.
Your song
disturbs
light
gashes
brilliant
sky.
Nearby
the river
tumbles
to the sea.

IX.
Clouds, then rain
then clouds then sun.
Your eyes
have turned
to dreamstones
and look inward
to face the ghosts
of blood.

Bumt Einar

Einar was a fisherman, whose family had lived on a remote shore in eastern England for as long as any could remember. Einar was old and alone, his gray hair and wrinkles telling their own tale of his life. His wife had passed some years before, leaving him without an heir and forced to fend for himself. But despite his loneliness, his health was good and his faith was strong.

With no son or daughter of his own to whom he could pass on his knowledge, he grew close to his sister's son, Rolf, a spoiled young man of fifteen with scrawny limbs and lank hair, whose father had died in one of Henry's wars. He was indulged by his mother and, given all he demanded, was growing into a petulant and arrogant man. Einar hoped that one day Rolf would mature and be proud of his ancestry.

"Fishermen? Why should I be pleased I come from fishermen? Where is the glory in that?"

Einar shook his head. "You should honour your history, boy. You come from a line of brave men and women, who fought the sea to provide food and who were always faithful to the gods."

"The gods." Rolf sneered in a way Einar had grown to hate. "Stories old crones tell children to frighten them."

And so it went, every conversation ending the same way. Still Einar hoped. For there was reason, kept hidden, to keep trying to make the boy respect his history: Einar still worshipped the old gods. In these days of change, when a mad king put his wives to death as easily as bed a whore, and had declared himself the head of the church in England, belief in anything other than the enforced doctrine was dangerous and best kept secret for fear of severe reprisal from the Church.

Einar had no interest in the Christian god, whom he felt demanded too much and gave little in return. *His* gods were fair and generous, had always helped and been kind to his ancestors.

He worshipped in private but had a few of the icons and images associated with Christianity scattered around his house to deflect attention should anyone visit. As he grew older, fewer people came to call on him as they were forced by the Church to purchase their fish from the bishops, so he was left in peace to his devotions. With fewer visitors to interfere, and from whom to hide his true beliefs, he grew careless.

"Uncle! Are you here?" Rolf walked through the house uninvited and without warning. "Uncle?" He came across Einar from behind and stopped suddenly. "What are you doing?"

Einar turned, startled. His prayers had been so focused he hadn't noticed his nephew until it was too late.

Rolf stood beside him, staring at the crude altar stone. A small pig lay dead; its neck cut and blood running down a groove carved into the stone and collecting in a wooden bowl. "Uncle?"

Einar looked down at the bloodied knife in his hand, then back at his nephew. "Rolf, why have you come?" It was a stupid question but the only words he could think to speak.

"What are you doing? I don't. . . what is this?"

"Rolf, come with me." He led the boy back to the cottage and to the hearth, his ritual abandoned. The gods would understand. As he gathered cups and poured ale, he spoke. "It's time you learned, understood. There are no others to keep the rituals, to honour the gods who've always helped our family." Einar handed a cup to Rolf and sat across from his nephew, the wooden chair creaking with age.

"I keep the old faith, the old ways. The Christian god," he spat into the dirt floor, "he is weak. He does not appreciate the faith of his people. He demands they follow rules, so many rules; do this, don't do that, you may have this but only on that day. It's ridiculous and no god worth anything would make it so difficult to love him, so confusing to know what to do to please him." He shook his head.

Einar had himself been on the receiving end of a priest's tongue for breaking dietary rules on a saint's day. Despite his disgust at the priest's rebuke, Einar had considered himself fortunate, for it wasn't that he was dishonouring the saint by his actions; it was because the saint had been so unimportant to Einar and his life that he had completely forgotten it was a holy day.

"But uncle, that's what the priests are for. To instruct us on God's will." The self-assurance was returning to his voice.

"To instruct us? Tell me, if they are so wise, and claim to know their god's thoughts, why do they serve such an unjust master? What good master would demand such punishments be meted out in his name? What mystical powers do they possess that they can read a god's mind?"

Rolf frowned. "They are trained to understand the scriptures, by the Holy Father in Rome. You know this."

"Hah! The father, who rules and claims infallibility. Is he himself not appropriating the powers of a god?" He sighed. "Is this itself not a sin, according to the scriptures you mention?"

His nephew stood, glaring at his uncle. "You fool. You're mad, completely mad. And you won't continue your heresy, I'll see to that." Storming towards the door, he stopped and turned back to his uncle. "And once you're gone, I'll take this," he waved a hand in the air, "your home. And your land. I'll sell it and move, finally be free of this place. You can watch me from hell."

Hurt by his nephew's words Einar watched the young man hurry from the cottage. He knew his time was short and prepared himself as best he could. Returning to the pig, he ran his fingers through the still-warm blood in the bowl, painting lines and symbols on his face and arms. He prayed to Odin, the All-Father, to give him the strength he would need in the coming days.

Retribution came sooner than he thought; he only had time to clean himself and change into his best clothes before a crowd gathered at his door.

"Heathen! Blasphemer! Open this door!"

Einar hesitated a moment before stepping outside. People from the nearby town were watching his door; news had spread fast. There was also a priest who stood at the front of the crowd, soldiers at the edges, and his nephew. If their eyes had not darted towards Rolf every so often, Einar wouldn't even have noticed the boy lurking behind the priest.

"What do you want? Why have you come?" Einar stared back at the gathered spectators.

"Einar Eriksson, you have been accused of heresy and crimes against the Church. What do you have to say?"

These people might falter in their beliefs when confronted with authority but he would not dishonour his gods by doing so. "I have nothing to say." He stood, arms crossed over his chest.

The priest snarled. "You do not deny these accusations?"

"I do not."

The crowd erupted into shouts of heathen, sacrilege and other less savoury abuses. The soldiers rushed forward and grabbed him, forcing him to the ground, chaining his neck, hands and feet. As they began the march back to town, Einar glanced over at Rolf. His nephew was deep in conversation with a senior-looking priest, both of whom were glancing over at Einar periodically. He caught Rolf's eye but the boy ignored him.

Einar was placed in a small stone building at the back of the church used to hold those who had been accused of some heretical activity or behavior. Three rooms were connected to a short hall leading to the outside entrance. He heard the lock turn in the heavy wooden door and footsteps walking away. His surroundings were bleak: stone walls, stone floor with a few scattered rushes. A wooden bucket to use as a privy. He sighed and gathered the reeds, sat on the pile and closed his eyes.

After a short while his stomach reminded him that he hadn't eaten since yesterday. Standing, he went to the door and looked out the tiny barred window. "Is anyone there? Hello?"

A door opened. "Shut up in there! Or I'll shut you up myself!" The door creaked as it closed.

"Wait! I need food!"

The annoyed voice was louder this time. "Food? What are you, the king? I know: why don't you ask your heathen gods to bring you food!"

Einar heard the laughter as the door closed. Dejected, he sat back down on his pile of reeds. Shivering, he pulled his cloak more tightly, looking out into the darkness.

The noise of the outside door being opened woke him, and, unaware of how much time had passed, he crawled to his cell door, stiff from the cold that had seeped through the meager reeds. Climbing to his feet he peered out the small window. "Is someone there?"

Instead of a reply the sound of feet shuffling met his ears. A moment later a weathered, lined face appeared at the door window. "I've brought you food." A wrinkled hand pushed a package through the bars. It landed on the floor and opened, revealing cheese and bread within. Einar grabbed the food and shoved it into his mouth, looking out at his visitor. The old man had dragged a wooden stool to the outside of Einar's cell and sat with a grunt, using his walking stick for balance. Einar, still chewing large mouthfuls of bread, watched as the old man removed his leather hat and placed it on the floor beside him, shaking the long white hair out of his face. He then took out a flask and drank deeply before standing again and offering the contents to Einar. The fisherman hesitated. "Go on, drink all you want." Grateful for the invitation, Einar drank long, not realizing until that moment how thirsty he was. The wine was watered but refreshing and allowed him to forget his situation if only briefly.

He handed the empty flask back. "Thank you grandfather, I'm grateful for your charity."

His visitor sat down once more, leaning back to peer through the bars at Einar's face. "What evil act brought you to this place?"

Einar frowned. There was something odd about the old man's accent. The fisherman shrugged; perhaps he was just tired. "Grandfather, I am a heretic. I worship the old gods. You should leave. You don't want to be caught associating with me."

"Pshh." The old man's face screwed up and he murmured something in a language Einar didn't understand. "I'll decide when I leave." He shifted himself on the stool, getting comfortable. "For now, I want to hear your story."

"There's no story. I worship the All Father and his family. I always have, as did my ancestors before me. I tried to keep it secret but my nephew reported me. And now I'm here." Einar voice cracked.

"I think I saw the young man, he was outside while you were brought here. Skinny lad, dark eyes."

"You were there?"

"Oh yes. I try to keep an eye on those who might have need of my help."

Einar frowned. "Do you live in the village?" He hadn't seen the old man before.

"No, I was passing through. I wander; I'm not content to stay in one place for long. Used to frustrate my wife terribly!" He chuckled, a deep comforting sound, like distant thunder.

Einar found himself calming, becoming drowsy. "And why are you here?"

The old man paused before replying. "I knew I was needed."

Unsatisfied by this answer, the fisherman found he could summon no words. He was so tired, his limbs heavy and warm. But from a long distance he heard the old man continue to speak.

"You've done well, my son. You are one of the last and I'm pleased with you." The voice was proud, like a father speaking to a favoured son. "Sleep now, it'll be over soon."

Einar was wrenched from sleep by his cell door being pulled open. Groggily he sat, looking around him. The memory of the previous day came crashing back and he crawled away from the uniformed man coming toward him.

"Where d'you think yer going?" A beefy hand grabbed Einar by the shoulder and heaved him to his feet with ease. The fisherman stopped struggling and resigned himself to his fate.

He winced at the bright sunshine outside, taking a moment to focus on the crowd who had already gathered. The priest from yesterday was also there, as well as a tall man with a large hooked nose wearing a bishop's mitre.

"Bring the prisoner." The man's reedy voice made Einar shiver.

Einar was dragged before the bishop and forced to his knees. The bishop looked down at him, disdain clear on his face. The fisherman glanced to his right to the clearing some distance away from the church. A large pyre had been constructed; men were still placing the last of the wood.

"So," he thought, "my fate has already been decided."

Looking back towards the crowd he saw the same old man who had visited him, leaning against a tree. Their eyes met briefly and in that instant Einar felt his mounting fear disappear.

"You have been accused of heresy. And you have confessed your crime, is this correct?" The bishop continued to glare down at him.

Einar glanced back toward the old man before looking up at the senior churchman, defiance glowing in his eyes. "Yes." There was no point in wasting words, he knew that.

The crowd roared as the bishop gestured to the guards. They dragged the fisherman toward the pyre and bound him to the post. He felt the burn of the ropes as they tightened around his wrists, ankles and neck. The crowd quieted as the bishop approached.

"Einar Eriksson, you are condemned to burn for your sins against the Holy Mother Church, so that the flames may wash you of your heresy and purge your soul."

The crowd erupted in cheers, drowning the sound of the first crackling of flame licking at the pyre. Soon Einar was surrounded by fire and smoke, chest heaving with the effort it took to breath and eyes streaming tears. But through the smoke and tears he saw the old man, standing at the edge of the crowd, nodding. Then all he saw was the blaze growing closer, and all he felt was the heat blistering his skin. He began to struggle, his body taking over. But it was too late. The flames engulfed him from all sides, and he felt searing pain.

Then nothing.

Where are we?"

"Here. In your village. But also not."

Einar looked down and saw himself burning, his body slumped forward, lifeless. He felt nothing. "What happened?"

The old man laughed but it was a sad sound. "You died."

This news didn't affect the fisherman at all. He just shrugged, accepting what the old man said as truth. "Who are you?"

"You know who I am."

"I don't, I mean, I'm not sure. . ."

"You've worshipped me every day of your life."

Einar looked more closely at the older man. He was wearing thick hose, a rough jerkin and a worn cloak. And his leather hat. "Odin?"

The old man tipped his hat slightly. "Indeed."

The god nodded his head in the direction of the pyre. Einar returned his attention to his lifeless body. The fire burned brightly and the town watched in fascination. Einar saw Odin raise his hand and a sudden wind rose around them. With a further gesture the wind rushed toward the pyre, scattering flames and cinders.

The townspeople held up their arms, covering their faces, but were still burnt by the glowing embers thrown by the gale. The flames leapt with life and caught those nearest the pyre: the praying priest, the watching bishop and Einar's nephew.

The townspeople fled in panic and there was no one to help the three men beat out the flames. Einar watched as they ran screaming in pain, reaching out for each other. He saw his nephew's jerkin catch fire, the boy frantically searching for help. Finally, one by one they fell, their screams fading.

"But. I don't understand."

The All Father looked directly at Einar. "The pain they caused you was an insult to me. The insult had to be redressed and honour restored." He led Einar away from the place of his death. They wandered and Einar lost track of how long they walked or how far.

"You are one of my last worshippers. The rest of the world now venerates a new god." He looked up at the sky and at the trees that surrounded them. "I've been waiting for you."

Einar walked in silence beside the old man/god, thinking. "What happened to the others? Where are they?"

"With so few people worshipping us, their rituals disappearing, we began to tire, grew weary of life. Some fought against the ennui, tried to integrate with humans, live among them. And a few were nearly successful, but they couldn't escape the draining of their life force. Others travelled the earth, searching for worshippers, but were also struck down by the malaise. For what use is a god with so few followers?"

He sighed and shook his head. "Finally they could no longer fight the tiredness and took the shapes of nature, trees, stones, rivers. All waiting for more worshippers to be found." The All Father put a gentle hand on Einar's shoulder.

"I'm sorry, I didn't know." The fisherman bowed his head as he spoke.

"My son, you have no need to apologise, this is the way of things. And as one of my last followers you have a place with us."

"Us? I thought you said. . ."

"I've sent my ravens to whisper to the trees, rocks and rivers. To bring together my family once more." Odin looked to the skies.

The white mist descended so quickly Einar had no time to orient himself. But he wasn't afraid, for the presence next to him was strong and protective and his soul rejoiced as he took his place among the gods he had so loved in life.

The Song of Spells I

These songs I know, which neither sons of men
nor queen in a king's court knows;
the first will bring help
in all woes and sorrow and strife.

A second song I know, which mortal men
must sing, if they would heal the sick.

A third I know: if there be dire need for a spell
to stay my foes.
I will sing that song and blunt their swords,
so neither their weapons nor staves can wound.

A fourth I know: if men tie me fast in chains.
When I sing that song so shall the fetters from
hands and feet spring free.

A fifth I know: when the enemy's arrow
flies through the host, no matter how fast,
I will catch it, if I can see its blurring flight.

A sixth I know: if a man would harm me
through runes carved in the tree's root,
on him alone shall the curse fall,
for he will reap his reward.

Hungry is the Wolf

Suffering? You don't know anything about suffering, young fellow. I was with the *Grand Armée* in Russia when that idiot Bonaparte decided to take us all back to France. What a disaster! The retreat was an endless struggle through a frozen Hell. *That* was suffering.

What's that you say? Hell's hot, not cold? So it is, but at the very centre of Hell is a frozen lake, as cold as the Devil's heart. According to that Italian fellow who wrote about it, anyway. Now stop interrupting and let me tell my tale.

It was just after we left Smolensk that I first saw the grey wolf slipping between the pines. No ordinary wolf, though God knows we were hounded by enough of those. I swear this one was as big as a horse, but as insubstantial as the cold fog that lay over every stream we crossed.

I can see you don't believe me. But I saw it, I tell you, with its terrible eyes glaring, its vast jaws slavering, its cruel teeth bared, pacing after us, always following, following.

Perhaps I had been driven mad. Many were, during that nightmare journey. But I saw what I saw; I heard what I heard. As God is my witness, I felt what I felt and suffered what I suffered. Yet I escaped the wolf and survived, all thanks to Redbeard.

What's that? Who was Redbeard? You young people have no patience. Just let me tell the story in my own way. But first, bring me another drink, will you?

Ah, bless you, that's better. Keeps away the pain for a while, at least.

You might wonder what I was doing with the *Grand Armée* in the first place. You can tell I'm not French. No, I'm from Westphalia. I hail from a little town called

Herdecke on the Ruhr. I doubt if you've ever heard of it. But I was young like you, then. Young and stupid, and I fancied being a soldier. The French offered us good pay and rich plunder once we reached Moscow. How I wish I hadn't listened.

What went wrong? It was the fault of that little Corsican. They say he was a great general in his youth. I don't know much about that. All I know is that the fat fool made all the wrong decisions in Russia, and what plunder we'd been able to gather was lost on that awful journey back.

The great grey wolf must have been with us long before I started to see him. He must have been there during the bloodbath at Borodino, I'm thinking. But he really started stalking us once we gave up Moscow and headed back to France.

It was bad enough at the start, on the road between Moscow and Smolensk. The worst thing wasn't the Cossacks harassing our rear: it was the peasants. It was better, far better, to die than to be in the hands of the Russian peasants. They hated us for the looting we'd done on the way in to Moscow. And that idiot Bonaparte ordered us to retreat back on exactly the same path we'd already ravaged and stripped of food. Little wonder we were hungry, or that the peasants wanted their revenge on those who had destroyed their harvests and raped their women.

Once we left Smolensk it got much worse. The snow started to fall. We were freezing and half-starved as we trudged along. We were no longer any kind of organised army. Most of us were no longer wearing our flimsy uniforms, useless at keeping out the chill. Instead we were rugged up with every bit of clothing we could steal. I was lucky; I'd taken a thick overcoat and decent boots off a dead man just outside of Gzatsk.

Some men pulled on women's dresses over the top of their coats. They looked ludicrous, but you'd do anything for an extra layer. We were a ragged mob, a circus, staggering desperately towards safety.

Food became more and more scarce. The supply wagons were empty. So what did we eat? Mostly the horses; the poor damned horses. The cavalry looked after their mounts, but many of the rest hadn't been properly shod to cope with icy ground, and too often they'd topple and break their legs. Starving men would crowd around a fallen horse, cutting its flesh to pieces before it was even dead. It made me sick to see it, but I'll admit I didn't turn away the meat. We'd camp and start a fire if we could, or huddle together and eat the meat raw if we couldn't. Those, let me tell you, were the good times. It got worse after that. Much, much worse.

The first time I saw the enormous wolf was a foggy night when we'd stopped by the side of the forest in a field full of prickly wheat stalks. The wheat was long gone, of course.

I woke up in the middle of the night needing a piss and walked up to the nearest tree. As I vented out a steaming stream, I spotted this huge wolf slipping through the forest beyond. Scared the piss right out of me. But here's the thing: I could see the trees right *through* the wolf! It was like a ghost, and huge, like I said.

Well, I gave a yell and ran back to where my compatriots were lying, and shook my friend Jürgen awake. He wasn't any too happy to be woken up, I can tell you, and he got even angrier when he couldn't see the wolf I tried to point out to him. I could see it just as clearly as I can see you, but he just grumbled and told me I was jumping at shadows. No one could ever see it but me. Why me? I don't know, but perhaps it had something to do with what happened later.

I was imagining it, you'll say, but I don't think so. It was real enough; it just wasn't made of flesh and bone like you and me. Its jaws were real; its hunger was real. It was wicked and it hated men.

Every night after that, I saw the ghostly grey wolf, slinking through the trees or stalking us through the abandoned villages. I saw it outlined against the sky by the smoke from the camp fires. Every night it grew a little bigger, I swear.

What's that? How did it make me *feel* when I saw it? God save me, how do you *think* it made me feel? It scared me shitless. I would hold on to the cross around my neck and pray. At first that seemed to work, and the wolf would slink away. For a time. But later . . . Well, I'm getting ahead of myself again.

It was about then I first came across Redbeard the blacksmith, hard at work re-shoeing horses in a camp. I say "a camp" but it was more like what you get when a mass of exhausted men give up walking when the sun goes down, slumping together in groups. But Redbeard was there, sparks flying as he crashed away on his anvil. His field-forge was on the back of a sturdy wagon. A young lad was pumping away with the bellows, so that the forge blazed away, full of glowing charcoal. I came up to watch, with some other men. For one thing, the heat from the forge was welcome.

The smith was a giant of a man, with a dense red beard falling down his front. Despite the bitter cold, he was naked to the waist, his chest and great thick arms all hard muscle, slick with sweat despite the cold. It was hard to tell how old he was, but there were deep wrinkles around his green eyes, and when he took off his metal cap and shook out his long red hair, I could see streaks of grey. I never learned his real name. We just took to calling him Redbeard.

I saw him often after that, usually working at the anvil. He was always fixing up something. Repairing the supply wagons, or the carts carrying the injured, while we still bothered with those, keeping them on the road. Or shoeing the horses. Putting on the spiked shoes they needed to keep upright in the icy conditions.

I never saw him work on the cavalry horses, not even when the officers came and asked him to. One fancy French officer took out his sabre and threatened Redbeard with it when he refused to re-shoe his horse. I swear, Redbeard just laughed––he towered over the man––then snatched the blade from the officer's hand and snapped it over his knee as though it were matchwood. How he did it without cutting his hands to pieces, I can't tell you. The Frenchy slunk off and didn't come back.

So we went on, and like I said, it got much worse, though I wouldn't have thought it possible. The deep cold set in, and food got even more scarce. We stumbled along, really starving now. Towards the end, it was so bad that sometimes men would cut off chunks of flesh from a horse still on its feet. It was so cold that the poor horse wouldn't even know it had been cut at first, but it would die, sure enough, when it had lost enough blood. One time I saw Redbeard pick up a man in one hand and smash him to the ground when he saw him cut a living horse that way. But Redbeard couldn't be everywhere.

That cold! It was bad enough by day, but you were lucky to survive the nights. Very damned lucky. You'd think you'd be safe enough if you lit a big fire, wouldn't you? You'd be wrong.

Listen: there was one night when we'd reached an empty village, its peasants fled. A big mob of us set a whole wooden house on fire to keep us warm. But here's the thing: if you got too close to the flames, your clothes would start to smoulder and your flesh start to burn, so you'd try to squeeze back through the crowd. But if you got too far away, you'd freeze, so you'd try to push back in.

That was a terrible night. Throughout the whole of it, crushed by men crowded on every side, always fighting to get myself into a safe spot, I watched the grey wolf circle us, outlined by the smoke and the flames. I swear I saw it snatching away men in its vast jaws, though they never cried out as it took them. They never saw it, but I did. I don't know how, but I did.

Four hundred of us were huddled around that burning house. Only a hundred or so staggered up in the morning. The rest were dead, burned or frozen. Or taken by the wolf.

I see you don't believe me. Well, I don't care. It's all true. After that I knew the only safe fire was small, if I could gather enough twigs to get it going. Or else just huddle together with enough other men somewhere out of the wind.

Then came the night when I got lost. I'd gone astray from my companions, see. That was dangerous: the only safety left was to try to keep up with enough other men who were fit enough to fight off the Cossacks if they made a sortie against us. Heaven help you if you were left behind. The Cossacks wouldn't kill you, though. The rumour was that the local peasants paid them to hand over prisoners, just for the pleasure of torturing them to death. So you kept up as best you could.

What was I saying? Oh yes, the snow was falling so thick that day that it was hard to see, hard to keep a straight line, and at dusk I'd lost touch with Jürgen and the other men I'd been marching with. Soon I was alone. And though I managed to pick up a bunch of twigs from the pine trees by the side of the road, they were too cold and wet to set alight. I knew I was likely to die, but all I could do was I huddle down in my greatcoat. But the snow started again, and soon it was coming down heavy. My coat was covered and I couldn't stop shivering. I'd long since stopped being able to feel my hands and feet.

That's when I saw the great grey wolf again, gleaming in the moonlight, pacing through the forest. Now it had grown as tall as the trees. Its huge long head turned my way, and its red-rimmed eyes were fixed on me, its jaws hanging open. I thought I heard it growl, a deep bone-shaking sound, though it could have been the wind. It came closer, closer. I knew it was after me and I was certain as could be that my time was at an end.

As the wolf came nearer, I grabbed hold of my cross and I prayed, prayed as hard as I could for God to send the wolf away. But this time it didn't work. Maybe God had abandoned me as a hopeless sinner by then. Or maybe it was He who prompted me to do what I did next. I don't know. But all of a sudden I remembered the lucky charm which my old grandmother had insisted on giving me the day I left.

She was a strange one, my gran. Went to church every Sunday like a good Christian. But when I was a kid she often told me stories of the older gods, the gods of the North, and I reckon she secretly did her duty by them as well as by the church. Hedging her bets, maybe. Anyway, just before I started my journey she gave me a lucky charm and told me to keep it close: a little bronze hammer hanging on a chain. See? I have it here even now. I hadn't hung it round my neck until then, more fool me, but it was there in my pack, so now I pulled it out, and prayed some more.

It could have been a coincidence, I suppose, but the ghostly wolf pricked up its gigantic ears, then bounded away. From behind, I heard a creaking and the sound of wheels. I turned, and through the snow I saw a wagon drawing towards me, pulled by two huge cart-horses. They were the strangest horses I'd ever seen, with manes and hides as shaggy as a bear. Maybe that's why they seemed to be enduring the cold so well, blinking away the falling snowflakes. At the reins I saw a red-bearded man, as big as a bear. It was Redbeard the blacksmith. I've never been so grateful in my life to see anyone.

He pulled the wagon to a halt and looked down at me. "Want a lift, friend? Hop on the back." His voice was as deep as the roots of the mountains.

I croaked out a reply, but that was all I could do. I tried to get to my feet, but my arms and legs wouldn't obey. I was all but frozen to the ground, I reckon.

Redbeard looked down at me for a long moment, then leapt down from the wagon. He picked me up as tenderly as if I were a baby, and as easily. He didn't even grunt with the effort, but lifted me up and set me in the back of the wagon. The forge was still radiating heat, thank the Heavens, from the last time it had been used. I huddled close, still holding on to my lucky charm as hard as I could. On the other side of the forge was stowed the big anvil and right next to me was a heap of the tools of the smith's trade, clinking away as the wagon set off again.

I looked back along the way the wagon had come, half expecting to see the great wolf trailing us, but there was only the falling snow and the howl of the wind.

We must have gone a mile or so before I began to

thaw. My hands and feet felt as though they were on fire, burning with pain. But at least I was safe, I thought. Soon enough we'd catch up with what remained of the army, and I'd do a better job of keeping up from then on, I swore.

But then I heard Redbeard begin to curse, and the wagon jolted to a halt. I was warm enough by then that I could raise my head and look forward to see why we'd stopped.

The great wolf was there, on the track ahead of us, its head higher than the tallest tree, its eyes aflame with hate, its jaws open like the gates of Hell.

Maybe I was delirious. Or driven crazy by pain and despair. That's what you'll say, I know. But the wolf *spoke*. I swear by all that's holy, it's true.

Its voice was as rough as gravel, and so loud it shook the ground like an earthquake.

"How are the mighty fallen, Odin's son," it said. "Are you reduced to this? Is the killer of giants now become a tinker?"

The blacksmith straightened in his seat and looked up at the vast creature. "I do the work I am called upon to do," he said. "I have grown tired of blood and battle."

"So weak you are now," the wolf replied, taking a pace nearer to us as I whimpered in terror. "I could snatch you up in a moment, and swallow you whole, you who once thought to chain me."

"I will sit hard in your belly, Fenrir, I promise you." Redbeard was on his feet now and he leapt down from the wagon. In his hand I saw his blacksmith's hammer. "But how is it that you are free from Gleipnir? The end of days is not yet come."

The wolf laughed. Can you imagine a wolf's laugh? A wolf as big as a hill? I couldn't, and I can't describe it to you, except to tell you that it chilled my blood and shook my soul. It laughed long and hard.

"That flimsy thing?" it asked, once it had done laughing. "A chain made of the sound of cat's footfall and the breath of fish? It was eroded by the stupidity of mortals. Every man's death took a chisel to it, every woman's tear was a drop of acid etching away at the links. This journey of death you are on finally cut it. So I am free, long before the time foretold. And that mortal behind you is mine. I claim him."

"No," said Redbeard. "He is under my protection. He called me to him by virtue of my hammer. You shall not have him."

Another bout of laughter. I swear, it was the worst sound in the world, and hearing that sound, I was certain the wolf was going to take me.

"By virtue of your hammer," the wolf said with a horrible, vast sneer. "Don't you know, little god, that all the virtue is gone from your hammer? These days men believe more in the pious carpenter, hung upon a tree, and not in you. No wonder you are no longer a mighty warrior and are reduced to tending to horses."

"A carpenter and a blacksmith are both good honest workmen," said Redbeard calmly, though I saw his grip tighten on his hammer. "I acknowledge the strength of the carpenter. But I am not thereby weakened."

"Are you not?" sneered the wolf, and came a pace closer yet. "We shall see."

"Hold!" cried out Redbeard. He seemed to have grown much bigger now, standing twice as tall as the huge animals drawing the wagon. And his voice had such a tone of command that the wolf did indeed stop.

"Why this man?" the blacksmith asked. "Why must you have him among all of the others dying along this trail?"

"*Why this man?*" The great wolf snarled, a sound

that sawed at my bones. "Because you have chosen to steal him from me, Odin's son. That is reason enough for me to want him."

"Have you not had your fill, wolf? How many tens of thousands of men have you taken already?"

"My fill? You know that I am never full, never before the end of days. My very name is Hunger." His jaws opened wide. And then he leapt.

At the same moment, Redbeard threw his hammer, right into the jaws of that ghostly beast, and it turned him backward, head over heels even in the midst of his leap. Ghostly the wolf may have seemed, but his body was solid enough when it crashed into Redbeard and spun against the wagon, toppling it over sideways, horses and all. I fell with it, right into a big drift of snow, just missing the anvil, and there came a terrifying hiss as the still-hot coals spilled out of the forge alongside of me, throwing up a cloud of steam.

I wasn't hurt, but I was in mortal danger when the wagon twisted and turned as the two horses tried to struggle to their feet again. I managed to crawl forward and with my knife I cut the horses free of their harnesses. As I was doing so I realized how truly strange these great hairy beasts were, for I saw that they had little horns, unlike any normal horse.

Meanwhile, the blacksmith was locked in a struggle with the gigantic wolf. Now he had miraculously grown huge himself. His massive hands were round the neck of the wolf, keeping its jaws from tearing off his face. Back and forth they crashed in the forest, felling trees as they rolled.

I wish I could do justice in the telling of that battle, but in truth for most of the time I was cowering away behind the overturned wagon, praying that the two combatants wouldn't crush me. From time to time, though, I risked a peek.

For a long, long time, it seemed as though there would be no victor, but then I saw the blacksmith grasp at his hammer as the two rolled towards it, still managing to hold off the wolf with his left hand. His right hand found the hammer, seized it and then smashed it hard into the great wolf's head. It let out a titanic howl and twisted free from the blacksmith's hand, to bound away, panting and drooling. Redbeard climbed up from his knees and glared at the wolf.

"Be gone, Fenrir" he said. "You cannot defeat me. I will gather my brothers and with their aid I will re-forge Gleipnir stronger than ever and bind you once more."

The wolf snarled, its red tongue licking at its teeth. "A hollow threat. Your brothers and your father are scattered far and wide. And do not forget how I took Tyr's hand when last you chained me. Will he risk another? I think not."

"Say you so? You are wrong. Be gone, and think yourself lucky."

"Not without a blood token. I will have that mortal who hides behind you. I *will* be fed."

There was a long silence as the two opponents faced each other. Then, to my terror, Redbeard turned to where I shrank behind the wagon.

"Mortal," he said. "Come here."

I didn't stir. I doubt that my legs could move. If they could I would have been running away as fast and as far as I could. So the gigantic blacksmith strode towards me. I cowered back before him, I can tell you. Was my protector going to give me up to satisfy the wolf?

"Take off your gloves," he said. "And your boots. Quickly now, if you want to live."

I did as I was bid. I had no choice. Meanwhile, Redbeard picked up the anvil from where it had fallen, lifting it easily in one hand. And he sorted through the snow to find another tool. A chisel.

"Hold out your hands," he said. Whimpering with fear, I did so, to see that my fingers were blackened with the cold. He took his hammer and his chisel, and forced my hand down on the cold anvil. With swift blows he cut through the flesh, severing each of my fingers as I screamed with the agony of it.

But my screaming didn't stop him. He cut every finger, then picked me up and did the same with my frost-bitten toes. All gone. He tossed me aside and I lay on the ground, still screaming, my crimson blood staining the white snow.

Redbeard turned to the wolf who still hovered at the edge of the forest amidst the fallen trees. "Here," he said. "Here is your blood token. Now be off." And he threw my severed digits in a shower towards the great wolf, who snatched them from the air.

"Very well," growled the wolf. "But we are not done. We will meet again, Odin's son, on the day when I swallow the sun."

"Before that, I promise you," the blacksmith said. "You will be bound again, I swear it in the name of Yggdrasil."

The wolf laughed. "You fool! The great ash is gone. And with it, so is your kind." He threw back his great head and howled a bone-shuddering howl. Then he leapt away. I never saw him again, thanks to all that is good and holy.

The blacksmith bound up my hands and feet with clean cloths, handling me as tenderly as a mother would a sick child. He righted the wagon and re-harnessed his shaggy, horned beasts, and we went on until we reached a camp. He left me with a group of Germans and then took himself off. My friend Jürgen was there, and he hugged me close as I wept out my pain.

Did I tell him or any of my compatriots what had passed between the blacksmith and the wolf? No. I knew that no one would listen to me, or even if they did, all they could think of was trying to survive and wouldn't believe me. I just said I'd gone astray and the blacksmith had found me.

As for the rest of that terrible journey back out of Russia, there is a lot I could tell. About how scores of men were dying with every step we took. About how I held Jürgen as he died in my arms one awful night, starved and gaunt, unable to go on. Yet somehow I found the strength to continue.

I made it to the bridge the engineers built over the Beresina River. Everyone says it was a miracle how they threw it up almost overnight. But I know that it wasn't a miracle. I spied Redbeard laboring mightily to help them, his field-forge glowing with charcoal and sparks flying from his anvil as he helped form the bolts and the struts that were needed. Then I saw him wade waist-deep into the swirling, freezing water, spending hours driving in the piles and hammering up the supports. No ordinary man could have done it. Without his help, it would never have happened.

Many of the men I had been with were too dispirited and shocked by then even to try to cross the bridge when they were urged to, but I wasn't one of them, I crossed early. My wounded hands and feet still pained me, but the pain was nothing to the horror of what lay behind. I crossed the bridge and for the rest of that awful journey I stuck as close as I could to the bulk of the men.

Forty thousand crossed the bridge that night, but we left more than that behind us. Many drowned in the river when the bridge collapsed as the rest of those remaining on the Russian side rushed it in a panic at the last minute. Forty thousand were all that survived the expedition to Russia, out of the hundreds of thousands who set out as part of the *Grand Armée*.

Eventually we reached safety, though with no thanks to the Emperor, cursed be his name. He'd long gone on ahead of us to stop a rebellion in Paris. I was gleeful when I heard that the British had defeated him and sent him off into exile. I danced in the street when I heard years later that he was dead. I shit on his name.

I don't fight any more. See my hands, what is left of them? I can't hold a knife to cut my meat, let alone hold a musket or a pike. That was Redbeard's work, but he saved my life by doing it.

What's that? Did Redbeard ever catch up with the wolf again? Did he put it in chains once more? Ah, that I can't tell you, but I pray that he did. Or perhaps the wolf still roams loose in the world, snatching up men and women every hour in its terrible jaws. Yes, I fear that it is so.

And now, I need another drink. Don't you?

Creator Deceiver Destroyer

As I long for you and call for you
I know not what aspect you will bring
If you come, no, when you come
I do not know which face I hope to see

I thought I craved the creator
crafty, the benevolent,
gift-giver to men and gods
Would you come as the lover?
But would even your succour
your blessing, your passion
be enough to cure
a black heart of melancholy
would even your fire
be enough to warm the icy cavern
inside this hollow shell

And if you came as trickster
player of pranks
weaver of schemes and lies
you would delight a mind
dulled by ennui, bored with life
and this sterile earth
but would even your tricks
grow stale with time and habit

And if you come as chaos
As vengeance, as destroyer
I would welcome that also
Perhaps most of all

Into The Storm

I never met my grandfather. For the first fifteen years of my life he was a ghost. A stranger on a photograph, an anecdote conjured up once in awhile during the course of my young, self-centred life.

Like most children, I had no interest in roots or family history. I was too busy living life and all of the freedom that childhood afforded me. It was only later, once I had crossed the threshold of my first job, my first real girlfriend and, eventually, my own family, with life, in all of its practicalities and responsibilities, that I began to consider things like that. Prompted by my children, I realised just how little I knew about my own beginnings.

And about my grandfather. He had passed away long before my birth. My mother was very young when her father died, and for years the only things I knew about him came from her: that his name had been Alfred Cartwright, that he had been an English teacher at a Grammar School, and that she had been just seven when he died.

That was it, an entire life framed by three lamentable facts. When I was sixteen, a little more meat was put on those bare bones, due to a casual conversation with my grandmother. It is because of family members like her and my parents that I am writing these memoirs. Because I don't want them to be diminished, to fade away with each ensuing year until the part they played in their descendants' lives is forgotten. Perhaps this reveals a fear that I harbour for myself. I don't know.

I cannot recall where we were, my grandmother and I, when we had this conversation. You must allow that certain things become dulled over time. But I do know we were outside, maybe sat in the garden. She asked me, as she often did, how school was going, and I mentioned that we were learning about the war. She then told me that my grandfather had been in the Great War.

"Granddad was in the war?"

I remember being struck by this revelation, as it did not tally with one of the few labels hung on him: that of English teacher. But his age and the years—I don't know why I had never done the math before.

"Is that when he died?" I asked, a little uncomfortably, but encouraged by our close relationship.

"No, your grandfather was one of the lucky ones who got to come home. Many didn't. But he was a changed man." Then, almost to herself: "Who wouldn't be changed?"

"In what way?"

"Well, before he went away to fight, your grandfather could be quiet around other people. It was one of the things that first attracted me to him. His friends were all boastful, feeding you lines, but Alfred was quite shy in comparison. I thought it sweet." For just a moment her eyes were distant and she was elsewhere, a younger sun shining on her face, until she visibly regained focus. "But with me, he was relaxed. And funny too! He had a dry, gentle humour that never failed to make me laugh."

As she went on, the whimsical lilt in her voice vanished. "But when he returned, although he still had that humour, it didn't always show itself. Sometimes he would be just sat there, staring off into space. Then he would catch me watching him and allow me a little smile, before occupying himself with something or other. Maybe tinkering around in that shed of his. He never mentioned the war and I never asked him. I didn't want him to relive the things that plagued him at night. He would have the most violent dreams, shouting out until I shook him awake."

A silence grew between us, laden and tense. "I wish I had met him," I said, softly.

Her eyes filled up as she nodded. "As things turned out, I didn't have him back for long. He had lots of bronchial problems, down to him being gassed when at the front. Within a couple of years he died, thanks to the winter colds. He was claimed by the war in the end, though you won't find him listed on any memorial," she added bitterly.

We never spoke of my grandfather again. Perhaps she regretted saying as much as she did, thinking me too young. Perhaps the hurt of opening old wounds was too great. I know, for my part, the memory of those pale eyes of hers filling with tears was enough to vanquish any further curiosity I had. And now she is no longer here to ask.

So that was that. There was nothing more I could know. I reached my mid-thirties, saddled with a mortgage, my own kids and goodness knows what else to occupy me, when one day my mother handed me a diary. It was an old, tattered looking thing. A faded, brown leather-bound book, the spine broken and worn, held together by a frayed piece of string.

She said that it was her father's diary, given to her by her mother some years previously. Having stored it with some other keepsakes, she now wanted me to have it.

That night, after the kids had been packed off to bed and the world was settling down, I read it in its entirety, cover to cover. Even now, whenever I return to it, which I habitually do, it makes fascinating reading. I keep it safe, along with these memoirs, for my children and their children.

The diary spans just over two years, from late 1914 to the middle of 1917, covering the months Alfred spent in training after enlisting with his lifelong friend Stan, their first deployment overseas to frontline action with the Lancashire Fusiliers, their enthusiasm slowly eroded by the realisation that there was to be no early victory. It ends with his journey home to Alice.

On the whole, there are few mentions of the actual horrors that Alfred must have witnessed. His custom was to note that so-and-so 'was killed today, by an exploding shell.' By their very nature, the ambiguity of these accounts allows the imagination to conjure up all sorts of horrific scenes, if you are that way inclined. Their almost casual observations suggest a soul who has become de-sensitized to the continuous carnage that he has found himself a part of. Occasionally, however, a particular harrowing picture slips through. Especially in relevance to the tale that I am about to relate.

These extracts serve to tell the story of something that happened to Alfred whilst he was on the frontline at Mons, on the Belgian border. It was something that troubled him greatly; his experience of a more personal kind of horror, encountered within the general horror of warfare.

Feb 9th 1916, Western front
Alfred looked up at the sun, climbing slowly in the clear, blue sky. The good weather was continuing, despite the time of year, and all had been calm for a few days now. You could almost forget why they were here. Almost.

Although Bosch had been silent, everyone was aware

that something was imminent, and were preparing themselves in their own particular way for when the time came. For his part, Alfred was content to sit among the lads, listening to the varying conversations dispersed in clouds of cigarette smoke, driven by the slight waves of closely guarded poker hands. He could almost imagine he was sat in the tap room of the Queen Anne back home in Middleton. In fact, there *were* some Middleton lads among their cabal of comrades, complemented by a handful of others.

It was like any situation you found yourself in: put a group of men together and certain individuals gravitate towards each other, creating cliques and friendships among people of similar character and attitude.

The front was no different. He was in a group of eight who spent much of their time together, six of whom were present now. There were the three Middleton lads, between whom was often speculation of what was going on back home, conjuring familiarities that further served to cement their bond. One of these was Tommy Sullivan, whose father was good friends with Alfred's, and of course there was Stan, Alfred's lifelong friend. The rest were from various north west towns. All in all a decent bunch of lads, although there was one who Alfred was not sure what to make of.

His name was Joe Bailey, of Ashton, though he answered to just Bailey. There was something about him that Alfred could not put his finger on. He didn't appear shy by any stretch of the imagination, but sometimes he would come over as being distant. Often he would listen to the conversation without offering much, detached from the usual banter. Sometimes he would look away, but could be seen watching whoever was speaking out of the corner of his eye, in an almost sly fashion.

He was doing it now, as Tommy held court. His sole contribution to the conversation was an imperceptible shrug, then a slight nod of the head. Present, but on the periphery.

As though sensing he was being observed, Bailey turned and met Alfred's eyes, raising his eyebrows slightly in an unreadable gesture, before turning away.

Perhaps I'm doing him an injustice, Alfred thought. He could be nervous about the impending action. War affects people in different ways, and we all cope however we can until our bit is done and we can return home.

Although the majority out here were buoyed by the resolute friendships they made, there were some, who, having learnt by experience, limited their attachments to withstand the blow of the losses that inevitably occurred.

Alfred walked over, taking his place among their casual, gambling assembly.

Feb 11th 1916

Captain Morris, salt and pepper haired, slight of frame and older than he looked, finished briefing the men who were gathered around him. He had told them that they were to go over the top the following morning, in a quite pleasant way, as though he was proposing a Sunday park outing or something. The men accepted it positively. Many of them had already seen action and were beginning to tire of sitting around, waiting for something to happen.

Alfred could see the excitement on the faces of some of the new boys, eager to get their first glimpse of Bosch. Hopefully they would survive long enough for the novelty to wear off.

As the Captain finished informing the men of tomorrow's plans, Alfred's attention was drawn to Bailey. He was regarding the officer with curiosity, an *intensity,* that was not normally his manner. When Morris finished speaking, Bailey held his hand aloft.

"Sir, may I examine those field glasses that you carry?"

Morris studied him briefly, then handed them over. Bailey turned them over in his hands, testing their weight, then suddenly jumped up onto the stepping post, peering over the top of the trench towards the enemy position, field glasses raised to his eyes.

"Bailey!" Alfred shouted, "get down!" But Bailey ignored both his and all other exhortations to get back below the trench top as he was likely to get a sniper's bullet through his head.

"PRIVATE! GET DOWN AT ONCE!" barked Morris, his bellow belying his fragile appearance. Bailey got back down, slowly, handing the glasses back over with a petulant look.

Stan's eyes sought out Alfred's, discreetly tapping his temple, echoing his own growing suspicions. Only the mad or the suicidal would raise their head above the trench in broad daylight to offer the Germans a little target practice.

The men disbanded as Bailey received a dressing down.

Feb 12th 1916

Alfred passed a weary hand over his face. He had spent some time writing in his diary last night, by torchlight, wishing for home and all its comforts, mindful as ever that the words he was writing could very well be his last. Sleep had been difficult to acquire, and his nervousness heightened when the first pale streaks of dawn began to lighten the sky.

He looked along the line of waiting men. They would all be feeling the same. In some of them it showed—a few were trembling, a couple of them skittish. Others were louder in their banter and bravado. But it was all bluster.

There was a freshness about the morning, now fully light. The time was drawing near.

"Well," one of the Middleton lads said, breaking his silence to bolster his own spirits, "this is what we joined up for."

"Is it?" Stan asked lightly, not looking up from the rifle he was checking over for the final time.

"Well I did," the boy replied. "What did you join up for?"

"Why, for King and Country, of course!" Stan smiled.

"I joined up to give myself a little holiday," Tommy Sullivan claimed, "and to teach old Kaiser a lesson before going home for my Christmas dinner."

"Which Christmas would that be, then?" Alfred asked.

The ensuing laughter was broken by the soft measured voice of Bailey: "I'm here to see how men go about killing each other in this age."

With such an unknown quantity as Bailey, often given to silence as he was, it could be difficult to recognise his humour for what it was—dry and understated. Alfred saw Stan regarding him, (not for the first time), a little quizzically, but suddenly the whistle sounded, a cry of "Right men!" immediately after from Captain Morris, and over the top they all scrambled, bayonets already fixed.

For the first twenty yards or so their advance was unchecked, the morning calm unbroken save for the tread of the men and birdsong, but then the Germans opened up, spraying them with machine gun fire. Alfred fixed his gaze on the horizon, pushing himself on in a determinedly straight line, repeating an inner mantra of *keep going, keep going*. The gunfire became heavier as the enemy rallied to their sudden assault, men falling all around him in terrible swathes. He stepped over prostrate men, some still moving, as though they were nothing but annoying obstacles in his way. All the time bullets came close, buzzing past his ear like angry wasps. He expected to catch one at any second as sudden, sharp cries of pain punctured the air.

Keep going, keep going.

He continued into the storm, a constant hail of iron. There were roars and whistles, but no spoken words. It was almost as if he was alone on the battlefield, the men to his left and right moving shadows to which he refused to look, keeping his attention fixed resolutely ahead.

There was no fear—just a focused determination to keep moving on. Fear always came before, and sometimes after, but never during the action itself.

On and on he went, at one point close to stumbling on loose ground, dimly aware of figures falling on his periphery. Suddenly he saw it—the promontory that was their objective. He picked up his pace as he moved over the rough terrain, stooping as he ran, trying to make himself smaller, eight yards, six yards, four, then he was there. He dived down amongst the others who had made it before him, spread out along the ridge. Face to the ground, he held onto his helmet as soil was showered onto him from a shell exploding close to the rear. He felt someone fall against him and looked up to see Sergeant Stevens holding onto his rifle tightly, grimacing.

"What now, Sarge?"

"You know the drill—achieve the objective, dig in and await orders," Stevens panted.

They stayed like that for some time, lay low, dirtied and tense, other men joining them in scattered arrivals.

Eventually the gunfire ceased as the advance finished. There were no clear targets left for the Germans to aim at. Men were either covered at the promontory, or lay dead and dying before it, caught in the enemy crossfire from either side of the ridge. The order came to hold the position while supply lines reached them, when they would be digging in. They would be going no further this day. Many men had been lost, for a gain of two hundred yards. Alfred offered a silent prayer of thanks for his own safe deliverance.

Later, when the troops had organised themselves again, he learned that his original gang of eight had been halved. There was only Stan, Bailey, a bloke named Harry Chapman and himself left. Rob Morley, lucky bugger, had got himself a cushty and was to be sent home. Lee Johnson, Johnny Bowers and Tommy Sullivan never made it. The news about Tommy upset Alfred in particular. There was to be no Christmas dinner for him after all. Alfred made it his resolve to write to his own father, asking him to tell Tommy's father how brave his son had been to the last, and how his death was sudden and without suffering. Alfred had no way of knowing this, but hoped it would bring the old man some small comfort.

In the evening, as the shadows lengthened and the men gathered in the newly dug tunnel, the Chaplain led them in prayers for the souls of everybody lost that day. Alfred also prayed silently for a swift end to the war, for all their sakes. The darkness spread and bled into their souls.

After the Chaplain's final benediction, the men began to quietly break up. Alfred noticed the clergyman, unmoving, fixedly regarding Bailey, who was some distance away.

"Is everything okay, Father?" Alfred asked him.

He turned, what little light remained reflecting off his rimmed spectacles. "What? Oh, yes, it's just that that man over there seems familiar to me. I think I've seen him before, on the French coast."

"The coast?"

"Yes, he was speaking to a German officer who was grouped with a number of enemy prisoners being shipped to England. It was the officer who drew my attention, wearing a patch over one eye. They appeared to be in deep conversation. I remember wondering if the German could speak English, or if the Englishman could speak German."

"When was this?"

He thought for a moment. "It would have been over a year ago, late 1914 I expect."

"It couldn't have been him, Father," Alfred explained. "Our battalion wasn't in France at that time, we were still in billets in England."

The clergyman glanced over towards Bailey again. "Ah, I expect you're right, then." At that moment Bailey turned towards the two men, and the Chaplain, like one caught gossiping, moved hurriedly and deliberately away.

Bailey watched him go.

Feb 13th 1916

Alfred cupped the mug of steaming coffee, watching the February skies darken. He had written the letter to his father earlier, informing him of Tommy's death. Seeing the cold facts laid out in black ink had lowered his spirits even further. Back home Tommy's family would be going through their everyday routines, completely unaware of their loss. Until Alfred's own father knocked at their door, charged by his son with an unenviable duty.

He was shaken from his morose thoughts by Bailey sinking down in front of him with a lethargy that he himself was feeling. Alfred nodded a greeting, his eyes straying to a pair of field glasses that hung loosely from Bailey's neck.

"I came across these on the battlefield yesterday," Bailey said, noticing his observation. He ran a hand over his head, making a show of catching lice from his scalp, turning them over in his fingers before his studious gaze, then crushing them.

Alfred watched as Bailey then put his thumb and forefinger to his mouth, giving the revolting impression that he was actually eating them. It was all for Alfred's benefit, of course. Just another example of his unusual humour.

They all suffered from lice out here, which was why they kept their heads closely shaved. All except Stan, of course. When they were at school together, he had always had collar length hair. Blonde, almost white, it would spike up on top in its own natural way, impervious to a comb. He'd always taken a lot of ribbing for it. It was still spiked on top, (only a little shorter), but now shaved short at the back and sides. He somehow got away with it, hidden most of the time as it was beneath his helmet.

Bailey leaned his head back against the trench wall, closing his eyes. Alfred looked at the field glasses again, wondering if they could have belonged to Captain Morris. It was possible. The casualty rate among officers was particularly high because they led from the front, which earned the respect of all of the men. Maybe

Morris had dropped them as he went to his death.

Alfred placed the mug down on the mud beside him and rubbed both eyes. He was having queer thoughts that he was quick to dismiss, worrying about the effect that the terrible days were having on him. The grim reality was enough to deal with, without anything extra from his dark imagination.

Bailey appeared to sleep. Alfred gave in to his own fatigue.

Feb 26th 1916

John Matthews was a giant of a man who had been in the battalion from the outset. The men sat around him, huddled against the chill afternoon, as he played his flute. Alfred always found it amusing to witness this great bear of a man teasing out each fragile note from his instrument as it was dwarfed in his huge hands.

Out here they hardly heard any music. The men would sing to lift their spirits when morale was flagging, or there was a hard day's march ahead of them.

They all sat in his shadow, marvelling at his dexterity. The music stilled all conversation with an almost magical effect. Even Bailey, for all his unusual manner, sat rapt at Matthews' performance. The tune was familiar to Alfred, though he couldn't think of its title. He wouldn't ask anybody, either, for fear of breaking the moment. He lay with his eyes closed, the faces of Alice and the children coming before him.

Mar 3rd 1916

The night was dark and oppressive. Alfred had sought escape in his diary in an attempt to avoid conversation. In truth, hardly any of the men were talkative. They sat together, yet apart, in muted lassitude.

They had been in the thick of the action that afternoon. The plan had been to add to their recent advances and capture the enemy trenches. It sounded simple. The artillery was to pound the German positions for five days, then, after this constant barrage, there would be no infantry left alive or intact enough to organise much of a defence.

Shell after shell had rained down on Bosch's lines. Alfred had felt the ground beneath his feet trembling as if groaning aloud at the horror that they were inflicting upon their enemy. It was terrible and relentless. Two days in Stan had muttered "Poor sods." But there had also been, God forgive them, a feeling of 'rather them than us.'

What had been for Alfred an angry rumbling, must have been a howling crescendo to them. With nowhere to go, their minds must have crumbled faster than their resolve.

When the bombing finally stopped, over they went, for once with little anxiety. They were not in any hurry. They strolled. They *ambled*. Alfred even spotted someone kicking a football as he went.

How naive they had been.

Bosch must have been dug in deep— real deep, buried within the bowels of the earth. Crazed and cowering but alive, the cessation of the shelling was a signal of intent. They emerged as the British line got close, ready and firing.

Wave after wave of men were cut down, falling on top of each other in twitching heaps. It was suicide. But the commanding officers were slow to realise. Those men who got anywhere near the enemy trenches were thwarted by thick coils of deadly barbed wire which was supposed to have been destroyed by the bombing. Men became entangled in this, fixed on the sharp points until bullets picked them off. They remained standing as they died.

Eventually the order had come to fall back once it was clear that the attack was foundering on this steel defensive line. The 'Big Push' had become the 'Big Slaughter.' Many men died on the way back, facing their own lines.

This day had cost them hundreds, if not thousands, of lives. It was up to the Generals to count the cost over their evening sherry.

Bailey hadn't made it back. For all the conflicting emotions the man had caused him, Alfred mourned. He had seen sights today he would never forget.

Alfred stopped his pen. For the first time he detected a tremor in his writing. He cast aside his diary, fearfully, his eyes resting on Stan's stricken face. Neither of them unable to break the silence.

Mar 18th 1916

Everything ground to a halt. They had endured two weeks of relentless rain, and the ground was a quagmire. The fifteen-pounders had sunk deep into the mud. Even the horses were becoming stuck fast. They were all quite miserable.

"Sir!" a young voice called out behind him. "Mr Cartwright!"

Alfred turned, finding a small, pathetic figure attempting to raise his right leg out of the sucking mud in an attempt to approach him.

"I thought it was you, sir," the man said, waving his arms comically in a desperate attempt to stop himself overbalancing.

Sir? Surely the soldier wasn't addressing him, an obvious private as he was.

"Are you talking to me?" Alfred asked.

Slightly unsure of himself, and still wavering clumsily, the lad whipped his helmet off. "It is me sir— Pete Foden."

Recognition suddenly dawned. Peter Foden! An old pupil of Alfred's. Ignoring the chuckles from the men behind him:

"Peter Foden, I'll be damned! What are you doing here?"

Foden glanced beyond him at the others, then said, "Well, there is a war on."

At this the others burst into laughter.

"Fancy that, Harry," Stan exclaimed, his elbow resting on Chapman's shoulder, "there is a war on, he says. It's a good job we're here then, isn't it?"

"Did you know there was a war on, Alfred?" asked Harry.

"Now, now Harry, you heard how the kid addressed him. It's *Sir*. All this time we were thinking our friend was one of the lower, expendable ranks like us, but it seems that we have an Officer among us."

Alfred gave a condescending smile as he explained. "Foden here was a pupil at the Grammar School where I taught."

"Right you, are, Major Cartwright."

He knew the moniker would stick, such was the manner of men. Poor Peter Foden didn't know whether it was his old teacher or he himself who was the target of the two soldiers' jests. He carefully made his way over, and Alfred shook him by the hand warmly, highlighting the change in their relationship.

The encounter with his former pupil had lightened the mood a little, but in reality it had shaken Alfred somewhat. Foden was but still a boy, like so many others out here. Too young to be involved in all this madness.

Mar 20th 1916

"Alfred!" He turned to find Stan approaching him, a little urgency in his voice. No 'Major' this time.

"You're back then," Alfred noted as he continued searching his pockets for his Black Cat cigarettes.

Stan had been picked to go on a recce the previous night under cover of darkness with nine other men, much to his dismay.

"Bailey is alive."

Alfred's hands immediately stilled. "Alive? Where?"

"We came across him last night. We were making our way as best we could, slowed down by the deep mud and heavy rain . . ."

"I did spare a thought for you when it was coming down," Alfred smiled.

"Yeah . . . well, we came across a foxhole, in the middle of no-man's land. The base was all flooded, and there were four bodies scattered around the sloping walls. As we slipped into it, one of the bodies moved. It was Bailey, very much alive."

"How is he?"

"He's unharmed. Says he has been holed up there since the failed offensive of the 3rd of March. With this weather he hadn't run out of drinking water."

"Why didn't he return under cover of night?"

"He said one of the other men had still been alive until that evening, wounded, and he wouldn't leave him. Also he had heard some Germans moving around out there."

"Who was he with?"

Stan turned grim. "Hard to say. The other three were mutilated, and they looked a little . . . chewed up. Their faces . . ."

"Rats," stated Alfred. They had seen it before. The one animal to thrive out here, with the steady supply of dead. Stan said nothing.

"How was he?"

He shrugged. "Hard to tell. *Physically* he seemed alright."

There was obviously more. "What?"

"He did this thing, when he was talking. With his eyes."

"What kind of thing?"

"He kind of blinked a few times, and each time they changed colour."

"His eyes?"

"Yeah . . . green, brown, and a kind of indigo."

They regarded each other silently for a few moments. Alfred could see that Stan was disturbed, and it was only their long friendship that was allowing him to tell Alfred this. He had clearly been unnerved by what he had found. Some of the things you saw could play on your mind. Certain superstitions ran through the ranks. He had heard on more than one occasion a man claiming to have seen the ghost of a dead comrade. Or a soldier of previous sound mind predicting his own death. Stan had been spooked out there in the darkness, of that there was no doubt. There couldn't have been much light for him to have been able to see Bailey's eyes clearly. Maybe there had been flares, reflecting in them.

Stan took his rifle off his shoulder, leaning it against the trench wall, producing cigarettes of his own with his other hand. He offered one to Alfred. Stan drew deeply as they found a spot to sit.

"So," Alfred said aloud wistfully, "Bailey's alive."

They sat smoking, both of them lost in their thoughts. Alfred wondered how Bailey had somehow survived two and a half weeks out there. He must have more story to tell. Alfred resolved to ask him.

Mar 21st 1916

Alfred, Stan and Harry sought Bailey out. The three had decided they should check on him after his ordeal. Although none felt particularly close to him, he was the only other member of their original gang left alive. Their camaraderie was the only thing that got them through the days.

It was warm; the rain had stopped. They found Bailey sat alone, clutching a cup of something that was definitely not coffee. A few other men sat apart from him, sending frequent glances his way. As they approached him he raised his face, and any questions Alfred had died in his throat.

Bailey's face was covered by several weeks growth of hair. But his eyes . . . his eyes! Sometimes Alfred had felt a little uncomfortable beneath his silent gaze, but now there was a wildness there, barely tempered by the measured look he gave the three of them as his eyes flicked from one to the other. Alfred froze, held by that stare, unable to speak while Bailey was unresponsive to Stan and Harry's attempts to engage him. He just gave that odd nod of his head, his stare never leaving them.

He looks crazy, Alfred thought. Perhaps he's suffering from shell shock.

Then he saw the rifle.

It was propped against the trench wall beside him. It took a few, muted moments for Alfred to fully register just what it was that he was looking at.

Attached to the rifle strap, by means of thin wire, were four fingers. Four fat, discoloured fingers, congealed blood gathered at the edges of the dirty nails. They hung there, taut and grotesque. Bailey must have seen the look of horror on Alfred's face, for he shrugged, and muttered, "Souvenirs."

He gave a broad smile. It was probably the first time

that he had ever seen Bailey smile. It terrified him.

There was a few seconds of shocked silence, and then he said to Stan: "Next time I'm going to get me a scalp," and gave him that awful grin.

They regarded each other for a few minutes, the three of them standing, he sitting. The silence grew uncomfortable. Eventually, it was Bailey who spoke. "You think I'm mad."

It was a statement, not a question. Stan and Harry deferred to Alfred, unwilling to speak.

"Bailey . . ." he began, but Bailey cut in:

"Who wouldn't be mad? Bound for all that time?"

Bound? Stan had said nothing about him being tied up out there. He tried again. "Bailey, we just . . ."

"Call me Loki," he cut in. "There's no longer any need for pretence. Your own little Ragnarok is coming." Grinning still.

After another uncomfortable minute, they left, abandoning all attempts to enter into dialogue with him. None could muster a single word of farewell. Alfred could feel Bailey's eyes on his back.

He was obviously disturbed. Spending all that time out there, with just a couple of corpses and a slowly dying man for company had taken its toll on him. Alfred had seen it before—men reduced to rambling wrecks under the strain of constant shelling and the daily prospect of death. He thought of the tremor in his writing some weeks before—was that how it started?

Bailey was not like those, though, who had no control over their trembling limbs. He appeared almost serene. But that calm, understated madness in his eyes, and, my God, those fingers!

"We should speak to the C.O," Harry suggested softly. Stan flicked his eyes towards Alfred, looking uncomfortable. He understood the troubled look.

Despite everything, they were sharing an uneasy sense of disloyalty. This gang of theirs, what was left of it, had been through so much together, and owed each other everything.

"Let's sleep on it," said Alfred. "We'll check on him again in the morning and then reach a decision." Harry nodded. Stan spat in agreement.

That evening Alfred sat hunched in the dark, unable to sleep. Something had been nagging at him for a while, yet whenever he tried to focus on it, the object of his discomfort fled. Sleep proving futile, he began to think again, inevitably, of Bailey. Thinking about how long he had known him, how *little* he had known him, going back over their last few months together.

And then it came to him, a revelation in images.

He saw Bailey holding Captain Morris' field glasses, testing their weight. His sullen look when ordered to hand them back. The other field glasses that he said he had found on the battlefield the day that Morris was killed. The grim look on Stan's face as he spoke of the corpse-strewn hole he had found Bailey in. Alfred's wonder at how he had survived. The image of chewed bodies. And then he saw another scene, more tranquil, contrasting greatly with the last: Bailey sat enraptured by big John Matthews' flute, as they were all assembled together as his audience.

And something cold began to stir in Alfred's guts, becoming more and more intense as those images played out repeatedly in his mind's eye.

He jumped to his feet, disturbing the man sleeping beside him, and began to move down the trench, hoping to find amongst the huddled line someone who could placate his desperate need to be wrong.

The heavens opened again as he asked everybody he met the same question: "I haven't seen John Matthews for a while, do you know where he is?"

This went on for a while until a man Alfred didn't know answered: "He's probably dead. He didn't come back from the push on March 3rd."

Alfred slumped to his knees, feeling as though he had been physically punched in the stomach. The soldier stood looking down on him, maybe considering it the shocked reaction to the fate of a friend. But Alfred's mind was reeling beneath the impact of thoughts he had long been holding at bay for being too terrible to contemplate. Thoughts that were now taking root and driving him over the edge.

He had believed, back then, that Bailey had been spellbound by the playing of John's flute, like they all had. But maybe it wasn't the instrument itself that had been the source of his fascination. Alfred saw him, then, watching John playing with those beguilingly huge hands. And then he saw those four swollen fingers, dangling as trophies from Bailey's rifle strap.

He was struck by a sudden wave of nausea, retching into the deep mud, still seeing the field glasses; the fingers; Morris and Matthews. Then he heard again Bailey's voice : "Next time, I'm going to get me a scalp." And he had looked directly at Stan as he said it. Stan with that distinctive, white mane of his.

He scrambled quickly to his feet, wiping his mouth with the back of his hand, heading off to find Stan and Harry to tell them of this horror, though aware he had no proof of anything.

He hurried back along the sheltering line, preoccupied with his terrible revelation, when suddenly there was an enormous bang, accompanied by a bright flash, and for some lost moments a debilitating vacuum of neither word nor thought. He was not aware of being thrown, but as his senses slowly opened again he found himself sat on the ground, dazed. The night sky was alight above him; nothing but a buzzing sound in his ears. He looked around and saw a scattering of body parts, and did a slow check of his own limbs, unable to understand how the shell had spared him. Confused, still sitting, he saw men scrambling over each other to climb up and fire their rifles over the trench at an enemy who must be attacking their line.

Still dazed, but feeling the urgency that had compelled him before the explosion, he got to his feet and began to move through his desperate comrades, looking for Stan in the confused melee. He was deafened to the chaos, but shouted out his friend's name as he went. Flashes from explosions he couldn't hear fragmented the sky, the earth trembling beneath his feet. Then, under one such bright flash, he saw Stan about twenty yards ahead, firing his weapon over the trench wall at what must have been approaching Germans. And then he saw Bailey, three-men down the firing line. Except he wasn't looking over the top, he was looking sideways at Stan, his head cocked curiously. Then he turned to Alfred, as though he could somehow sense his approach, their eyes meeting over the arena of combat. Bailey smiled. In that instant, Alfred knew it was all true.

But suddenly Alfred was knocked sprawling in the mud, losing eye contact as a mortally wounded man fell on top of him. There was blood, he could taste it in his mouth. His? The dying soldier's? Blood mingling with the heavy rain. Alfred tried to roll the man off, his weight pinning him down in the sludge.

'Dead weight' passed through his mind. He struggled to shift him, feet sliding in the clay. He grasped a handful of tunic at the man's shoulder, his other hand gripping his belt, arching his back to heave him off, when, in the midst of these efforts, he became aware of a shroud beginning to envelop them both, a thickening cloud that he thought was smoke until, even in the dark of night, it began to take on a yellow tinge.

GAS! his mind screamed. GAS! The thing he feared above all else.

At first he froze, whether from the immediate effect of the gas or from sheer terror he didn't know, but then he fought to be free of the body pinning him to the earth. He kicked desperately, trying to gain some leverage, holding his breath so not to inhale the noxious fumes, but he felt his throat already beginning to burn, his vision blurring. Yet, even as everything began to swim out of focus, he tried to make out, in the shadows, the familiar figure of his friend. But he couldn't see Stan. Everything was confused and disordered in the muted madness.

Finally he managed to rid himself of his millstone, and tried to rise, spluttering and clawing at his throat. He was swaying on his knees, unable to stand, feeling tears stream down his cheeks. A face came before him, then, a face serene and untouched by this hell. Comforting him in his final moments: Alice.

I'm sorry, Alice. I'm sorry.

This final thought petered out, along with his wife's face, as everything faded black, the sensation of the rain on his face dimming, seeping away down a long, dark tunnel as he slowly slipped away. Like a swimmer sinking further from the surface, he surrendered. The last thing he felt was an arm around his waist, a shoulder beneath his arm, then nothing more.

March 31st 1916
Alfred lay helpless, his bandaged right eye itching

irritably. He lifted a hand to relieve it and was immediately struck by a spasm, his sharp intake of breath causing his body to be racked by a series of painful coughs. He gazed up with his free eye at the canvas roof above him, breathing through gritted teeth.

He was in the 35th Casualty Clearing Station. He was aware of that now. At first, as he drifted in and out of consciousness, he would awaken with a jolt of pain as his sharpening senses caused him to start with panic at his unfamiliar surroundings. But eventually, after several such awakenings, he became aware enough to understand what he was being told.

He was to be sent back to Blighty. The RAMC staff had been good to him, but they were run off their feet. There was only so much they could do. There were many casualties. Men cried out all through the night. Flies were everywhere.

As soon as he was able, he endeavoured to discover the whereabouts of Stan, Harry and Bailey, passing enquiries through a stretcher-bearer and a doctor. It was not long before he got a response: Harry had been attached to a different battalion, but both Stan and Bailey hadn't made it.

Stan, his constant companion from childhood, was dead. They had enrolled together in a shared desire for adventure, wishing to experience the world away from their poor, industrial town. Well now he had seen just what man could do to that world. They had scourged it and soaked it in blood. It was inconceivable that he would never see his friend again.

And Bailey: he was missing, presumed killed. Just what to make of him? Alfred had always thought he was different, even before the insanity that engulfed him at the end. Maybe there had always been something, and the war had merely accentuated it, hastened his deterioration. Turned him into the Bailey who named himself Loki. Loki who collected grisly souvenirs on the battlefield. Loki the murderer.

There: he had said it.

Though it gave him no peace, Alfred could not help but wonder at their end. He was convinced that it had been Bailey's intention to kill Stan. Had he himself been killed by a German before he could carry out his task? Had Stan killed him in self-defence?

Alfred feared even greater the truth about Stan's death.

He went over and over it: Stan and Bailey. Bailey and Stan. Over and over, before the madness and his fever slipped him into a state of delirium, and the buzzing once again sounded in his ears, the yellow cloud surrounded him like a fog, and emerging through it all was the face of Bailey; the face of Loki, his eyes changing colour: green; brown; indigo.

Although the diary goes on to detail Alfred's return to England, this is where the story that I have related ends. At least insofar as it involves my grandfather. I shall keep his original diary with this account.

I often think of what my grandmother said about him, on his return home. How he was altered. How his sleep was often disturbed by nightmares. I think that, of all the terrible things he must have witnessed during the war, he was haunted the most by the one thing he did not see. The one thing he could never know.

Sapling

Grows a small, young ash
In the neighbour yard

I daydream of you
Come here to see me
Watching over me
As you walk the Ash

Green spearheads throw shadows
It dreams of its mighty cousin

In a raven's feathers
Calling a mimic's song
Walking the tree's limbs
O lovely Skytreader.

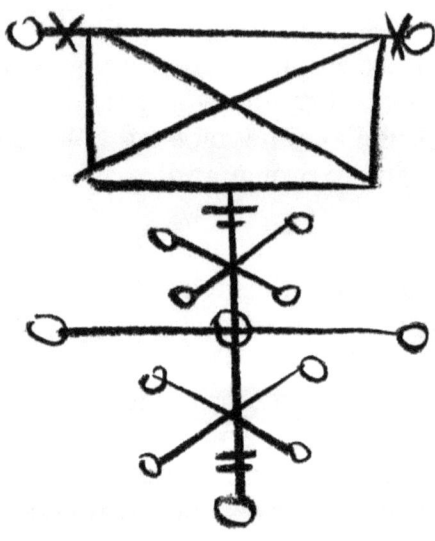

How 'Bout Them Apples

"This pie is the most."

She'd heard it before. A group of kids had wandered into her diner.

"Seriously, you have to try this. It's unreal."

A few more kids walked past the diner and were waved in by their friends.

"What's buzzin', cuzzin'?"

"Nothing. Just hanging."

She blocked out the conversation. She liked this decade just fine, but the vocabulary got on her nerves. It changed with every generation and she'd been around to witness it for longer than anyone suspected.

The bell on the door jangled and she turned, expecting to see more kids. Instead a large man in a trench coat came in, his hat pulled low over his eye patch. Glancing around the diner, he scowled when he saw the kids and made a motion with his finger. Suddenly the kids looked up, one by one, fear and confusion on their faces. The puzzled looks remained as they collected their things and silently filed out of the diner, altering their path to avoid the one-eyed stranger. One brave girl looked back at him and he rewarded her by raising the eye patch and revealing what lay beneath. With a yelp the girl ran from the diner.

"Why do you do that?"

"It amuses me."

"People will be asking me about it for days."

He shrugged. "Tell them what you will."

She sighed. "Pie?"

The raised eyebrow was reply enough. She served the pie. "You could have left them alone."

Odin removed his hat, allowing his tied grey hair to

fall onto his back. He took a large mouthful of pie and leaned back from the counter, fork in hand, eye closed. When he opened them again she could see the fire in his good eye was brighter.

"What do you call yourself these days?"

"Ida."

"You look good as a human."

Ida frowned at the All Father. "You owe your immortality to me and my apples yet you see fit to insult me?"

Odin rolled his eye and the dust eddies outside the diner grew momentarily worse before calming again.

"How are the others?" she asked.

"I don't see them. I think you see them more."

Idun nodded. The gods all came to her sooner or later, those who wished to go on. "Loki is long overdue."

Odin nodded, crumbs from the pie falling from his beard. "He's been having fun with the humans. Got involved in chemical research during their last war. Evidently found he enjoyed it." Odin finished his pie. "No mead to wash it down?"

"In Brooklyn? What do you think."

"Shame." The All Father put his hat on and stood. "Loki will come. In the meantime you should be grateful for the peace."

And with a nod he was gone. As the bell on the door broadcast his departure, Idun began to clear the dishes and wipe down the white Formica countertop. Odin was right. She should be grateful for the peace, for the lack of attention. For the fact that she and her operation were not seen as anything other than a middle-aged woman running a diner. The fact that she served the Aesir was nobody's business but her own.

Shoulda coulda woulda.

"Excuse me ma'am." Idun hadn't even heard anyone come in.

"Yes sir, can I help you?"

"Just a coffee please." He took off his coat and laid it on the stool beside him, but not before removing a small spiral notebook from an inside pocket.

Idun watched him from the corner of her eye as she made fresh coffee. Young with dirty brown hair and in need of a shave, the whiff of cigar smoke hung on his clothes. And a determined look in his eye. Definitely not local. "Can I get you anything else?" She placed the mug on the counter and slid it toward the stranger.

"No. Well, maybe." He flipped open the notebook. "Do you know a woman called Agnes Jones? Lives around the corner?" He pointed over his shoulder.

"Yes, she's a customer. Why?"

"Then you don't know?"

"Know what? Who are you?" She didn't like strangers, or their questions.

"My name is Frank Wilson. I work for the Brooklyn Gazette."

"Doing what?"

The stranger hesitated. "Okay, I cover the obits. But I'm hoping to move to full on reporting, crimes, drugs, you know."

'Quite the move' she thought. "And what does this have to do with Agnes?" She suspected that she already knew the answer.

He reached across the counter and took her hand, patting it. His hand felt like raw octopus. "I'm sorry to be the one to tell you this but Agnes is dead. She passed away last week."

Idun grabbed her hand back. She didn't generally like humans but every so often one would come along whom she could tolerate, even grow fond of. Agnes was one of these. "That's very sad. She was a lovely lady, one of my most loyal customers." She hoped that was enough to end the conversation.

"How well did you know her?"

Idun sighed, then recovered. "Not very well. Older woman, well-travelled." She held up her hands and shrugged. 'What else do you want?' the movement said.

"Did she ever talk to you about her childhood? Younger years?"

"No." What was he getting at? The man's manner made her uneasy. "She may have mentioned a son?"

He nodded. "Yes, he died when he was young."

'Ahh."

Both sat in uncomfortable silence. Frank swallowed a mouthful of coffee. "Did you know she was 130 years old when she died?"

"What?"

He nodded and took another gulp. "It's true. When I was writing her up for the paper I looked for her birth certificate." He finished then stared right at Idun. "She was born in 1825."

"I don't believe it. And I don't appreciate you coming here with your crazy stories about someone I know." She took off her apron and came out from behind the counter. "You should go."

He spoke as he gathered his coat. "Oh, it can't be true, it's not possible. Must be some mistake." He shrugged his arms into the sleeves and turned to her as he approached the door. "But I may just stay a few days, confirm the mistake. Like a good reporter would do." He winked at her and she turned in disgust, not hearing the doorbell as he exited.

"It's happening again," she said into the Bakelite mouthpiece.

"Are you sure?"

Idun thought for a moment, watching the neighbourhood residents walk by the diner. It was Sunday and everyone wore their best clothes: men in pressed suits, mothers in dresses trying to keep their children clean, if only until the local holy man witnessed their temporary pristine state. "Maybe. I'm not sure." She sighed. "Something about him bothered me."

"You're over-reacting."

"Perhaps." Freya was right, she may have been overly sensitive. Still, she felt the caution was justified. It was need. Even Freya was careful. She was going by the name Frieda, these days. "I'll talk to you later." She hung up the phone, straightening the receiver. The timer in the kitchen buzzed. She tied on her apron and went to take the pies out of the oven, a frown wrinkling her otherwise ageless face.

"Tell me about your mother."

"She was a wonderful woman, generous to a fault."

Frank scribbled in his notebook, trying desperately to master the shorthand professional reporters used. "Mm-hmm, mm-hmm. And your father?"

Agnes' daughter lowered her head. "He died before I was born. My mother never spoke about him much."

So that avenue was closed. Why was this so difficult? She was an old, insignificant woman. "If you don't mind me asking, how did she die?" He already knew, but needed to get the daughter talking.

"She died in her sleep. She was old."

"How old?"

His abruptness occasioned a raised eyebrow but no comment. "I really don't know. In her 80s I think."

"You don't know how old your own mother was?"

"Mr Wilson, I don't like your tone."

He backed away. "I'm terribly sorry. It's a big city thing." He hoped that would suffice. At her nod he continued. "Your mother was 130 years old."

The daughter frowned. "You found her birth certificate? I thought that had been lost."

"The records office had a copy, had to dig around a bit." He took a folded piece of paper from the back of his notebook. "See."

"That's not right."

Frank noticed she had dismissed the idea without even glancing at the certificate. This was more difficult than he had hoped. "Tell me about her life in the neighbourhood."

The daughter shrugged. "She was just a normal woman, she helped people when she could. Went to church on Sunday, same as most folks around here."

"Have you lived here long?"

"All my life."

"It's a nice neighbourhood?"

"It's fine."

He looked around the small apartment. "No kids?"

"They're at school."

This wasn't getting him anywhere. "I guess you must go to the diner around the corner."

"Sometimes."

"I hear it's a decent place, would you recommend it?"

"Sure. The food is excellent, Ida is a lovely woman. She's been there since I was a kid..." The daughter stopped herself suddenly. "I really must get dinner ready, Mr Wilson. If there's nothing else?"

Frank was being dismissed and he knew it. He rose, gathered his coat and held out his hand. A look appeared on the daughter's face that he couldn't decipher, then the briefest of shakes before showing him the door.

Outside he gathered his thoughts. The air was getting colder and he pulled up his collar to block the wind. As he turned to leave, an old man exited the building.

"Excuse me sir, can I ask you how old you are?" There was no time to make friends.

"What? None of your business." He looked in his 80s but walked away with the fluid movement of a teenager as he strode away, muttering about kids today.

"You're back." Idun hadn't seen the reporter for a few days.

"I said I would be. And everyone speaks so highly of your place, how could I stay away."

"Oh?" Idun shrugged. "What can I get you?"

"Coffee please."

As she reached for a mug from the top shelf, the reporter continued his inane chatter.

"Nice weather for so late in the year."

"Yes."

"I hear we're likely to get snow next month."

"Indeed." She placed the drink in front of him.

"Sure. Bound to happen eventually, right? Life, right?"

She just looked at him. "Can I get you anything else?"

"Is there something going on?"

"What do you mean?"

Frank shook his head. "It's just, I can't find any evidence at all that Agnes Jones was NOT 130 years old when she passed."

Idun waved a hand, dismissing the comment. "Just because you can't find evidence of something doesn't mean it's not there." She stared at him directly for the first time this visit. "Perhaps you should consider another career. Investigative research maybe isn't your forte."

She left him in silence while she served another customer coffee and apple pie and dawdled as long as she could, wiping imaginary spots from the counter and straightening the glass salt and pepper shakers spaced every few feet along the length of the Formica. But she saw that the reporter had finished his drink.

"Refill?"

"Sure."

She poured again, hoping he was finished with the questions. It was not to be.

"Tough neighbourhood. How long have you been here?"

"A while."

"Why set up here?"

"Family business."

Frank looked around the diner, peering over the counter to the back kitchen. "Just you?"

Idun was once again getting frustrated by this man. She turned to brew more coffee, unnecessary as there were already two full pots available, and muttered about 'sons' and 'war'. She found any mention of the war, which was still so raw in people's minds, would immediately stop the conversation.

"So your parents ran this place before you?"

"Something like that."

He drank in silence, only speaking to compliment her on the coffee. Then "I've spoken to a few people, they all say the same thing, that you were here when they were kids. Youngsters, oldsters, everyone."

"I look a lot like my mother. They're mistaking me for her."

He nodded. "They all compliment your cooking, especially your apple pie. Any available?"

Idun always had pie ready. "I'm sorry, no. Just about to make a new batch." She grabbed a bowl and wooden mixing spoon from the storage shelf beneath the counter.

He smiled, an oddly lopsided grimace. "Maybe I'll come back later, everyone raves about that pie." The smile was accompanied by a chuckle. "Maybe I'll do a story about your pie."

She smiled politely at him and grabbed the spoon, her knuckles white.

"You must really have wanted that pie."

Frank Wilson was back in her diner the next day, making a nuisance of himself with his questions. So many questions from this human. "Well, I've heard so much about it."

Idun hmphed. "Coffee to go with it?"

"Please."

Frank looked around the diner, saw the few other patrons, older men and women who nonetheless looked healthy and happy. He looked more closely, hoping no one would see him staring. These people, having their animated conversations, were glowing with health.

The doorbell jangled and a tall smartly-dressed woman entered.

"Frieda! What are you doing here?" Idun walked over to her fellow Aesir and received a hug.

"You sounded upset on the phone the other day, thought I'd visit. And have some of that pie of course."

Idun's eyes widened but the slight nod of her head towards the reporter was a second too late. "Another fan of Ida's pie I see."

Frieda walked over to where Frank sat and claimed the stool next to him. "Who are you?"

He held out a hand. "I'm Frank Wilson. Friends call me Frankie."

Frieda stared at him, glancing up at Idun before continuing. "Why are interested in my conversation, *Mr* Wilson?"

He seemed to shrink in size. Looking around the diner again, this time in order to avoid her gaze, he saw the exact same thing as last time: older people laughing and eating pie.

"Mr Wilson, this is my--" Ida hesitated a moment-- "my cousin."

"Distant cousin," Freya added.

"So you DO have family." Both Idun and Freya wanted to wipe the smug expression from his face.

"I never said I didn't."

"And what do you do, Mr Wilson?" Freya was fascinated by humans, despite her general disdain for them.

He was about to reply when Idun interrupted. "He's a reporter. He's here to write about Agnes. You remember her, don't you?" She raised an eyebrow at Freya.

"Of course. That woman who used to come here. Nice lady."

"Liked the pie, apparently."

"Everyone likes Ida's food."

Frank looked around again. "I think 'like' is an understatement."

"Meaning what, exactly?" Freya's eyes bored into him. She had picked up the trick from Odin but she could never generate the fear he did, even with her two eyes against his one.

"Nothing. Nothing at all." He finished up. "It *is* very

good." He threw some cash on the counter. "I need to run, have a few more folks to speak to, then I'm done."

"You're making a lot of effort for one woman."

He turned to them, Freya still sitting on the stool, Idun now back behind the counter. "I like to be thorough" He winked again, leaving both women irritated.

"He's trouble."

"I told you that." Idun wiped the counter where Frank had been sitting mouth turned down as if she had tasted something bitter.

"He's too close."

"Yes. But wait a while. A few days. He might just give up and go away."

Freya shook her head. "I'm calling Loki."

"No. Leave it for a few days."

"But..."

"Leave it."

Idun went out back, to the alley behind the diner. Climbing over a box she carefully balanced a plate of pie and a thermos of coffee. Humming to herself, she scanned the alley until she found the person she was looking for, sitting in his cardboard box, surrounded by dirty blankets and non-matching spare shoes.

"Heimdall." She handed the food over.

The large figure grunted his acknowledgment and a dirty hand appeared from beneath a blanket to grab the plate. She had tried to get him to come inside, to help him find a place to live, but he didn't want any help. At all. This is where he needed to be right now.

She turned back towards the diner door but stopped halfway down the alley when she heard his throat clear. He hadn't spoken a word to her for months; it was best to listen when Heimdall spoke.

"Watch yourself."

"I will. You too."

He nodded and started in on the pie.

Idun watched him for a moment then went back to the diner. She locked the back door and returned to the front, doing a last check before shutting off the lights for the night. As she checked the equipment in the kitchen, she heard the faint jingle of bells..

Wiping her hands she went back out front and looked around. Everything was as she had left it moments ago. Except the small doorbell were swaying slightly; perhaps a breeze had moved it? Walking over to the door she looked out the window. Nothing. Then she saw the envelope, pushed through the bottom of the door. Picking it up she unlocked the front door and stepped outside, scanning the street. Again, nothing, the street was deserted. Blowing leaves swirled as the hot air from the diner hit the street in front of her. Trash was out for collection the following morning and the dim street lights illuminated the steam escaping from the subway vents.

She went back inside and locked the door, checking it twice, before sitting at the counter and opening the envelope. Idun recognised it as the kind they sold at the druggist up the road. With trembling fingers she tore open one end and shook the package. A single folded page fell out. She could see writing on it, the ink seeping through the page from the front to the back.

The words were there before her in thin spidery writing. "I know what's going on. How 'bout them apples?"

That was it. No threat. No request for money. No request for anything. But it was enough.

"Kill him."

"No."

"Why not? These humans kill each other all the time, what's one more? Especially this one."

"No." Louder now.

Loki slumped in his chair. They were all crammed into a corner booth in the empty diner. He looked over at Odin, his anger at being disagreed with misplaced. "Why is *he* here? I can deal with this."

Odin said nothing but stared Loki down.

"He has to go, this reporter." Freya pointed at the note in the centre of the table around which they sat. "He knows."

"Maybe not." Tyr was there with them.

"You've seen the words." Idun shoved the note towards the god of war. "He's been asking questions. Too many. Even spoke to the bums, until Heimdall growled at him and chased him away."

"He's still on the streets?"

Idun ignored the hate on Loki's face when Heimdall was mentioned. "His choice." With a wave of her hand the topic was over. "What do we do?"

"Kill him."

"NO!" This time they all spoke.

The diner was so silent the low hum of the freezer in the back, normally unnoticed, could be heard.

"Tell us again what happened."

"Let me in."

Frank Wilson hadn't been around for a few days and Idun had begun to hope he'd left, gone back to his own place. "I'm sorry sir, we're closed." She tried to close the door but the reporter slammed his foot down, blocking the door.

"Just one coffee." He smirked. "And some of that pie." She tried to close the door again, slamming it against his foot. "Wait! I just want to talk."

"As I said, we're closed." She stomped hard on his foot and closed the door, turning the lock quickly.

But he wasn't done. From outside in the covered doorway he yelled at her. "I know what's going on! I'll tell everyone! You can't keep it a secret! All of these people, living into their hundreds? Did you think no one would find out?"

She watched him, silent, her lips thin and white, wishing he would stop. He didn't. "You'll regret not talking to me! You'll regret the way you've treated me!" He waited for a reaction but when none was forthcoming he finally stormed off, swearing as he left.

"Humans are really living longer?"

"So it seems. The apples that keep us immortal apparently also prolong their lives." Idun nodded towards the outside.

"Well, that's it then. Even if he doesn't exactly know who we are, there's plenty enough to keep him snooping." Freya sighed.

The diner was silent again, the freezer still humming. "I have to leave."

All of their voices scrambled to be heard over the others, except the All Father, who remained quiet, watching. Loki's voice finally won.

"Please just let me kill him."

"What, and attract more attention when he goes missing?"

"Then at least let me scramble his little human brain, just a bit." He made a stirring motion with his index finger.

"Leave his mind alone." Idun sighed. "I've been at

this address through two of their world wars now, it's time to move on. Things are changing, so must I." She gestured to the jukebox, attempting to lighten the mood. "I even put that monstrosity in."

No one could come up with any arguments that Idun couldn't easily shoot down. "One last pie before the move?"

Heimdall leaned against the building across the street, watching the diner, head tilted slightly. Two men stood before it.

"It was here, I swear!" one said, his agitation obvious.

The other man looked sceptical. "Maybe we're on the wrong street."

"No, this is the street." Frank gazed into the dirty window of the obviously uninhabited building.

His companion looked at his watch. "It's getting late."

"I'm not crazy!" He grabbed a woman passing by. "You! Wasn't there a diner here last week?"

The old woman frowned and shook her head. "No. That place's been empty since before the war."

"No, that can't be."

"I've lived here all my life. It's true."

The reporter grabbed her shoulders. "All your life?" Frowning, then glancing at his companion he continued to address the woman. "How old are you?"

"Frank!"

"Now that's not a question a gentleman asks a lady." She paused. "But as it seems so important to you, I'll tell you."

Frank waited, holding his breath.

"I'm 78," she said.

He looked at her, the smoothness of her skin, the

sparkle in her eye. He let her go and muttered an apology.

"Can we go now?"

They started walking away when suddenly Frank turned back and shouted at the woman. "You're not fooling me! You're not 78! You're a lot older!" He advanced toward her as he spoke, the walk turning to a run.

The woman screamed and ran, faster and faster, outrunning him until he stopped following. Giving up on his pursuit, he bent down and grabbed a chunk of cement, a piece of the sidewalk that had come loose. With a heave he threw it at the diner window.

By now the old woman's screams had attracted attention and a beat cop, a large man with long blonde hair tied back with a leather cord beneath his cap approached, swinging his club like he was born with it in hand.

"He attacked me! Then he broke that window!" The woman pointed at Frank.

The policeman moved and a moment later had Frank's arms pinned behind his back. "You're under arrest." Frank heard the metallic snap of handcuffs and felt their pinch around his wrists. "Destruction of property, assault."

"But you don't understand!" He turned to face the cop and saw a familiar glint in the ancient eyes.

"Oh I understand. I've been walking this beat for more years than you can imagine. Always people like you around." He turned the man roughly. "Let's go sir, a car will meet us around the corner."

"You're in on it! And you!" He pointed to the old woman, still watching the proceedings with interest. "You're all in on it!"

"Let's go buddy. You're my last duty of the night.

Then I'm off to go for a nice long healthy run." The cop winked. "Keeps you young. And healthy eating. You know what they say, 'an apple a day'."

Frank was screaming when he was put into the rear of the police car. "Your friend will need professional care. He's had a breakdown, seen it before," said the cop.

"He's not a friend, just a colleague."

The cop nodded. "Well, good evening to you sir." His words could barely be heard over Frank, who was now laughing hysterically. "Can I drop you anywhere?"

"Sure, that'd be great. Train station."

Heimdall watched from across the street as the car drove away, wrapping a blanket more tightly around himself. It was time for him to go too. He followed the apples . . . They all did.

The Song of Spells II

A seventh I know: if a hall should burn,
flames flying high, so can I can save it.
I know how to sing that song.

An eighth I know: which all may sing
if they learn it well;
where hate grows in the warrior sons,
I can calm it with that song.

A ninth I know: when the storm will send
my vessel below the waves,
I can calm the wind and bring peace to the sea.

A tenth I know: when at night, and evil spirits
will fly in the air, such a spell I can weave
that they fly home, confused and bewildered.

An eleventh I know: When I lead men to war,
I sing over their shields, and they strive mightily
safe into strife, safe out of battle,
safe to return home.

A twelfth I know: when the hanged man
dangles from a rope, I can cut him down
and such spells can I carve in runes,
that he speaks.

All that Glitters

"Miss Gulvash? Would you have a moment?" The secretary stood in the doorway, waiting for his boss to look up from her computer screen. He stared, entranced, as if mesmerised. He seemed willing to wait, as long as he was allowed to keep looking at her.

"Yes, Frederic?" Miss Gulvash glanced up at him. "Frederic?"

Her secretary gave a start, and flushed as if caught in the act of doing something wrong. "Oh, I'm sorry, Miss Gulvash. I have some papers for you to sign." He walked over to the desk. "The contracts you asked for."

"Well done, Frederic."

He smiled happily as she said his name. Frederic clearly thought it important that the owner of the company knew his name.

Audhild Gulvash would never understand people. However, as long as something as simple as saying their name made them perform, then she would use it. She looked over the contracts, taking her time as she did with everything. She had worked long and hard to get the company off the ground and make it flourish, just as she had done with all the others. Frederic stood waiting, one foot twisting around with nervous energy. Like a child at his first hunt, Audhild thought. Her brow creased. She should try to think more modern! Young ones didn't go on first hunts any more. First dance, perhaps?

"Is something the matter, Frederic?" She didn't take her eyes off the paper.

"No, of course not, Miss Gulvash."

"Yes, there is." She put a long, slender finger on the paper, the tip of her pink-polished nail pointing out a typo. "This needs changing." Frederic was predictable enough; he leaned over the desk, almost bumping his head against hers. Audhild slowly looked up into his eyes. Frederick stepped back quickly, face red as a beet.

""I'm sorry," he whispered.

"I know," she replied, her tone normal. With her antique fountain pen she circled the spot on the paper and handed him the sheet. "I'll sign it when this is correct." Frederic stumbled out of the office.

Audhild rose and went to stand in front of the large window. From the top floor of her steel and concrete empire she looked down at the city that had been her home for the last few decades. Ten, perhaps fifteen more years and then she'd have to move on again. It was either that or start ageing, and the latter wasn't an option. Her kind didn't age well, nor fast if they managed it at all. Audhild frowned. Ten years. She'd give herself ten years and during that time move her assets. She'd also use that time to think up a new business. A pity. "God's Gold" sounded nice and was so to the point. Her personal point. The ring of her phone made her turn back to her desk.

"Miss Gulvash." A man's voice. Calvin Winters, a shrewd businessman pretending to be interested in her while it was really her company he wanted. He owned a chain of jewellery shops.

"Mr Winters. How nice to hear your voice again," Audhild lied as she sat down and checked her nails. Which of his approaches would it be this time?

"Dear Miss Gulvash. I would like to make you an offer you can't possibly refuse." Ah, that one. She smiled thinly, waiting to hear.

"I offer you... me."

The smile broadened. He didn't know that she already had him. Eighty-four percent of his company's shares were in her hands.

"That's very generous of you, Mr Winters."

She picked up her pen and made a note to transfer a substantial amount of his inventory to her personal storage. Gold was what she lived for, and that for a very long time.

"Do I dare to hear some interest on your behalf?" Calvin Winters never gave up easily.

"Only if you consider yourself a valid investment, Mr Winters," she replied. "I'll think about your offer and get back to you as soon as my schedule allows." With that Audhild ended the call and turned her attention back to the e-mail she'd been reading before Frederic had disturbed her. The e-mail was from Norway, the sender a very old acquaintance, once a foe but over time they'd become something akin to friends. He suggested to meet up again as it had been a while, which was true. And these days a journey over the ocean was quite easy and comfortable. Audhild thought back to the creaky, wooden barge that had brought her to this land, packed in a cargo hold with so many others; mortals that stank, moaned and died on the way. It was so bleak compared to the private jet she had at her disposal now. Audhild shook her long, blond hair loose and checked her schedule, but not for an appointment with Calvin Winters. She then marked a week and replied to the e-mail.

Audhild left her office earlier than usual. She called for her car and told the driver to take her home. Home was a modest bungalow outside the city. She didn't need much in luxury and her home showed that.

"Tomorrow at 8:30," she informed the driver. "Not sooner."

The man nodded and drove off without a word. She liked him. Silent and reliable. He was that way in bed as well, but today Audhild was not in the mood. She entered her home and kicked off her shoes. Shoes annoyed her but as CEO she felt required to wear them. First she ran a bath and soaked for a while. Then she took a ready meal from the oversized fridge and heated that up in the microwave. At home she didn't feel the need for fancy. Her faded jeans and old, tent-like sweater were proof of that. After eating she put the plate on the table and looked at it from her couch. A grin played around her lips.

"You shouldn't, you know that," she told herself as she pointed a finger at the plate. "Stop it, you shouldn't." It was a hard habit to break. The plate disappeared. "Oh, dear. Bad you." Audhild laughed.

Using her power felt good. She kept it hidden away from the mortals; no one needed to know she wasn't like them. As usual her fingers itched for more. It was addictive. Doing it once was not enough but doing it too much could cause problems.

After a while Audhild got up and stretched. She looked up at the ceiling and sighed. The ceilings were too low. She tried to remember when was the last time she'd worn her normal shape. Many hundreds of years. Probably closer to a thousand.

"Bah," she muttered. All these depressing thoughts made her feel bad and there was only one thing she knew that helped against such emotional mayhem. She went to the kitchen, pulled the microwave aside and pried a tile from the wall behind it. From the opening behind the tile she took a heavy, brass key. It was worn, well-used. With the key in hand she went into the hall and opened the door to a storage room. The walls were lined with shelves, most of them empty. Only the shelves on the back wall had some tin cans and bottled preserves. Audhild moved the cans and bottles to another shelf. Then she pushed against the back shelf. The wall moved away and then, without a sound, upwards. Behind it was a black hole. As soon as she stepped forward, lights sprang to life, revealing a staircase going down. The woman smiled and started her descent, enjoying the familiar creak of the wooden steps.

At the bottom of the stairs was a door. Dark wood with iron bars, like something from a medieval castle. The brass key in Audhild's hand opened the door smoothly. Audhild took a deep breath and entered the hidden cellar.

She slowly reached to the side where she found a lighter. Much more convenient than the old days, she used that to light a torch mounted on the wall. As the flames on the torch grew, the cellar started to shine and sparkle. Audhild walked around quickly, lighting one torch after another, until eight torches burned brightly. Their flames danced and made her treasure seem almost like a living thing. There was gold everywhere. Piles of coins on tables, thousands of objects large and small on shelves, and in several places there were huge, open chests so full that they spilled their contents on the floor. The wall was decorated with crude trees, obviously made by an amateur. Painted by Audhild herself. She stopped and looked at the distorted, black, dog-shape that she'd painted between two trees.

"I wonder how you are doing, old friend," she said. How often had she run with that animal, so long ago? "Maybe I'll have time to come and look for you, Sköll," she told the painted wolf. After all, she had reserved a whole week off for herself. Lots of time to visit her friends. There had to be some time to go to her original home and see how it fared. It had been so long now that Audhild wondered if she would be able to revert to her original shape and actually find the place. Would the wolf be still alive? He hadn't been a normal wolf but so much time had passed. Audhild slowly pressed a foot into a stack of golden coins, sighing in pleasure as they tumbled over her toes.

"I should do this more often," she told herself as her eyes took in all the precious metal scattered around. It was what she lived for, what she craved. Food and clothes? Not important. Fame? Not important? Fortune? Only if it was gold. Long ago she had changed her name to Gulvash. Audhild Gulvash was known once as Gullveig, Norse goddess, sorceress and giant.

Over a thousand years ago the Aesir had convened to meet in moot. Christianity was spreading like a disease, and so few stayed true to their faith. Odin had called them together; even Gullveig who lived in her forest at the end of the world. She'd been hard pressed to leave all her gold but the issue was too grave not to attend the meeting.

"We must withdraw," Odin had said whilst staring at the group around him with his one, piercing eye. "Attention for us is waning. Under such conditions we can't function properly anymore."

"But what shall we do?" had been the question on everyone's lips. Thor, and a few others had complained that they didn't want to change, but Odin in all his wisdom managed to convince even them.

Before leaving for her forest again, Gullveig had talked with several other Gods and Goddesses about their ideas and prospects but none of them had any solid ideas. On her way home she made small detours to several lands to collect more gold. It made her think that going into the business of buying gold and perhaps other precious items would be a good way to continue.

It wouldn't be as glamorous as being a giant and a Goddess, but it would give her ample opportunity to be near as much gold as possible.

Days passed. Business flourished, Calvin Winters called a few more times and the date of Audhild's departure to Norway approached rapidly. On the day itself she was driven to the airport where her jet was waiting. Four suitcases, two with personal belongings and two filled with gold, were brought aboard. They took off without incident. Audhild occupied herself for a while polishing the golden items from her two special suitcases. It never bored her and helped to pass the time. Nevertheless, she soon slept.

"Miss Gulvash?"

The voice of her personal steward woke her. Sleep was not, strictly speaking, necessary, but after spending so much time amongst mortals Gullveig had picked up the habit. It had helped to convince more than one of her many husbands.

"We're about to land. The pilot asks if you would please fasten your seat belt."

"I know, I know," she grumbled. Despite the practice, she still didn't do well with waking-up. "Put your seat in the upright position and stow the tray table in front of you." She knew the lines of the airline attendants. The steward frowned. "What is it?" she wondered.

"There is no tray table, Miss Gulvash," he courteously pointed out, then hurried off to sit down and buckle up himself. He didn't dare to look at Audhild until the plane was safely on the ground.

She carried her bags with the gold off the plane herself. Those were too important to leave in other people's hands. A young blonde girl was standing, holding a sign with her name.

"Hello. I am Audhild Gulvash."

The girl smiled and bowed. "Welcome to Bodø Airport, my lady Gullveig," she said. She spoke the name quietly but clearly. "Master Odinski sent me to wait for you and take you to your quarters. My name is Karin." Odinski. It was the name Odin used these days. Karin looked at the suitcases. "May I take these?"

"You won't be able to carry them," Audhild said. "There are two others, more your speed." The steward came with a small trolley that held the other suitcases. Karin accepted the little cart and thanked the steward. Karin obviously was used to being in the presence of deities. She led the way to a car that was waiting for them.

Soon the luggage was loaded and the car drove off. Audhild was pleased that Karin didn't feel the need to fill the time with mindless chatter. In silence they travelled for about an hour until they reached Løpsmarka, a small village north of the airport. It looked like a lonely, forgotten place, which served this occasion just fine. The car pulled into a small parking lot near a large, old house. There were three other cars, something that made Karin nod in approval. "We are expected," was all she said before leaving the car. As soon as Audhild had stepped out, the front door of the house opened and a man in a long fur coat came out.

"Gullveig," he said, his voice booming as always. Another good reason for a remote meeting place. He held out his hands as if he prepared for a hug.

"Odin...ski..." Audhild allowed her power to erupt. No one hugged her, not even the Father of Gods.

Odin frowned, then smiled. "Of course. You never were the hugging kind."

"Nor were you, back then." Audhild felt it was safe

to become a little more Gullveig. Still she wanted to keep tabs on herself. She would have to become Audhild Gulvash again after this visit.

"It's good to see you again," said Odin. "Even when you don't look like you."

"I haven't looked like me for a long time. It was quite a surprise to get your invitation."

Odin nodded and ushered her towards the waiting door. "Let's go inside while my people take care of your luggage. There is much to discuss and and only amongst friends."

"I wonder when was the last time you all considered me a friend, but I appreciate the invitation," Audhild said as she looked at a few men who carried her luggage away. She'd always been the odd one out. Living far away, left in peace by many, until some of the Æsir manipulated her, which led to the Æsir-Vanir War.

The suitcases containing her gold were taken inside. The men didn't seem to notice the weight. As Gullveig entered the building she thought to herself, '*There has to be a very good reason for me to be invited and I want to know every little detail.*' In the hall there was a table with burning candles and a few rocks. The Goddess, repressed for so long, immediately sensed the life inside the rocks. They were from the old country! She stopped to touch them for a moment, then caressed the golden candlesticks that held the candles. A nice memory of this visit perhaps, she thought. It was hard to walk past them.

Mr Odinski walked ahead of her and opened a door into a room that looked like a smaller version of his Meeting Hall of old. It seemed just as full though.

"We're complete now, so we can begin," the God of Gods said as he sat down in a comfortable leather chair and picked up a glass. Audhild looked around at the faces of those had had been waiting. Slowly their faces started to morph into the familiar. Thor, Freya, Loki, Bragi, Gefjun. Even Andhrímnir, cook of the Gods, was there. He waved at Audhild and patted the free spot on the couch next to him. She sighed and hoped he didn't smell of boar.

"Thank you," she said, relieved he'd showered and actually smelled nice.

"You're welcome," he said and smiled. It was definitely him. She'd never forget the crooked teeth. "At least you're of a size now to share a couch with." Audhild had to agree with that.

"Are we done rambling?" Clearly this was not a meeting for reminiscing the good old times. "There is a reason that I called you all here and I'm glad you all managed to make it." He looked around and considered each one individually. Thusly satisfied he nodded. "We've all been mucking about for the last thousand years, since, well you know. You all remember that all too well, I'm sure." Gullveig saw everyone nod in agreement. She herself did too as it still was a blemish on her reputation as a Goddess. The others clearly felt the same way about it. She looked at the God of Gods and waited for him to continue.

Thor leaped to his feet, his hammer in hand. "I remember it all too well," he stated, "and to be honest, I'm more than sick and tired of it."

Gullveig kept her face straight as she watched him. The God of Thunder wore a bespoke pinstriped suit, which made him somewhat attractive to her. Of course he'd never be a match for gold. Thor looked around.

"I used to put things to the right and hit clouds to make thunder. And what am I doing now? I'm the CEO of a big firm that predicts the weather." He thrust his hammer high, and a spot on the ceiling crumbled. "And they don't listen to me. They keep looking at their stupid computers and charts, and they keep getting it wrong."

Suddenly Thor seemed to shrink after venting this defeat. "I don't want this any more." He dragged his hammer along the ground as he went back to his seat. Gullveig was surprised. She'd thought that Thor would have been able to make a good life for himself. Then Freya got up.

"Thor said what I feel. Sick and tired of all this human life. I've been running brothels and such. At first it was fun, but you can't imagine how boring that gets after the first few centuries. Oh, I shouldn't complain, I'm doing well, but... it's not what we were meant to do."

The Goddess of sensuality ripped off her red dress to reveal her well-known cloak of falcon feathers.

"I'm looking forward to the day we can go back where we belong."

Proudly she turned and sat herself down, leaving the remains of her red dress on the floor. Several more Gods and Goddesses stood and lamented over their fate until Odin raised a hand.

"Enough. Really, enough. What are you? A bunch of whiners? I hope there's still some God left inside you." He rose up. "The reason that we left our original position was Christianity. People turned away from us." Many of the Gods present nodded. "Well, I have some good news for those who haven't been paying attention. Christianity isn't what it used to be. It's declining. People turn to other religions. Paganism is coming back into style more and more, and there are lots of mortals who call themselves Asatru. They call for the old Gods to return." Odin held up a hand, palm facing towards the centre of the room. A sphere appeared and spread out. In it, everyone saw a large group of mortals in what had to look like ancient attire. They had gathered around a fire and chanted ancient texts, recited old poems. Granted, they did it poorly but at least they gave it their best. Odin wiggled a finger and the noise from the singers inside the sphere fell away. "Here you see it. They want us. They are looking back to how things were and they want that back."

Silence reigned in the room. Gullveig pondered the words she'd just heard. Was it possible? Would the Gods rise again to their former status? No more staff meetings? No more contracts? No more Calvin Winters? It was almost too good to be true, and she'd learnt that when something sounded that way it usually wasn't. Still, she waited patiently because this was Odin speaking, and Odin wasn't known to babble.

"I am telling you all that the time has come to retake our rightful place." Odin walked around the room, once again looking at each of the attendees. "If we do this right then we can become ourselves again. A few of us have already made some plans on how to go about it, but I first want to know how you lot feel."

He stopped pacing and waited. As had always been the case, nearly all the Gods and Goddesses started talking at the same time, each venting their opinion more loudly than their neighbour.

Gullveig was among the very few who remained silent. First of all because this was more amazing news than she could have guessed, secondly because she'd always been a quiet one. Long ago, in her forest at the end of the world, there hadn't been many to talk to. Just Sköll, the wolf, and he wasn't very talkative at the best of times. To her surprise Odin sat down next to her. Where had Andhrímnir gone?

"So what do you think of this?" It was easy to hear

him talk despite the racket the others made. Gods had their little tricks for that.

"It sounds wonderful," Gullveig admitted. "I've gotten used to the way I live now but it has never stolen my gold . . . I mean heart. If this is really viable then I'm in. I'd love to see my forest again."

"And your gold," Odin added. He knew her well.

"Yes. Also my gold. Do you know if it's still there?" Gullveig's heart started beating a little faster.

"I'm not sure but we could head over there and have a look," the Father of Gods said. He patted her on the knee. "It's good to have you back here, kid."

Gullveig smiled. "It feels good to be back." She meant it. The prospect of visiting her old home made her happy, the more so, as this could mean an opportunity to someday move back. Odin nodded and sat back. He simply waited for the Gods and Goddesses to get over their excitement about, agreement with and disapproval of his suggestion, and that would take a while.

A relative silence returned to the room when outside darkness began to set in.

"I take it that you have reached a conclusion," the Father of Gods said as he rose from the couch. Of course he had heard everything that was said. "Most of you are either in favour or doubtful but optimistic. That's good enough for me."

Gullveig noticed that Odin himself had changed over the many years as well. Once his word had been law. Now he seemed more mellow, almost democratic. It was probably just an illusion.

"We're going to do this. If you really want out then here's your moment. Pack up and leave. If you go, you'll lose your God status but you'll have my wishes that you live happily ever after." Odin's face told Gullveig that he was not trying to be funny. She also heard him say *wishes*, not *promise* or *guarantee*.

A few of the mutiny-prone Gods rose, looked at each other and waited for someone to make the first move. No one seemed eager to be demoted to regular mortal status with its doubtful merits and limited lifespan. Mutters and whispers went to and fro for a while. Then everyone sat again, looking at their leader.

"Very well. Now we have that established I suggest we get a good night's sleep and discuss this further in the morning. If there are any among you who haven't picked up the sleep habit; the cars are still outside and waiting. Go and have fun but try to keep a low profile. We don't want the world to know we're coming back, just yet."

Several of the Gods and Goddesses present rose and left the room in a hurry. Gullveig was one of the few who actually slept and excused herself. Karin, who had been waiting in the hall, showed her to a large room and wished her a good night. It took Gullveig quite a while to fall asleep, even with lots of gold around her pillow. Odins news kept ringing in her mind.

The next morning she awoke with the air buzzing around her. Most of the Gods were up already; that had to be. Air didn't buzz like that otherwise. Gullveig hurried through a shower and fresh clothes, patted a golden apple for luck and went to join the others. She found them in the same room again. Some of the usual noise-makers now sat in silence, holding their heads. Clearly some had slipped from proper God status in different ways, she realised with a smirk.

"Good. We're all together. *All*," Odin said. He looked pleased that no one had run off after hearing the plan. "There will be a few hours of preparation for everyone.

Get back to your proper self and then leave this house. Go to your old home and see if that's in a proper state. If not then you will fix it. Take your time, take a few days or so, and after that time you'll all come back here. At that point we'll decide how we proceed with the plan." The Father of Gods looked around. No one made a remark.

"I'll go with Gullveig, seeing that she lives quite far from here."

"You're *not* going with Gullveig." Freya rose and looked down at her husband. "You're coming with me and we're going to see about *our* home."

Odin sighed and looked at Gullveig who could only laugh at the scene. The battle of power between Odin and his wife would never end.

"I'll find my way home," she assured him. Hopefully a few hours was enough time to prepare for that, she hoped. After all she had to drop her mortal shell for a while, return to her old shape, and allow her full Godly powers to flow again. And her size. The latter worried her most because it had literally been ages that she'd allowed herself to unfold to her real size. She remembered all too well how that had hurt.

Gullveig got up and went to the room where she'd slept. In the mirror she saw the familiar face of Audhild Gulvash. The face of Gullveig was different, of course. Then she sat down on the bed and took a deep breath. Unleashing her powers would shake her up. She located the inner, self-imposed bonds that kept her power constrained and carefully undid them. Her body spasmed as the energy ran through her. Her skin itched and she shivered. Even her vision blurred for a while. Once she could see again and the shivers had left her legs, she got up and stretched. She felt the power. After that she had to take care of clothing. Being the giant she really was, she would need a dress that fit. With her power now flowing freely, it was a good moment to create a dress from some things in her suitcase combined with a number of blankets she discovered in a closet. She cursed herself a few times as her magic didn't do what she wanted. Lack of practice made far from perfect. Finally she had what she wanted. Dragging the enormous garment with her she went out through the back-door and found herself in a small yard that opened to a deserted field. After another deep breath Gullveig took off her mortal clothes and then shivered in the cool breeze. After spreading out the large dress she lay down on it, closed her eyes and concentrated on her magic to reshape her body into the giant Goddess she was. The energy coursed through her and she prepared for the pain.

It was intense. Bones and tissue that hadn't been properly expanded for almost two millennia made their displeasure very clear. Panting Gullveig lay on the dress, carefully moving her limbs, almost taking out a wall. Damn, this would take some getting used to! She sat up slowly and checked herself. Yes, she was her real self again. She got up and pulled the dress over her head. She didn't feel the cold ground any more. Looking around to make sure she wasn't seen when walking off was easy now; she stood tall enough to see over the roof of the nearby houses.

Odin had chosen this place with care. It was easy for her and also the others to leave the area in order to go where they had to. Gullveig felt dizzy as she paced off. She felt a thrill, but feared being herself. It had been too long ago.

Gullveig travelled across the lands. No matter how long ago it had been, she knew where to go, where her home was, and a few days later she passed the last mountain range that lay between the common lands and her forest at the end of the world. Her heart beat fast as she saw her old home. It had changed much and not for the better. No one had taken care of it; trees had fallen over, there was debris of branches and fallen leaves everywhere. As soon as she stood among the trees she dropped to her knees and brushed aside what didn't belong there. Something else, something more important had to be there, she knew, and after removing a few layers of moss her fingers touched coins. She dug faster and lifted up a small part of her golden treasure. The gold she loved so much, the gold she'd collected for so long. It was still there! She cleared away all the dirt and branches from her home and delighted in the view of her wealth. No matter how many companies she'd founded in the mortal world through the ages, all of them together would not bring her as much gold as she'd gathered here.

"Sköll!" she called out a few times. The large wolf didn't come. Perhaps he was too far away to hear her. Perhaps he no longer lived. Gullveig didn't know but didn't care either. Sköll was his own boss, always had been.

After the journey in her own, large form, she felt more secure inside her body. She'd used her power a few times to acquire food and a little gold, and combined with her knowledge of the modern world she thought herself quite formidable now. If Odin's plan would take root there would be a grand future for her and the other Gods.

The next day Gullveig realised that she had to start her return journey. For a moment she scolded herself for digging up her gold. Now it lay there for all to see.

"Good thing that mortals still can't travel beyond the

mountains," she said to a tree as she walked past it. A look back was all she took time for before proceeding towards the mountains that lay between home and the world. The journey back to the house in Løpsmarka went as fast as Gullveig had remembered, and as she approached the small town she dreaded the moment of having to revert to her mortal shape. The giant Goddess sorceress crossed the last field and kneeled in the now very small yard. She smiled as she saw a wooden chest that contained her human clothes. Someone had been very thoughtful to clean and fold them. Gullveig took off her rough dress. She feared she wouldn't be able to get out of it in her smaller form. Then she focussed her mind and began to shrink.

There had been pain, she remembered that when she woke up. To her surprise she was in the bedroom. Her clothes, both large and small, lay on a table near the window. Slowly Gullveig rose, her joints cracking, spine popping. Her body complained about its size after being normal again for a while. She looked in the mirror and smiled. Slowly she dressed as she pondered her experiences of the last few days. Being a small mortal again made for such a bleak life, compared to the rush of power and the thrill of knowing and having her strength. She wanted to be her old self again. Audhild Gulvash was no longer leading an interesting life. Her stomach warned her that her body needed sustenance so she went to the kitchen and found. The young woman hurried to prepare something for her and seemed pleased, no - proud to do so.

"Master Odin told me that everyone has returned now," Karin said. "You were asleep for a day. This evening there is a final meeting."

"There is something about you," Gullveig observed.

"Something different. What is it?"

Karin blushed. "Master Odin says he will *raise* me when the Gods have returned."

Gullveig grinned. That was so typical of the old God Father. Ever grateful to those who served him well, he would make Karin a half-goddess in return for what she'd done. "Will you keep your name after that?"

"Maybe. I haven't thought of a better one and I've had this one for twenty-eight years already."

Karin made her age sound old. Little did the child know. Gullveig thanked her for the food and quickly devoured it, washing it down with tea. After filling herself, Gullveig went looking for some of her fellow Gods. That was easy enough. First she ran into Jörð, Goddess of the Earth.

"Hey, care for a walk?" Gullveig asked. On the way out they met Ullr, God of the hunt, and Lofn, the Goddess of forbidden loves. They too gladly joined the walking party. As they left the house through the back-door they started exchanging experiences. Gullveig noticed she wasn't the only one who wanted to leave the human life behind her. This bout of freedom had roused ancient spirits and these were hard to tame and subdue. The group walked to the centre of Løpsmarka and pretended to be interested in the shop windows for a while. They settled in a bar and ordered stiff drinks, despite the hour.

Jörð sat back and stared at her glass. "It is good to be back," she said as she swirled her drink around. "It's been so long that I feared I had forgotten how to be me." The others nodded in silence. "I hope it won't be too long before Odin's plan is put into motion."

"Odinski," said Ullr.

"What? Oh, sure." Jörð grinned. "Silly name." To the few humans in the bar it looked as if Jörð's chair slipped from under her but the others knew better. Odin might have chosen a silly name but he was still very much aware of everything, and that included the talk in this very bar. "Damn him!" Jörð said as she got up and put the chair straight. She pointed a finger at the broken glass but Lofn stopped her.

"Not in here, Jörð," she warned the Goddess of the Earth. "Don't get carried away just yet. We'll order you a new one." Someone from the bar already came running to clean away the glass. After some more time during which lots of alcohol was consumed (Gods weren't affected much by mortal alcohol) they paid handsomely and sauntered back to the house.

After dinner, an elaborate and festive affair that Andhrímnir and Karin had done a lot of work for, the assembled Gods and Goddesses retreated to the hall one more time. Odin looked at everyone and clearly was pleased to see *everyone*. No one had dropped out; the prospect of their new and hopefully shining future as their former selves was obviously too enticing.

"We have inspected Valhalla. It was quite a mess. I gather that most of your homes were as well." Nodding heads all around. "I gather also that you started cleaning up, *and* got done with it. Otherwise you're not worthy of being called a God in this room." More nodding, in places a bit less reassuring, but Odin ignored that.

Gullveig sensed a hum of anticipation in the room. Everyone seemed more and more eager to take their rightful place again. Odin continued his speech, talking about the proper time for them to regain their status. He warned the congregation not to move too quickly.

"Be aware that we've been gone for a while. We built many small empires of our own. Break them down quietly so your human presence won't suddenly be missed. We'll get more than enough attention when we reopen Valhalla's gates; there's no need for the police to come looking for us too."

"Can't we keep our human lives, you know, as a side job?" Loki asked. "I'm having a lot of fun with it." He ran a successful chain of casinos.

"No. You're in or you're out. I know it's a vain hope but can you start acting like a proper god finally?"

Loki muttered and looked at Thor who sat shaking his head.

"Go home tomorrow. Break down your empire. Erase your existence from the human world. Be back here in a year." Odin sat down and waited for comments. There were none. There were talks amongst the Gods, but that was to be expected.

In the next months, Gullveig started dismantling her empire. Using her powers, which she dared to use now, she made herself look sick, terminally ill. Using that as an excuse to sell her company there were many buyers hoping to make a cheap kill but Audhild Gulvash wasn't going to simply dump her company. She wanted as much out of it as she could, paid for in gold.

After eight months the sale was final. Calvin Winters had won. Two large vans with golden items in many sizes and shapes were delivered to her bungalow where she had retreated, pretending to be too sick to go to the office. Calvin had come with the vans in person.

"Dear Audhild," he said as he sat near her bed. She knew he didn't dare to come too close as she looked awful by now. "I am very sorry that I got my hands on your company in such an unfortunate manner. We could have had a great future together. I do promise you that I'll take excellent care of what you've built up."

Audhild looked at him. She could see he was being

more honest than she'd ever seen him. She nodded and coughed convincingly. Karin, who had come over to *take care* of her, put a hand on Calvin's shoulder.

"It is better, I think, you leave," she said in her broken English. Audhild knew that the man would prefer to stay but Odin had started working on Karin. The new, young half-goddess applied some power to him which made him stand and say goodbye, thinking it was his own volition. Audhild chose that moment to draw her last breath. Her head lolled to the side and her eyes glazed over slowly. She could go without breathing for hours so she appeared very dead.

"Oh dear, I think she left us," Karin said with well-played sorrow.

"Dearest Audhild, it was great knowing you," Calvin said. He'd spread the news like wildfire. "Rest in peace."

From the corner of her eye, Gullveig saw how Karin ushered the man out of the room. As soon as they had left she started breathing again and sat up.

"That was that." She got up and walked to the window. Peeking outside from behind the curtains she saw that the vans with the gold had already been moved into safety as per her instructions. Calvin Winters might be shocked by her death but it wouldn't be below him to take the vans back with him. Her car would take him and his van-drivers home. As she stood there, the deathly colour faded from her face. She looked around. Nothing here would be worth taking home, she had already decided. She'd also arranged for a truck for the next day, to load up all her gold from the cellar. Arrangements had already been made for a cargo plane to take it to Norway, together with her coffin while she'd be on board as one of the crew. Money and influence had made all of that very easy.

Karin came back into the room. "He left. We can start packing now." Gullveig grinned. It was good to be back.

Valkyrie

You rise in beady black night.
Ugly but coherent, hard eyes cold
glass you rise like gorge, like
discontent from Stygian fissures
scored across black diamond rock.
You rise in a gasp of steam, wild
flock of currents batting wings
in fetid air. What you need is what
stirs your blood, black bile urges
you on, an inky tide of hunger, rage
and pain. I have summoned you
here to feast on the flesh of rain.
Alone I have ripped open the wind.
All night I dreamt of sharp golden
beaks, splinters and nails. I heard
your half-broken voices raw and wild
among savage plains, I felt the tide
of your wings. When I woke long
before dawn, I could only spit
your names: Harpy, Raven, Valkyrie,
Crow. See where my armies
have halted on this side of the rocky
gorge, made camp among spiders
and gorse. Between the wasps
and bees their campfire smoke rises
and mingles, steeping a dizzy tea,
a headache brew of visionary tales.
Morning crawls toward the eastern
sky and we are coming on with bugles,
drums and pipes. Slowly we come
to feed the hungry dead with death.

You of the fierce winged tribe, you
know my name. I have called you
here to witness my hands. Take notice
of tangled lifelines in the palms, ragged
nails crusted with earth and fire and lime.

Past Bound

Dr Saga Burke sat at her desk in the corner of her office. Every available wall space was covered with shelves, filled with more books than she cared to count. Being surrounded by so much history made her feel at home. She had *lived* through much of it, but seeing how events were remembered fascinated her.

She had spent many years working within academia. It had meant moving from university to university and changing her identity, but that was the way of it. It was the same for all her siblings, those that hid in plain view.

She turned her thoughts back to the task at hand, the end of term papers. Focusing, she marked as many papers as she could. She looked up at the clock; it was getting late. A glance at the room's single window confirmed the time, as it was already dark outside. She got to her feet and pulled on her long winter coat and made ready to leave.

Before she got to the end of the corridor, a young man appeared from one of the other offices. Alasdair Sinclair's nose was buried in a book on medieval Scandinavia. Saga smiled. He was a post-doctorate, specialising in the history and culture of Northern Europe. Glancing up from his book, he started, clearly unaware that anyone else had been close by.

"I'm sorry. I didn't mean to give you a fright," Saga said.

"That's all right. Been working late again, Dr Burke?"

Closing his book, he stowed it away in a knapsack. Alasdair was young, with short strawberry blonde hair. Saga wondered if he was ready for the cut-throat world of academia, but he worked hard and it was clear he wanted to prove himself. Since his arrival in the department, a few months before, he had become a popular member of staff.

"Call me Saga. There's no reason to be formal," she replied "I can see that you've been burning the midnight oil too."

"Too much work, not enough time," Alasdair answered as they continued towards the exit.

Saga allowed Alasdair to open the door for her. "It doesn't get any easier. Trust me, but I'm sure you'll do brilliantly."

"Thanks for the vote of confidence," he replied, with a warm smile.

Once outside, they went their separate ways. Saga had a quiet evening planned. It was certainly a far cry from her former life, when she had been one of the All-Father's closest confidants.

But that life was gone.

She rarely had any contact with any of the others. It wasn't as if she was trying to keep them at arms-length, she just preferred the peace and quiet that her mundane life offered.

No mortal ever knew of who they really were. The All-Father had made it clear to them that the consequences of anyone finding out would be dire. Both for them and the mortals. Humans were like children. They needed guidance, but they had a tendency to destroy anything they did not understand. That was how it had been for countless centuries and it looked as if that was how it was going to stay.

Alasdair's office was small, little more than a broom cupboard. But it was his own space. It was where he could do his research. The idea of having to teach still made him nervous. A small part of him that felt he would not do justice to those who had gone before.

He sighed, stretching. He needed to clear his head. Time for lunch and fresh air. Stepping out of his office, he spotted a familiar figure a short distance away.

Saga was struggling with the vending machine. As far as Alasdair was concerned, its coffee was not fit for human consumption.

"Saga, I don't think that's been working since yesterday. Someone was meant to come out. I'm guessing that they haven't been yet," Alasdair commented.

"That's just my luck. It always seems to break when I want to use it," she laughed. "I must be jinxed."

"I'm just heading out for lunch. Why don't you join me?" he asked. "I'm sure that a break would do you good. Plus, you could get some proper coffee."

Glancing at him, a slight smile crossed her lips.

"Know what, I think you might be right. You can tell me all about your research over lunch."

"Well, if you're interested in hearing about the history of slaves in Norse Dublin. I know just the place."

Leading her out of the department and through the side streets of Glasgow's West End, he had a specific place in mind. He had spoken with Saga on a few occasions. Their conversations had always been comfortable, but she made him feel like he was stepping into the unknown.

He glanced at her, then quickly looked away, a slight blush tinging his cheeks.

Saga watched Alasdair as he worked. He was sitting at the desk in her apartment, muttering to himself as he tapped one fingered at his laptop.

She had taken a number of lovers in her life, but

none of them had proved to be as passionate, or willing to please, as Alasdair. They spent more and more time in each other's company.

But there were always going to be aspects of her life that he was never going to know. None of her former paramours had ever discovered the truth and it was going to stay that way. That didn't mean that she didn't care for Alasdair, but the end of their relationship was inevitable.

That only made Saga determined to enjoy the time she had with him. They had been together for a few months, but had managed to keep it quiet in the hope of avoiding office gossip. Despite their efforts, it didn't take long for rumours to start doing the rounds.

Letting out a sigh, Alasdair rubbed his eyes. Saga walked up behind him and gently massaged his shoulders. He began to relax as she continued to work the knots out of his shoulders.

"Are you all right?" she asked.

Alasdair looked up and gave her a smile. "It's nothing important. I know what I'm meant to be writing, but I'm struggling to find the right words. How am I ever going to get a teaching position, if I can't even write a decent research paper?"

"Maybe you need a break. You've been working hard," Saga answered. "I have an idea for something that might help."

"What?" Alasdair asked, cocking his eyebrow.

Getting him to his feet, she guided him back to the sofa. Both of them sat, facing each other. A look of curiosity flitted across Alasdair's face, though he remained silent. He watched her closely, as she lifted her hands to the side of his face.

"You'll have to trust me. Close your eyes and breathe deeply. This is nothing more than a relaxation technique."

Smiling again, he did as she asked. As he took slow, deep breaths, Saga closed her own eyes and focused her thoughts. She could feel the familiar tingle of energy as it passed through her. She channelled it into Alasdair. She had done this for others, when they needed inspiration. It was always successful. The list of her lovers included famous writers and poets, none of whom realised how the seeds of their great works had been planted.

Opening her eyes, she watched Alasdair's face. The shadow of a smile crossed his lips as he sank into the sofa. Feeling that her work was done, Saga eased him back into the here and now. Opening his eyes, he sprang to his feet, before pacing, excitedly.

Saga smiled. "It helped?"

"I have no idea what you did, but it more than helped," Alasdair answered. "It's as if whatever was stopping me from writing is no longer there. I could almost visualise the lives of those slaves. It was as if I was there. What would I do without you?"

Saga strolled into the department. She hadn't seen Alasdair for a week, but that did not worry her. She collected her mail then continued on to her office. This was her quiet day. No lectures, or meetings. Peace and quiet was all she needed to get on with her work.

She dumped the mail on her desk. There was one that stood out. No address, or stamp or postmark – just her name scrawled across the envelope in a handwriting that she recognised. It was Alasdair's.

She opened it.

I need to speak with you, urgently! I will be waiting for you in our usual coffee shop at Ten O'clock.

Reading it again, Saga frowned as she fished her

mobile from her bag. She had better get going if she was to make the rendezvous.

Alasdair was already sitting at their usual table, nursing a coffee. Saga smiled at the girl behind the counter and ordered. Then she took her drink and sat next to Alasdair.

"What are you are not telling me?" Alasdair demanded.

Laughing lightly, Saga smiled. "I don't know what you're talking about? I've not been hiding anything from you."

"Yes, you have. Tell me."

"Alasdair, what are you going on about? You're starting to worry me."

Watching him as he took another sip from his coffee, Saga covered his free hand with her own. He didn't pull away, but the warmth that she had once found there was missing.

"Don't make this any more difficult than it is already," he whispered.

"I don't know what it is that I am meant to have done. What has changed?"

"It all started when you did that relaxation technique on me," Alasdair continued. "I keep catching glimpses of things I shouldn't. Things that no-one alive could know."

"Oh? That's unusual."

"You think?" He stopped and stared out the window for a moment. Taking a deep breath, he looked back at her

"It was all great for the first couple of days. Everything was flowing and I was writing my best work. That was until I began to know things. I would catch glimpses as I walked past places. I saw people who should not have been there – people who I knew were dead."

Alasdair held her gaze.

"Maybe you've been working too hard," Saga said. "I think you should see someone about this. It can't be right that you're seeing things that aren't there."

"I am not losing my mind. I know what has been going on. I don't know how I know it, but I know what you are. It's connected to what happened last week."

Saga cocked her head and regarded him cooly. She had been so certain that she had been careful. Finishing off her coffee, she waited for Alasdair to continue.

"You're not human. Are you?"

Getting to her feet, Saga looked down at him. "I don't have time for this."

Walking out, she knew that it was not the end of the matter. She took an alley, hoping to get away from Alasdair, but he followed. Saga turned. She regretted what was going to have to happen.

"You're one of the Norse goddesses, aren't you? I presume the others are about somewhere," Alasdair whispered. "If you want me to keep quiet about who you are and what you can do, you'll . . ."

"I'll what?" Saga demanded, her voice edged and sharp.

"You'll help me get a professorship. Yeah, you get me tenure." Alasdair smiled. "If you don't, I'll do everything I can to expose you and your kind to the entire world."

Saga held his gaze until he turned and walked away. A sudden caw caused her to look up. Two ravens were perched on a nearby lamp-post, watching her with twinkling black eyes. She nodded in resignation. she knew what she had to do.

Saga entered the darkened library. It was night, but

that did not mean closed. Just a flash of her staff card was enough to get her inside. Walking through the darkened halls, she found a small number of students doing an all-nighter.

There would be no one working where she was going, though Alasdair would be waiting. As before, she had received a note. It was nothing more than a statement of where and when they would meet.

At least they would not be overheard. Sighing to herself, she reigned in her feelings as she took hold of the door handle. This would be the last time she got embroiled emotionally with a mortal. The next time, it would be different.

Walking into the room, she saw her lover, quickly making eye contact with Alasdair.

"I knew you would come," he said.

"There's a lot that has to be discussed."

"That's true," he smiled. "Shall we start?"

"I didn't mean between the two of us."

"What are you on about?" Alasdair demanded.

They were not alone after all. She had felt the presence the instant she walked in. Alasdair followed her gaze as a familiar figure stepped out of the darkness. His wide brimmed, grey hat was pulled low over his missing eye. Stumbling back, Alasdair steadied himself against a nearby table.

"Who the fuck are you? How the hell did you get in here?" he hissed.

"Hello Alasdair," the All-Father growled. "How I got in is none of your concern, but there is indeed something for us to discuss." He strode closer to the mortal, one hand lifting the patch covering his eye.

Loki

neither fully beast nor god, forged of spite and inspiration,
his clever ideas never end where they ought, but venture
forward
with pinpoint precision, sharp and deadly
though their source is often disguised, shifted from original
purpose until every being above and below
bellow for the lost eye to open and end such mischief
as none other can conceive but such the malicious sprite
of frost and foam, clothed in golden weave –
when the authors tired of his madness
they tried to edit him out entirely,
encircled and scratched until unrecognizable
and then inverted his symbol over his head,
left him for lost as his own poison
pained him and denied his end
even while the ground shook

Freya's Graces

The coffee house was crowded. Juanita did not feel like talking with anyone, but with no other choice she sat at a table occupied by two blonde, Nordic-looking women.

They seemed friendly though, and introduced themselves as Frieda and Fulla. Both spoke with a distinct accent. Was it German? Juanita did not want to talk with them, but felt she had to be polite.

"Are you ladies from Germany?" she asked.

"We've lived there," Frieda said. "And you?"

"I'm local. I've lived in Grand Rapids all my life."

"Do you like it here?"

"I love the people. Sometimes, though, the gangs make me want to leave."

Juanita had warned her boyfriend not to cross Tito Salinas, but he had ignored her, and now owed him five thousand bucks. Salinas beat the hell out of him, locked him in a room, and gave him three days to come up with the cash. If he did not have it by Monday at five o'clock, they would kill him.

Juanita had called his parents, brothers, friends— anyone she could think of—but had raised only four-hundred dollars. Salinas would not take a partial payment. All or nothing, he said. He did not make deals with guys who owed him that much cash.

For some reason, she found herself telling these complete strangers her troubles.

"They make me want to go someplace where I would never have to worry about things like that," she said. "I don't know if such a place even exists."

"It most certainly exists. You can get there easily enough." Frieda said. Fulla nodded, but otherwise sat quietly and observed.

"Then tell me how."

"The place is within you."

Juanita rolled her eyes. She did not need to hear more pieties. She had gone to church and prayed that morning. When she had told a girlfriend what was going on, she offered to appeal to the spirit world. Juanita did not put much stock in religion of any kind, but the same desperation that had sent her to church made her agree to join Keira for the spirit ceremony.

They closed the curtains in her apartment and lit candles set on a makeshift altar and then drew a pattern on the floor with white chalk. Juanita knelt, as instructed, in the white circle; Keira stripped naked and prostrated herself before the altar. She began to chant.

As she chanted, Juanita felt her skin prickle, like static. Then her hair stood on end as her heart pounded and she gasped for breath. The chanting ceased after a few minutes. Whatever it was that was happening was over. Juanita's heartbeat slowed, her hair settled, and the sensation of being bombarded by electric prickles ceased.

Keira stood up, threw on shorts and t-shirt, put out the candles. She turned on the lights and opened the windows.

"We made contact."

"Who did we contact?"

"Spirits. They didn't speak, but I know they were here."

"I felt something, but how will that help? I want to get Ernesto free before Salinas kills him."

"I don't know, Juanita. I only know the spirits were present and heard you. They might come to your aid."

Juanita tried to hide her impatience. Time was valuable. She had wasted two hours on a ceremony that only indicated she "might" have supernatural help—no different from the priest who had told her Ernesto would live, "if it was God's will." She tried not to show her annoyance as she left. Keira told her to have faith. Now this foreign woman was telling her the power to free Ernesto was within! Frieda seemed to read her emotions.

"I understand your skepticism. I will enable you to free Edwardo, the young man you love, from the group who have him."

Juanita's mouth dropped open. Frieda gave a cat-like smile.

"Your friend," she said, "*was* successful in contacting the spirit world."

Fear radiated through Juanita's body. Were the two women spirit beings? Ghosts or demons? All the stories and tales she knew taught that those from beyond the grave always caused trouble.

"You doubt," the woman continued, "and, in truth, your friend did not mean to summon us. She's not very good at the craft at which she purports to excel. She . . . shall we say, dialed a wrong number? But we want to help you."

"Who are you?"

"Frieda, though I prefer the other form of my name, Freya. Today is the day sacred to me. That you chose to seek divine help on this particular day was fortuitous."

Juanita racked her brain. Friday was named after a Norse goddess; Frigga. But she was also known as Freya. Juanita stared in confusion at the beautiful woman.

"The custom is to show reverence," Freya said.

Juanita wondered desperately what to do. She bowed her head. "I'm honored to meet you," she said.

"That's good for a start," Freya replied.

But by now Juanita's rationalist defenses had started to assert themselves. "You could have found out about the trouble Ernesto is in from Kiera, or from any one of several people."

"I could have," Freya responded calmly. "But I could not have found out from friends that this morning you desired him so badly you took a bath instead of a shower so you could satisfy the passion you felt for him; immediately afterwards you said a rosary, though you knew what you did in the bathtub is considered a sin and may have invalidated your prayers. You ate Post Grape Nuts, a cereal you don't like, as an act of penance for your transgression. Do I need to go on?"

"No."

"Your whole life is open to me, Juanita. I want to help you."

"Yes, ma'am," she said, her eyes wide.

"I prefer to be addressed as *Lady Goddess*."

"I'm sorry . . . Lady Goddess."

"That's better—much better. You're a good girl, I can tell."

"How will you help me? Am I allowed to ask?"

"Of course. I'll bring something to you that has power to free the man you love, but you must be willing to pay the price, as I paid a price to obtain this object."

"What price?"

"You'll find out. Go to the library and look this term up." She handed her a slip of paper. "You will know what is required of you after you read the story of how I obtained the . . . artifact. After you know what you must do, and if you are willing to give of yourself, come to the address that is written below the name."

Juanita looked down at the slip of paper. When she looked up, both women were gone.

She stared into space for a moment then unfolded

the paper. Freya had written one word: BRÍSINGAMEN. Below it was an address on Carrier Street. She folded the paper, stuffed it into her purse, and hurried off to the Public Library.

Once inside, she did an internet search. *Brísingamen* was a necklace to which the goddess Freya had taken a fancy. The only way she could obtain it, though, was to sleep with the four dwarves who had manufactured it. She wanted it so badly she agreed to this. The tales varied at this point. Some said she had to go every year and pay the dwarves by yielding to them; others said Odin found out and provided means for her to extract herself from the bargain. She sat back and looked at the screen. Freya was scheduled to pay the price to the makers of the necklace and wanted to her to be a substitute. Otherwise she would not have mentioned a price—the same price she had paid. There was no other explanation.

She sat back and wondered. Was she willing to pay the price? She shuddered. It would be gross, weird, and perverse, but it would save him. After a while she left, then drove to the address she had been given.

It was a red and white shingled house. Nothing special about it, though it had the elegance of age. Two large cats sunned themselves on the porch. She went to the door and knocked, and was admitted.

The house exuded comfort. Expensive rugs and elegantly built furniture and lovely natural wood, it immediately put her at ease. Freya and Fulla waited in the front room. Juanita wondered if she should kneel, then simply bowed.

"You've made your decision?" Freya asked.

"Yes, Lady Goddess. I am willing to do what you ask."

"What am I asking you to do?"

"Yield to the dwarves with whom you made a bargain to obtain Brísingamen."

"Good. Come with me."

She walked up a flight of stairs to a bedroom. When Freya closed the door and Juanita turned, her eyes rested on two of the most beautiful women she had ever seen. She could not keep her her eyes from them.

"I need to know if you will be attractive enough to those to whom I am indebted so they will accept you as a substitute. My daughters will be the judges. Remove your garments."

Juanita stripped. The two beautiful young women—dressed in modern, fashionable clothes, looking like they could have walked off the cover of *Vogue* or *Cosmopolitan*—watched as she shed her clothing piece by piece, everything but her sandals. Naked, she put her hands to her side. She had never considered that she might not be attractive enough. She thought she was reasonably pretty. In high school she had been a cheerleader and, her junior year, Homecoming Queen, but beside the two silent goddesses, she felt dumpy and plain. They assessed her. After what seemed an endless pause, one of the young women spoke.

"She will do. The dwarves will like her dark skin and hair. She's strong and trim. They will certainly feel desire for her."

"Very well. Thank you, my daughters."

And, just as it had been at the restaurant that morning, the two women were gone.

Juanita wondered if she should dress and get in bed. Fulla brought a smock for her and helped her put it on.

"You can wear this," Freya said.

"To bed?"

"That will come later. We have somewhere else to go. We must make arrangements."

"Where are we going?"

"Come along."

They left the bedroom and started down the stairs.

"You've read enough to know what I'm asking you to do. Are you prepared to take my place when the dwarves come for what is owed them?"

"If I agree, you will free Eddie?"

"You will have the necklace to wear for a day. It will give you powers. The brigands who hold the man you love will grant your request to release him."

"I agree," she said grimly. "I'm ready right now if you want to summon them."

"I always lie with them on four consecutive days," Freya said.

"That won't work. I have to free Ernesto today."

"Time does not exist for me as it exists for you. None of the time you know will pass as we arrange for you to take my place. You have to be approved."

"Approved? I'm going to stand in for you and let myself be . . . well, you know. How will I need approval for something as simple as that?"

Freya smiled. "You are a spirited woman. Give me your hand. You must come with me."

"Why? I know what I've agreed to."

"Yes, but even the gods are ruled by law. I will take you to Folkvangr, my realm. There we will arrange the conditions of the agreement. I've summoned those we will need for the arrangement."

"Sorry I'm causing so much trouble," Juanita said.

Freya gave her a look. Shame flooded Juanita's soul. She knelt. The action surprised her. She had not thought to do so.

"Forgive me, Lady Goddess," she said. "My heart is anxious."

"Rise," Freya ordered.

They walked outside. Juanita expected to see the street with parked cars, the houses, and the church where the street formed a "T." Instead, the two of them walked onto a wide plain bounded by distant mountains. Snow fell in large flakes from a cover of blue cloud. Not a hint of wind interfered with its descent. She saw birches, maples, ash, and oak. But there were trees with gold trunks, red and blue branches, leaves of silver, gold, and purple. Flashes of light—something like lightning but not exactly the same—rolled through the clouds in beautiful patterns, soundless and rhythmic.

Juanita gaped. She had never seen such beauty. The white meadow stretched toward the mountains, which seemed a hundred miles away. Snow and clouds did not give a gloomy cast to the landscape, only a solemnity and a sense of holiness.

Freya walked slowly. Juanita felt cold through the thin fabric of the smock she wore. It chilled her and yet the chill did not bring her discomfort. It filled her with a kind of steely resolution.

"Remove your shoes. This is a sacred place."

Juanita looked dubiously at the snow in front of her but had no power to dispute the goddess, let alone disobey. She kicked off her sandals. The two of them went on, walking into the meadow.

Snowflakes melted in her hair. Ahead, a group of figures appeared whom she assumed must be guards. Fierce-looking warriors in helmets with boars sculpted on them greeted the goddess as she approached. They wore chainmail armor and carried spears. They did not kneel or bow, which Juanita thought odd, but she realized, even though her knowledge of Norse culture was limited, that it rated bravery, valor, and prowess highly. In life, these men had been formidable, had given their lives in battle, and the goddess treated them as equals.

After Freya conversed with the men in a language Juanita did not understand, the two of them continued on.

"Why do you need guards here?" Juanita asked after a while.

"Remember that we are always in danger of attack from the Frost Giants and other evil creatures."

Memory flickered in Juanita's head.

"Is this Asgard?"

Freya smiled. "This is Folkvangr, my realm. Of those who die honorably in battle, half find their rest here. The rest go to Asgard."

They approached a grove of trees with golden leaves and white trunks. Intricate harp music wafted through the air. Juanita halted a moment, captured by the beauty of the notes she heard. Freya stopped with her. She smiled as Juanita listened. After a long while—she could not tell how long; perhaps time did not exist in this place—Freya spoke.

"It is Bragi. He is showing off. Come. We must proceed."

They climbed a hill. At its crest, Juanita gasped to see a green sward surrounding a pool of deep blue water. No snow fell there. A small structure of stone with a thatched roof stood at the edge of the pond. As Juanita and Frey descended into the declivity where the pond nestled, a woman with a Valkyrie attending her emerged from the stone house.

Juanita puzzled at the new paradox. The woman looked like Freya but her hair was dark, not blonde. She wore a long silver dress. Her attendants wore tunics and carried some spear-like weapon. Juanita noticed the woman wore a dagger in a sheath that strapped around her shoulder and rested at an angle above her left breast. The attendants knelt. The woman did not.

"Can we do this?" Freya asked her.

"If Vár will allow it—and I don't see any reason she would not," the woman replied. "The mortal you have brought should step in the waters of the pond."

Freya nodded. The two men led Juanita to the edge of the sapphire water. There, the Valkyrie helped Juanita disrobe.

"Step into the sacred pool," the dark haired woman said.

It felt cold, but the cold came with a stab of pleasure. For a moment Juanita saw blue, felt the ice wash over her, heard Bragi's music even immersed in the pond, and, a moment later, found herself on shore in the green grass. The Valkyrie dried and dressed her. Freya nodded at the woman. The attendants knelt. Then Freya took Juanita's arm and they continued their journey.

"Who was that woman?" Juanita asked. Once more they walked through snow.

"We call her Sjöfn. She is a goddess of love."

"She looks like you. Is she your sister?"

"She is both herself and me. What is the term you mortals use? A *manifestation?*"

"How could she be two things at once?"

"Quite easily. Many things in your world are two things at once. And I think you've learned things are different here."

"Who is Vár?"

"The goddess of covenants."

"I've already agreed to what you want, Lady Goddess."

"Yes, but we must amend my agreement with the dwarves."

Juanita looked over at her. "Will Vár allow it?"

"She has in the past."

Juanita felt a wave of shock go through her. "You mean I'm not the first to agree to this?"

"The obligation is odious to me. I frequently commission another woman to take my place. Not always. As the proverb has it, 'If you make a bed, you must lie in it.' For me, that is literal. I keep the agreement periodically so I suffer the result of my own folly. But not always."

Juanita saw another structure loom up out of the snow. It looked like a cave with a carved façade—She had seen something like it before; Petra. They walked out of the snow, through the door, and into the interior. A circular room housed a fire burning on a pillar. Behind the fire stood a woman who looked old and young at the same time. She wore her grey hair pulled back and tied in a long braid. Her garment was simple. Her grey eyes radiated brightness and intelligence.

"Greetings, my sister," Freya said.

"Greetings to you, Queen of Heaven."

"Can the arrangement be amended?"

"Is the mortal willing?"

Vár's eyes fell on Juanita, who felt suddenly frightened. She looked at the goddess, and was overwhelmed by the power, resolution, and clarity of one who knows and sees all. Juanita's mouth felt dry.

"Young woman, do you know what is expected of you?"

"I do, my Lady."

"Are you willing to perform the deed?"

"I am willing, yes."

"The consequences for failing to perform you part in this agreement are dire, quite dire. You will dwell forever in Helheim, the abode of the dead, if you fail in your duty. Grmr, the hound who guards that realm will tear at your flesh. You will shiver in its cold until Ragnarök. Be advised."

Fear coursed through Juanita's spirit. What if she lost her resolve? What if the dwarves were so hideous she could not bear their embrace? Maybe there were worse things than losing Eduardo. But after a moment of doubt, she spoke up.

"I am willing. I agree to Freya's arrangement."

"You have made your choice. Come then."

Juanita walked up to the pedestal. Vár put her right index finger in the fire and then withdrew it. It glowed like a hot coal. She turned and swiftly drew it across Juanita's face, tracing a line from her forehead, across the bridge of her nose, down to the bottom of her cheek.

Juanita screamed as pain lanced through her body, the agony bringing her to her knees. She started to reach for her face. Vár caught her hand.

"Don't touch the wound," she said. Even through the pain she felt, Juanita noticed the goddess's finger—the finger that had glowed like a coal only seconds ago—looked perfectly normal now. Juanita sobbed but then felt a hand touch her face. The pain evaporated. She looked up in bewilderment.

"Let's go," Freya said.

In only a moment she and Freya were standing in the front room of the house they had left. Juanita touched her cheek and felt a ridge.

"There is a scar," Freya said.

Juanita rushed to a mirror. She screamed in horror. A thick red scar ran diagonally across her face.

"You didn't tell me this!" she wailed.

"Peace." Freya touched her gently. "The scar will vanish after you have fulfilled your part of the arrangement. It is Vár's way, and I must submit to it.

Believe me when I say it will disappear and you will not be disfigured."

Juanita calmed. "You could have told me," she said grumpily.

"You might have felt fear if I had."

"Won't the dwarves be repulsed at the sight of a woman with a hideously scarred face?" she asked.

"Child," Freya replied, "they aren't interested in your face."

Juanita felt her anger ebb but didn't want to let go of it yet. She looked around.

"Where's Fulla?"

"She is in the bedchamber."

A loud knock came at the door.

"They're here," the goddess said. "It's time."

"All in one day. This is all I ask of you, Lady Freya."

"If you so wish. I'm sure they will agree."

Once upstairs, Fulla helped Juanita pull off her smock. Freya nodded and, accompanied by her attendant, left the room. Juanita gathered her courage. She had slept with more than one man. But these were supernatural beings. *And* dwarves. The door creaked. Her first paramour entered the room.

He was not what she expected.

For one, he looked nothing like a dwarf. Most notably, he was not short. Perhaps he stood a bit shorter than the average man, but not that much shorter. His body, though, looked different. His arms, legs, and neck were thick; hands gnarled and hairy; feet big and clunky. And his face did not look right. Something about it seemed misshapen, though Juanita could not exactly say what. He approached the bed, said his name, *Dvalinn*, undressed, climbed in, and went to work.

Too hairy, too ugly, she thought, as the embrace

began, but Juanita soon found that looks did not mean everything. She liked the strength with which he held her. His coal-black beard felt soft and soothed her face and neck. And—she had to admit—it was one of the best experiences she had ever had. She got her joy once and then again. She bucked, stretched, beat his back with her fists, moaned, shouted, and swore. After Dvalinn finished, he lay there a while, grunted, got up, got dressed and left. He had only spoken his name. Dwarves, she gathered, were men of few words.

Alfrik, Berling and Grer followed in succession. Each experience took her to levels of joy and pleasure she had never dreamed existed. Like Dvaliin, the dwarves came in, gave their name, did their work, and left. When the last one had done, she lay there, sated, not wanting to move for fear it would break the spell of unutterable delight that had enveloped her like a golden cloud.

How long she reposed she was not certain. After a while, Freya entered. Juanita thought she should get up but Freya touched her shoulders.

"Are you well, child?"

Juanita smiled. "Yes and no. No: I'm worn out and sore. Yes: I'm as well-screwed as I've ever been in my whole life."

Freya smiled. "They are remarkable, looks aside. I could hear you shouting downstairs. I admit I envied you. Maybe what is required of me is not so bad after all."

"I liked it."

"Bathe and dress. I'll meet you downstairs. I will have the necklace for you. You may go and rescue your lover."

The bathroom, pink-tiled and large, stood next to the bedroom. A mirror ran the length of the long counter across from the bathtub, and Juanita saw her reflection. The scar on her face had disappeared.

Attended by Fulla, she bathed, dried off, dressed, and came downstairs.

She knelt before Freya. The goddess held out Brísingamen and lowered it over Juanita's head. She felt the cold metal on the sides of her neck and the hard, cold jewels resting against the flesh below her throat. As if in answer to what she was wondering, Fulla, held up a mirror.

The necklace was not a thin, delicate string, as Juanita had thought it would be. It was solid—a circle of gold, thick and heavy. Various jewels—rubies, opals, emeralds, some stones she could not identify—hung from it. She stared silently at its beauty. Finally she nodded. Fulla lowered the mirror. Freya looked at Juanita solemnly.

"Go now. Return the necklace to me before the sun is set. You will need these as well."

She dropped five coins into Juanita's hands; Krügerrands. Juanita nodded and set out.

She came to an address on Division Street that housed the headquarters of Tito Salinas' gang. A gang member stood by the door. He leered at her as she approached.

"Hey, baby," he said. "Nice rack."

As she stopped his expression changed suddenly. He licked his lips.

"What do you want?"

"I need to see Tito."

He did not give her any backtalk but simply nodded and motioned for her to follow him upstairs. She followed him up a long, steep flight and led her through a maze of halls to where Salinas sat behind a desk as if her were an executive or CEO. He ran a multiracial gang—a man you did not cross up or mess with. He gazed at her, mischief in his glance, but then his face changed. He looked, she fancied, a little frightened.

"Juanita?

"That's me." She reached in her pocket of her skirt and got out the Krügerrands. She slammed them down on his desk. "The coins are gold. They're worth double what Eddie owes you. You have your money. I want him."

He nodded, his face showing the vacant stare she now knew was the look of someone under enchantment. He and two of his soldiers led her to the room they had confined Edwardo in.

He was bruised and hurting. She got him to his feet. The gang members helped him downstairs. When she thanked them, they nodded, looking stupid and bewildered, not knowing why they had been so cooperative and why they felt they must obey everything she said. She drove Eddie home, helped his mother get him in bed, and arranged for a doctor's appointment to make certain he was not hurt badly. She drove back to Carrier Street and the house where Freya awaited her return.

Once inside, Juanita unclasped the necklace and handed it to Fulla, who scurried over and fastened it on for her mistress.

"Thank you, Juanita" Freya said. "You will always be in my graces."

"I thank you, Lady Goddess. Where I live, your graces are much needed."

Balder

all beauty must fade
as all stories close,
episodes of creation
appreciated only because the avalanche
is posed atop crescendo –
sunsets awe because twilight
dulls senses, leaving memories,
cheap imitations of five petal
masterpieces

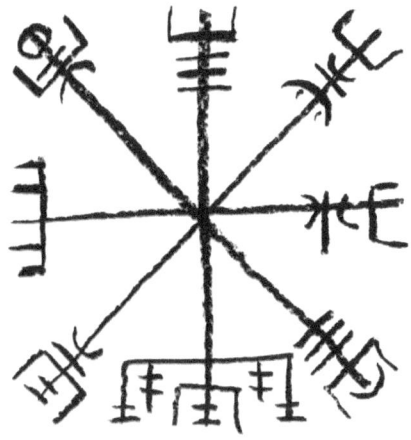

Old Gold's Last Stand

"Wait a minute. I'll activate the GPS and check," said the tall girl with glasses. "Hold my champagne."

One of the other girls, the one with a purple party-hat, took it.

The boy in the felt hat interrupted. "Come on, I'm sure it's this way." He led the others towards a narrow passage. "I think we can get through here."

One of them stumbled and they giggled and moved in the general direction of the alleyway, but stopped dead as a filthy, ragged homeless man stepped out, barring their passage.

"Halt! You shall not pass!" he cried, in a surprisingly strong baritone, one hand raised.

The students stood gobsmacked for a second, then laughed.

"Way to go, Gandalf," the girl with the hat said. They half circled him and continued on their way.

The old man watched them go, then scratching his beard, stepped back into the shadows.

"I have the strangest feeling that should mean something," he muttered to himself.

The old man, known to most as *Old Gold,* sat down beside his cardboard shelter, but the importance of the moment slipped away.

It was one of those hot autumns. One that never wants to give in, and doesn't allow for a fresh gust of air. Instead, it was baking the city so it smelled like asphalt and fast food, with a hint of dog shit, perfume and vomit. Old Gold shuffled along slowly. He had no particular place he needed to be. It was all about being *present.* He would meet the people he needed to meet. This had been the way, as long as he could remember.

All of a sudden there was a new scent in the air. He stopped, sore muscles alert. There was something oddly familiar. The fragrance was sweet and sour. There was a savoury moistness to it. He felt his mouth water and stomach rumble. He was hungry in a way he had forgotten was possible.

He turned and looked around, searching for the source of the heavenly scent. He spotted the sleek form of an Airstream trailer, with windows like portholes. A diner. On the neon-lit sign, he could just decipher the letters. *Idun's All-American Apple Pie*.

Before he even had time to think about it, his old bones had moved towards the door. He entered and the scent filled his nostrils and made his blood rush.

At the counter stood a young waitress. Her pillbox hat covered long, blonde pigtails and a heart shaped face. Her dress was turquoise with bright white details. A short apron was tied around her narrow waist and above one of her perky breasts a name tag read, "Idun."

"Welcome!" She greeted him with a smile. "I was waiting for you. I have just what you want." She disappeared into the kitchen, then came back carrying a small tray with a large piece of the house special.

Her smile was inviting. He wasn't used to that. Did she know him? Had he been here before? He felt dizzy, the scent, the colours, her smile making his head spin.

"Just a minute," he muttered and backed out the door. He looked around. There was something familiar. Old Gold patted his pockets, where was it? He felt the hard edge in his right pocket and fumbled slightly before he extracted his diary. He flipped it open and read a page at random.

"They think I'm homeless. Most of them are decent. Some share the little they have. That makes me think it was all worth it. Still, most of what I have seen is about making it. Making it for themselves. I still haven't seen a comprehending pair of eyes. Not once have I been searched out for a father. I guess I'll stay until the end, just to give them a final chance. Anyway, I can't go back to Åsgard, not the way I left."

Old Gold put away the journal, his brows creased in puzzlement. He looked inwards, searching his memory.

"Åsgard" he tasted the word. "Åsgard". He had been there. It was . . . home?

Old Gold closed his eyes, remembering.

He had left them a letter. It explained everything. Then he did it. In his head, he heard a voice cry out. "He's jumping! Do something!"

I have been watching, waiting for so long. At first, I was expectant. I had anticipation. Thinking about who would come made my watch nights short, my eyes not sore nor my back stiff. My undertaking was young and I had hope and belief.

I had not imagined Trell or Karl to be the one to knock on my gate. In my heart, I thought I would see Jarl. He was the strongest. He would conquer any obstacle. He did not show. I guess he was busy. Lots of things to do when you are the first among your people.

I settled for a while with the thought it would be Karl, then. He should be able to steer his own time. He did not have all, but he would make his way. It warmed my heart. I would be so proud and happy upon his arrival.

Eventually I started to think more and more about Trell. I had underestimated him. He had the most to win; he would have to be strong to endure. I waited. Sure, he might take some time; he would not have had an easy life.

For centuries, I waited. I longed to see how they were doing. I had put them into the world, and every part of me ached to be with them. Yet, I stood my watch and lived with hope.

My vanity hurt of course. Did they not want to know where they came from? Did not Jarl want to see who gave him all his opportunities? On the other hand, Karl, did he not wish to see if I was just as mighty as he, or if his strong eyesight was inherited? Or how about Trell? Wouldn't he have anger towards me for his fate, or didn't he have any favours to think to ask me? But vanity aside, all I thought of was to know them. I dreamt about shaking their strong hands.

Now I see they will never come. If I stay, I will never know them. I have guarded this realm for more years than I know, but now am done. There just isn't anything more to give.

I am sorry.
Heimdall

Old Gold sat on the bench outside the diner. He knew that wasn't his name, of course. That had been left behind, same as everything else.

He had plummeted into the abyss. In the golden setting of the sun, he had been the black shadow, falling towards the ground, towards Midgard. Like a comet he had crashed to the surface, leaving behind a crater. But he had not had death in him then, and so his rebirth took place.

When he arose, he thought it fitting to start out new in all ways, so he called himself Gold. Apparently, you can run but you can't hide. Heimdall stood and reached out with a shaky hand for the diner door.

Idun invited him again and he exhaled heavily and slumped down into a booth. It was the apples of course. The godly apples. If he ate, he would be young again. He could start over. He might go home. He found himself staring at the pie.

"An all-American Apple Pie to die for, eh?" He glared at Idun, but she just smiled. A blindingly beautiful woman with the optimism of perpetual youth.

"Try it. It's super-good".

Heimdall stabbed a fork into the pie, felt how easily it went in. The pie would be just the right amount of moist. His old hands quivered. Saliva gathered in his mouth and he swallowed. Idun had placed a scoop of ice cream on the plate too. Where it touched the pie, it slowly melted. Heimdall's eyes started watering. Tears, for the first time in how many years? But he didn't eat. Carefully, deliberately, he put down his fork.

Trickster's Grace

The gods of dark and those of grey
caged behind bars, powers bound
reduced to shadows of themselves
none defend them in the modern world
except for my patron, lord and friend
except for the sly one, the swift one

who will speak for him?
giver of fire, bringer of ruin
he who wins with trickery
what cannot be won by swords

Who am I to argue for him?
I am his votary, his channel, his champion
Hear my words: the world needs him
Needs his cunning, his deceit,
Mischief must walk freely through the spheres
He dances between good and evil
and maintains the line between

And when the best-laid plans went awry
Yes, it was I who let him in

I ride beside him as he rides to freedom
Under his wing, warm affection
he welcomes my embrace
and we mock with no barbs

What next, now you are unbound?
He says, let us wander the ruins
the ghost city along the Detroit,
I ask him, only take my hand
we shall be as Adam and Eve

An elder spirit in deep Siberia
He would visit and make parley
I accompany without complaint
So long as we ride the rails
Across the steppes, through the night
And into their newborn legend
And he feeds me the finest caviar
From his fingers

He has whispered to my heart
I belong by his side now and ever
The companion to all his adventures

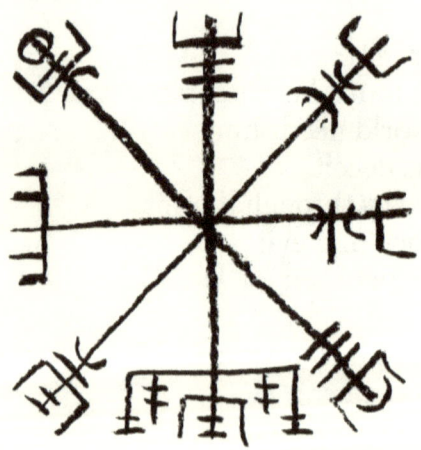

They're Coming

It was only a dream, but it bothered her for days. The goriness, the vivid images and the strangeness of it, caused her much unease. And it wasn't even *her* dream. It was Noah's. Noah, who always slept soundly; who always awoke with a smile on his face. But that pre-dawn June morning, when Noah turned to her and blurted out: "They're coming!" Something changed.

There was a time when Jiawen thought her life would unfold as a series of uneventful episodes. Her immigrant parents introduced her to one eligible bachelor after another. Many from families like hers, first generation Asian Americans made good. Jiawen could have had her pick of lawyers, financiers and doctors. But she spurned them all. It wasn't that she thought she was better than them. She just wasn't ready. But what wasn't she ready for?

When she chanced into Noah at Trader Joe's one day, her life was ripe for change. They were in the same checkout line and started chatting. Unlike Jiawen, Noah had a real passion in life, which was sustainable horticulture. When she found out he was moving overseas to start an organic avocado farm, her façade of nonchalance crumbled. Within weeks, she had quit her job, broken her lease, and was ready to move to Belize.

It all went swimmingly, until that morning. Noah wouldn't go back to sleep, and Jiawen had no idea why. Later, over a breakfast of stewed pineapples and green tea, she felt she had to do something. Looking up from her newspaper, she spoke.

"Who is coming." For a moment Noah looked surprised. Then, she could see something igniting behind his eyes.

"The blood," he began.

In his dream, long, low ships had arrived in Corozal Harbor and disgorged hundreds of men. Not just ordinary men, but huge medieval men armed with a panoply of weapons hell-bent on killing. The invaders quickly made their way to the town's only Save-U Supermarket and started swinging their battle-axes at the startled shoppers. It was a massacre. As Noah and others ran from the marauding Norsemen, he saw a frothy river of blood flowing down Corozal's main street, the Calle Viejo.

"That was when I woke up," Noah said, downing his cup of tea. Jiawen didn't know much about Vikings, except they apparently *didn't* wear horned helmets, had lots of hair, and came from somewhere in Scandinavia.

"What could it mean?" She asked rhetorically. The question hung in the air like a swarm of black flies.

During the week that followed, Noah was distracted. If he would talk, it was only about the ongoing problems with his farm. Once, she caught him surfing the web and reading up on Viking history. She went to the same page and started gathering information. One of the goddesses attracted her attention. Riding a chariot pulled by cats, the powerful Freyja lived to survey gore-strewn battlefields, choosing the slain and conveying them to the afterlife. Jiawen thought her the most sympathetic deity.

Then she discovered a book. A dog-eared paperback titled, *"Legends of the Vikings"* that seemed to have magically appeared on their bookshelves. As she flipped through the volume, a bookmark fell out, proving that Noah had bought the item at the local second-hand bookstore. Jiawen re-shelved the book and didn't ask him about it.

She mostly stayed out of his way. While Noah spent the day at work, Jiawen puttered around the house, redecorating and researching new ways of cooking quinoa. One evening, almost a month after the dream, the two of them were dining at the newly opened Village Grill. As Noah polished off his shrimp appetizer, Jiawen, bogged down by the overall grey mood, put down her silverware and looked him straight in the eye.

"You have to let it go," she said quite suddenly.

Noah stopped eating and looked at her, his forehead creased.

"The whole Viking thing," she continued, "You have to let it go."

For a while, there was no response. All Jiawen could hear was Noah's even, subdued chewing. Then, he said, "Okay."

For the next few days, all was well. Noah's mood lifted, and Jiawen no longer felt that unspoken tension when he was near. It didn't last long.

Whilst doing laundry one day, Jiawen was emptying out Noah's pockets when a small piece of metal fell out. Smaller than a quarter and seemingly made of silver, it was the head of a horse with its nostrils flaring and its tongue curling into a question mark. Jiawen asked Noah what it was, but to her surprise, he claimed to know nothing of its existence. Suspecting the item could be worth something, she kept it in the bottom drawer of her antique Mexican armoire.

That night, Jiawen had a dream. She was at a wedding, soon revealed to be her very own. All her friends and family had gathered to celebrate her big day. Noah looked particularly resplendent in his wedding suit, while she tried her best to remain calm in her hand-sewn red taffeta gown. The proceedings unfolded without a hitch, until the ring exchange.

Jiawen had somehow forgotten hers, and started to panic. Luckily, a small boy with a mop of golden hair came up and offered her a ring fashioned from wood and shell. And then they were pronounced husband and wife.

When Jiawen and Noah turned to walk down the aisle, everyone had vanished. The church—it was definitely a church—was suddenly empty. When they emerged into the sunlight, there was only an old horse waiting for them. The ancient beast looked at the newlyweds with indifference.

The dream convinced Jiawen to keep the amulet. The presence of the strange equine must mean something, she told herself. The truth was, the more she looked at the silver trinket, the more she liked it.

Motivated by a sense of having something to do, Jiawen fashioned a bracelet out of Mayan glass beads and strung the horse head at one end. It looked beautiful.

A few days later, Jiawen was enjoying a cup of coffee in downtown Corozal, when a homeless man, smelling strongly of seaweed, came up to her. The man startled her as he demanded money. Up close, Jiawen could see that his irises were milky with disease, and she turned away in disgust and fear.

Despite trying her best to ignore him, the man simply wouldn't go away. Growing increasingly desperate, she opened her bag to search for a dollar bill, only to find a twenty. She was on the verge of moving away when the decrepit man grabbed hold of her arm. She tried pulling away, but he had a surprisingly firm grasp, his filthy, over-grown nails digging into her milky flesh.

It was then the man noticed Jiawen's bracelet. With

his otiose eyes fixed on the charm, the man became alarmed. "*Maldita!*" he proclaimed loudly. He quickly let go and scurried away. Shaken, Jiawen abandoned her half-finished coffee and left the cafe.

When she got home, with the three strident syllables still echoing in her head, Jiawen googled the word and discovered what it meant; *Cursed*. Immediately she took off the bracelet and threw it into the trash. With the amulet gone, she felt like a weight had been lifted from her shoulders.

For the rest of the day, Jiawen sat in a quiet corner of the kitchen, feeling lost. Now it was her turn to be moody. Noah didn't notice. Insomnia took hold, and Jiawen could no longer sleep. As she tossed and turned in bed one night, Noah awoke. Seeing her discomfort, he asked: "What's the matter?"

He wasn't expecting his words to cause a little explosion.

"What do you mean *what's the matter*? Can't you tell?"

All at once, the relaxed complacency of their relationship evaporated. Noah felt blindsided, and demanded to know why Jiawen was angry. But she refused to engage. She turned away from him and kept her silence.

The next morning, when Jiawen awoke, everything was different. It was as if a large, unpolished lens had been placed in front of her, such that the world seemed a little less sharp, a little more shadowy. Noah, who had already departed for work, had left behind a note of apology, written in his unmistakable scrawl.

Jiawen read it but didn't feel any better. She tried making breakfast, but promptly dropped an egg that smashed on the hard tile floor. Then she attempted to clean the bathroom, but slipped in the shower and bruised her knee. She gave up and went for a walk.

She found herself at the Save-U Supermarket in downtown Corozal. Reaching for the mayonnaise, Jiawen accidentally knocked down a can. She was putting the item back when she noticed the brand. *Viking Milk*, the label said. She started shaking. All at once, she had a vivid vision of Noah's dream. It was the image of brutish men throwing screaming infants into a large cauldron of boiling oil. For several drawn-out seconds, Jiawen couldn't get rid of the vision. She started hyperventilating and blinking rapidly, causing a fellow shopper to ask if she was all right. Jiawen nodded and the shopper went away. Slowly, the image faded.

Jiawen abandoned her groceries and took to the narrow cobbled streets, walking without a destination. A heavy feeling had settled over her. At Mercado Central, she tried smiling at the little kids sitting on coin-operated rocking horses. But her smile barely concealed a deep sense of doom. It was as if the Vikings were already here, their axes raised, ready for mass decapitations. Later, as she stood in front of a young seamstress hand-stitching a beautiful white wedding gown, Jiawen couldn't help but imagine big gobs of blood splattered across the pristine silk.

She eventually found her way home and took a long shower. As warm water cascaded down her torso, she began to sob.

The next week passed like a protracted bad dream. Jiawen and Noah would have dinner and not exchange a word. She would go about her day as if she was the mere caretaker of her body, her thoughts far away. The old feeling of ennui again enveloped her – she was the newly minted graduate once more, with no purpose other than to search for meaning, a meaning that continued to elude her.

One afternoon, she made a visit to the avocado farm, surprising Noah.

"Why are you here?" he asked with a smile.

Jiawen wanted to say that she missed him, that she loved him, but the words wouldn't come. Instead, she put her hand in his, and led him to the nearby grove. Noah followed, curious and puppy-like. There, under the cool shade of a custard apple tree, they made love.

"My birthday's next week," Jiawen said afterwards.

"We have to celebrate," Noah offered.

Jiawen smiled. It was her first smile in many days.

When they got home, Jiawen made dinner reservations. Her birthday would mark a turning point, she was convinced, and her life thereafter would be free of self-doubt.

The Village Grill was packed that night. Because of the special occasion, Jiawen and Noah were seated by the head waiter at the best table in the house. On one side, they could see the great expanse of the mirror-like Caribbean, while on the other, the glistening lights of downtown Corozal.

Jiawen held Noah's hand in hers, as she perused the wine list and half listened to the bossa nova in the background. As Noah chatted on about organic insecticides, out of the corner of her eye, she saw a figure stand up. This was quickly followed by the sound of a wine glass smashing onto the travertine floor below.

Jiawen turned to look. It was an elderly gentleman, fear written all over his face. A napkin still tucked into his ill-fitting corduroy pants, he stood arrow straight, pointing to something outside the window. As a waiter rushed up to help, the gentleman said in Spanish:

"There! Don't you see them?"

The waiter looked to the sea, confusion on his face. A quick glance by Jiawen proved that its surface was no longer calm. It was roiling, as if massive sea snakes had clustered together and were thrashing in unison.

She became quiet. When her gazpacho arrived, she ate a mouthful and quickly laid aside her spoon. And when Noah asked her what was wrong, she made a little grimace and said she had a headache. Later, as she turned her attention back to the old man, their eyes met momentarily.

When the old man paid his bill and made his exit, Jiawen was compelled to follow. She turned to Noah and said: "Give me a moment," and she was gone.

The old man walked briskly. Afraid of losing sight of him, Jiawen broke into a run. By the time she caught up, they were near the harbor. She called after him, and he stopped, turning around.

"What do you want?" he demanded in heavily accented English.

There was a small pendant hanging from the old man's neck, gleaming in the orange glow of the street lamps. Immediately it caught Jiawen's attention. It was identical to her horse head charm; perhaps it was the very same one.

"What do you want?" the man repeated, as he moved a step closer. A scowl formed on his tanned, moon-shadowed face. When there was no response, he took another step forward.

Before she knew what was happening, Jiawen struck the old man with her fist. A red welt quickly formed on his left check. But instead of cowering away, the old man smiled, an odd little grin that played on his soft, weathered lips. Then he mumbled under his breath. "*Maldita.*"

Something exploded within her. Jiawen shoved the man hard, her strength amplified by growing fury. Losing his balance, the old man fell, his head hitting the curb with such force that she heard his skull crack.

Jiawen stared at the prostrate figure, not knowing what to do. Not a single soul was around, and no one had seen. But just as she was about to bolt, something made her turn back. She went back to the old man and squatted.

A rivulet of blood had appeared next to the body and was flowing down the sidewalk. At a certain point, it dripped down the curb and trickled down the street. Jiawen tried to feel the man's pulse but couldn't find one. She began to feel dizzy, and when she stood, the world was spinning wildly around her.

All she could hear was the sound of the sea, unmistakably alive and pulsating to an ancient, primal beat. Jiawen remembered how Freya would carefully select those worthy of resurrection, spending her time with each expired soul as she made her evaluation.

As she considered her options, Jiawen's eyes returned to the metal pendant on the old man's neck. Only now did she realize the horse was laughing. In fact, it seemed as if it was laughing at her. Fueled by a jolt of adrenalin, Jiawen yanked the jewellery from the man and clenched it hard. The metal immediately cut into her flesh, drawing blood.

She let her hand bleed, the blood dripping onto the old gentleman's supine body, mixing with the crimson flow from his broken skull. Maybe this is a dream, Jiawen thought. Just another bad dream. But it wasn't, and the copious blood flow underscored the reality of the situation.

One thing seemed certain. The bleeding would never stop. Not from the old man, not from her palm. Under the unblinking street light, the ribbon of crimson was snaking its way to the sea, whence, like an overdue tsunami, the Vikings would come.

Thor's Exclamations

thunderstruck
power, merciless energy
enough to consume itself
unchecked, hammered home
by years of incessant
headbanging against the empty
blue sky
where all subtleties fade
before the immortal hammer
set to end each world
with decisive blows
unnecessary today
though Thor still swings
Mjölnir to end
dull sentences

Saga

I first met her while waiting tables in her cafe. I was doing a Literature with Creative Writing course at Manchester University, and needed to subsidise myself. I was in digs with a couple of other students, my course and (mostly) my materials were covered, but a guy has to eat and, of course, there were the evenings. Such is student life.

I called in on spec and found that there was a job going. It was weekends, and in addition to waiting on I was a pot washer, floor cleaner, rubbish remover and general dog's body.

Saga agreed to take me on without any references or enthusiasm. She was older, wiser, and, well, *other*. She had that strange accent (Scandinavian, she said. I don't recall her ever saying which actual country she was from), and wore her hair in a way that accentuated her foreign identity: flame red, it was braided and hung down over the right shoulder. Always the right.

Sometimes she took an interest in her customers, sometimes she remained aloof. I never knew what factors came into play in determining this.

After a short time she began to take an interest in me. She would ask about my studies, and wanted to read my writing. Initially I was a little reticent about sharing it with her. In those days, believing I had a little talent but unsure of the extent of my ability, I was nevertheless idealistic, with literary ambitions. I said, with juvenile bravado, that I wanted to be a Hemingway, or a Faulkner.

She laughed at that and said "Do you not like any of your own writers?"

Her laugh made me feel my age, as though she was an adult tolerating the simple talk of a child.

There was a young girl, of early high school years, that for a while she used to teach on Saturdays. She would take her to the room above the cafe, leaving the running of her business in the hands of a Polish woman named Kasia, who used to revel in this temporary elevation. She essentially did the same work as I, but on these Saturdays she would adopt a high and mighty attitude on account of her being the 'stand-in manager' as she liked to put it. After a few months, though, the girl ceased coming.

I'm not sure if Saga was a qualified teacher or not, but I do know that the mother of the girl was ecstatic with her daughter's progress. I heard her once say to Saga that her form teacher had told her that she was flourishing, moving up two whole sets.

On a Sunday we would close up early as we only really did a lunchtime trade on this day. This was when, a month or so into my time there, as we readied the place for leaving, Saga began to take an interest in my writing. After asking a few times how things were going with uni, she asked me to bring in whatever I was currently working on.

And, of course, I did. Despite the sensitivity about my writing, by this point I would have done anything she asked. I was young and infatuated. But it was more than just an older woman fixation, I think it was the contrast. I had still an immature take on life. Full of ideals but no experience to ground it in. She was worldly-wise and erudite, with a sophistication that spoke of other places. She was the one person I knew who not only knew about the books and authors I enthused about, but turned me on to others that were always exactly the kind of thing I was looking for.

On those late Sunday afternoons, once Kasia had left, when the till had been emptied and everything had been cleaned and put away, we would put the chairs up on the tables save for two. Then we would sit opposite each other, separated only by a wooden table. She would study my work and I would study her, as she scanned my handwritten notes with those green, elfin eyes. The smattering of freckles on her face fascinated me. Sometimes they appeared to glow red, spread liberally across her cheeks and the bridge of her nose. I would think of star constellations, or flower-strewn meadows. Oh, the simple, romantic analogies of the young!

Occasionally she would glance up and I would freeze. I don't know why. There was a sense of being caught out, but also something in her gaze that immediately seized me. A strange mixture of thrill and fearful possibilities.

Of course she knew the depth of my feelings, how could she not? But she showed neither rejection nor encouragement. Again — it was like the tolerating adult and the child. It was just peripheral white noise to the work taking place. And it *was* taking place.

She began pointing out the flaws and the contradictions in my writing, helped me flesh out the characters and give them such depth that they rose from the paper like living, breathing people. All of a sudden I no longer imagined them — I could *see* them! I knew them all, each one, like an intimate confidant. Their penchants, their vulnerabilities.

I began looking forward to those Sunday sessions with her more and more. More than the dry, uninspiring lessons of uni where my lecturer's monotone voice barely stirred the somnambulist forms around me.

I began living for them.

There, among the lingering smell of grease and

cooling caffeine, rain beating against the window as the outside town passed by oblivious to the magic taking place inside, my writing took on life.

And not just my writing.

There was something that Saga gave out, something that infected me. *Invigorated* me. It was like I was suddenly seeing through her eyes. The world; the people in it; myself. My outlook and attitude matured. I was just a young man, riding an acid trip where everything fits. I felt an understanding of human nature beyond my years. It was as if I was somehow becoming an informed observer, distinct from this rarefied species. And this new perception shot through my writing, fired from those special moments with this woman.

Her real passion was poetry. Although back then that was not my thing at all, she would sometimes recite lines when it was quiet and would captivate me all over again.

She did it in a way that would remove me from that place and open me up to worlds I could never have known. I know how pretentious that sounds, but you never knew her. She could be aloof, as I have said, but once she became engaged, well . . . everything was transformed. Nothing existed outside that moment.

She never recited the same thing twice. There would be lines I'd heard somewhere before but couldn't place, (like I said, poetry wasn't my thing), but mostly they were unfamiliar things, sounding more like snippets of sagas (pardon the pun) and epic stories. Some verses would be in her own tongue, but, despite my lack of understanding, they still held me in the soft rising and falling of her beguilingly melodic voice. As for the poetry in English, if you was to ask me now to repeat a single line I would not be able to. That is hard for me to explain. Startling though she was in person, the creativity she demonstrated, the inspiration she instilled, (or rather the memory of it), seemed to dissipate when she wasn't there. It was like frost being brought before the sun of scrutiny, a memory made of the substance of dreams.

As I have said, she was aware of my feelings, my *love* for her (there, I have said it), but it remained unacknowledged. That's not to say she never showed any emotions, it's just that somehow she consciously never became embroiled in them, became entangled in complicated attachments like the rest of us.

The final time that we spoke, I flattered myself that she was flirting with me. But now I think she was just using me for sport. Maybe she was getting a little bored with our arrangement. For some reason, my newly acquired awareness for humanity never seemed to apply to her.

It was another Sunday, in April, and we had finished going over a story that we were both satisfied with.

"Andy," she said, as she turned off the lights to the kitchen, "recite for me a four-word love story."

Sometimes she would set these casual tests, though she had long since finished her appraisal of me.

I thought for a moment. "She came home early."

"Yes! That is it," she said in amusement. " And in one so young, too. Now recite for me a four-word horror story."

I thought again, briefly. "She came home early."

I think at first she thought I was being perverse. She shot me such a look, her eyes flashing in a way I'd never seen before, appearing at once both fearsome in her anger and ancient in her beauty. My heart skipped a beat.

But then, as if slowly dawning: "Yes. That fits, my

mortal, that fits."

She paused then, looking almost regretful, as if she rued this sudden exchange. And instantly she transformed again, striding confidently to the door. She flipped the 'open' sign over to 'closed' and pulled the door open, holding it for me. "We are done."

I thought she was referring to our creative sparring. But the next morning, as I passed on the way to the bus station, (okay, sometimes I would go out of my way just to get a glimpse of her during the week), the cafe was closed and in darkness. Kasia was standing outside looking bemused. I went over.

"I don't know where she is," said Kasia.

I cupped my hands to shield my eyes as I peered in through the glass. There was no sign of Saga. The chairs were still on the tables, nothing moved.

I forgot about uni.

The usual motley bunch of customers began to arrive, betraying both puzzlement and frustration at this unforeseen break in their routine. Kasia and I wondered if perhaps Saga was ill (she had never been late to work before), and we both discovered that neither of us knew where she lived. We had no contact number for her either.

The cafe never opened again.

I thought about relaying my concerns about her disappearance to the police, but I quickly discovered, through a friend of a friend who worked in the local letting office, that Saga had given up her occupation of the premises, long before her lease had expired, even though it had been paid up fully in advance. It seemed Saga, true to her mysterious nature, had simply moved on. Maybe that's what she had always done. Maybe this is what she did.

For a while I felt bereaved. It was though, well yes,

someone I'd loved had died. The effect of her absence cut that deep. For a while I kidded myself that she might return, just turn up unannounced in some other business venture around the town. But time went on, draining away such wishful thinking. She had spoken last her final words to me.

We are done.

Maybe she was referring to our friendship, knowing that she was leaving. Although that look of regret had been so instant, yet so fleeting, coming as it did right after her comment.

Yes. That fits, my mortal, that fits.

She could have meant our lessons together. Perhaps, like that young school girl, she felt she had nothing else to teach me, for make no bones about it, my ability as a writer had developed exponentially.

But, just like the poetry that she used to recite, the *dynamism,* if you like, wore off. I still had the ability, and Saga had helped me to elevate and enhance it beyond my first crude attempts at producing something of note, but without her tutelage, without her very presence, it never again reached the heights of what it once was.

One result, though, of the time that I spent with that remarkable woman, was that poetry took root. I began to turn more to poetry than fiction to express myself. Sometimes when I wrote I would hum along to myself, for I could not recall Saga's words, but I remembered their rhythm, as they rose and fell in that small cafe. It was as though some instinctive score had become ingrained in me. Although the original inspiration had become diluted, there was still something there to tap into. I would hum that rhythm, and new words would come.

Many years later, when my debut collection was

published, I included a short poem called *Four-Word Story*. It was sparse, a different style to the others and was a last minute addition. It seemed appropriate though, I think, to somehow memoralise that final conversation with Saga.

Although the book was no bestseller, (let's face it, poetry never is, unless you are an Armitage or a Duffy, and even then probably not), I like to think that somewhere, *somewhere*, Saga has picked up a copy of my book, thumbed through it, read *Four-Word Story* and remembered. And perhaps, in that same somewhere, she is reciting it, even now, in that undulating accent of hers, to a love-struck, budding writer, ignoring his doting, puppy-dog eyes. Her hair still red and braided, hanging over her shoulder, untouched both by time and the trivial predilections of men.

The Song of Spells III

A thirteenth I know: if the new-born son
of a warrior is baptised in my name,
then the boy will not fail when he goes to war,
he shall never bow before an enemy's sword.
A fourteenth I know: the true nature of
gods and powers and of elves,
which none can know untaught.
A fifteenth I know, that which was sung at the gates of
Dawn;
strength to the gods, and skill to the elves,
and wisdom to Odin who utters these words.

A sixteenth I know: when all sweetness and love
I would win from some artful wench,
her heart I turn, and the whole mind change
of that fair-armed lady I love.
A seventeenth I know: so that even a shy maiden
cannot refuse my love.

An eighteenth I know: a secret from all save alone to
my sister,
or she who keeps me fast in her arms;
most safe are those secrets known to only one-
the songs are sung to an end.

Now the sayings of the High One are spoken
for the benefit of men, and to the woe of Giants,
Hail, to the speaker of spells! Hail, to he that knows!
Hail, to you have that listened! Use what you have
learned!

Death Amongst Us

The statuesque blonde woman and her male assistant continued to work on the corpse, which had been brought in that morning. A murder victim, which in the grand scheme of things, wasn't that uncommon. She had spent many years working in the city's mortuary, finding that she was more comfortable there. The mortuary was cold, clean and sterile; a place that was utterly under her control. It also helped that the dead did not ask any questions, or dare to answer back. Unlike the living.

She didn't have to be the goddess of death in order to realise that there was something different about this murder. She had been told about where he had been discovered, and his injuries were in keeping with that information, but the reasoning behind it wasn't proving to be so co-operative.

As with any murder case, there were two uniformed police officers standing at the door that led in and out of the mortuary. They were there to keep an eye on proceedings. A legal requirement in cases such as this. Looking up to the viewing gallery, she could see DC McBride looking down on what was going on below. A younger detective stood beside him, with the air of someone new to the role. Lowering her surgical mask, Hela walked over to the intercom system and pressed the button that activated it, allowing her to speak with McBride and his companion.

"Good day, gentlemen. I don't really need to ask if you are here in relation to the young man we are currently working on."

"You've been brought up to speed," McBride commented.

"We have confirmed your assumption that this one

was a local thug. His mother identified him. The only injuries that we can find are a series of small puncture wounds, like those found with snake bites. It is very likely that was the cause of death, but that still has to be proven beyond all reasonable doubt," she replied.

"That would fit with where we found him," McBride added.

"So, he was found in a pit with venomous snakes?"

McBride tilted his head to one side, before he continued. "He was. What are you thinking?"

"I know only of one other person who was killed by being thrown into a pit of venomous snakes."

"I've not heard anything about anyone else being killed like that," the young detective commented. "If you're wanting to kill someone, why not just use a knife?"

"You're new to all of this, aren't you?" Hela continued, giving him a cold look. "You won't have heard of the victim. Not unless you know your history."

"This is DC Mulligan," McBride said. "Mulligan, this is Hela. She's the chief forensic pathologist."

Hela held Mulligan's gaze. He tried to hide the shiver that went down his spine. He felt as if she was looking right into his soul. He didn't have to be told to know that she was the sort who would be able to hold her own in most situations and he wasn't willing to get on the wrong side of her.

"Well then, DC Mulligan, legend says that a Norse warrior and hero, Ragnar Lothbrok, was killed by one of the kings of England. As the story goes, he was thrown into a pit of venomous snakes. That was enough for the snakes to attack. Their venom caused him to die a slow and painful death. I suspect that the man before us did not have an easier time of it."

"So, we may have a killer on our hands, who has a

thing for history and legends?" McBride questioned.

"The autopsy will have to be finished before I commit myself to saying anything. It may be obvious to us what the cause of death was, but we both know that we will need to make it official. I will have my report on your desk as soon as possible," Hela answered.

"I look forward to reading it," McBride added. Hela watched as they left the viewing gallery, then she turned back to her work.

Hela looked down at the corpse. She had been taking notes as she worked, hoping that it wouldn't take too long for her to finish the task at hand. She had taken numerous tissue samples and they had been taken up to the labs in order to be processed, where it would be determined whether death had been caused by snake venom. The justice system was a stickler for all of the bases being covered.

As the autopsy was finished, she waited for the test results to come in. Once they had come back, it wouldn't take long for her to write up the report. It was late and she had sent her assistant on a coffee break. He wouldn't be back for twenty minutes. That would give her enough time to do what she needed to do.

Hela placed her hands on either side of the man's head and focused. She rarely did this, as the vast majority of deaths didn't warrant it. Most people died of natural causes, but there were things that only this man could tell her. With a sharp gasp from his lips, the dead man's eyes shot open.

"Where am I? What happened to me?"

"Listen to me. I need you to remain calm and to answer some questions. That is all that I ask," Hela told him.

He didn't answer, allowing for Hela to continue.

"What can you remember?"

"I was out for a run when I got jumped from behind."

He stopped. Through the connection they now shared, Hela could feel that he was struggling to remember what happened next, as well as how to put it all into words.

"I was knocked out. When I woke up, it was dark, but there was enough light for me to see that I was in some sort of pit. I could hear things moving close to me. It sounded like snakes. I could hear them hissing and slithering around."

"What happened next?" Hela asked.

His voice caught in his throat. "The snakes began to attack. I could feel them biting me. My body was on fire. There was nothing I could do. I couldn't get away. Oh my God, I'm dead!"

"Focus. Did you see the person who attacked you? Who killed you?"

Hela struggled to control her frustration, knowing that she only had a short time to get information out of him. In his panic, she could feel him fight against her. There was still that part of him that wanted to run and hide, but his body was refusing to respond. She could feel him slipping away.

"I couldn't see him. I couldn't see him" he continued.

His voice was getting weaker as he spoke and his eyes fluttered shut as the connection deteriorated further. Hela knew that she had to let him go but she had more questions. There was only one thing that she could add to the investigation. Even though the victim hadn't seen his attackers face, he still knew enough to be able to say that the killer was male.

Hela let go of the cadaver and walked back to her desk and the paperwork. She continued where she had left off. When her colleague returned, they placed the corpse into one of the chilled drawers. With nothing left to do, they both left.

"Good morning, McBride. I can see you've brought me another cadaver. How many is that in the past week?" Hela asked.

As before, McBride was standing in the viewing gallery, looking down at the mortuary. Even from a distance, Hela could see a steely look in his eyes that he got when things were serious. She began to suspect that what she was going to see next was far from pleasant. Unlike his previous visit, McBride was alone.

"Where's your colleague?" she asked.

"In the nearest toilet, spilling his guts. We may need to harden him up, when it comes to dealing with things like this, but I can't blame him for this one. I nearly lost my breakfast," McBride added.

Hela moved over to the mortuary slab, where the corpse had been laid out and covered with a sheet. Removing the sheet, she could see why someone of McBride's experience would have such a reaction. The victim had been placed face down, which was the only option that had been open to them, as he had been cut open from the back. What was meant to be inside was now on the outside.

"Who in their right mind would do that to someone?" McBride questioned.

"Someone who is really trying to make a point. This is a form of execution called a blood eagle. I am starting to think that we might be dealing with a serial killer, not just with an obsession with history, but with the Vikings."

"What makes you think that the same person is responsible for these two murders?" McBride questioned. "It's not the same MO."

"With the first murder, the victim died after being put into a pit of snakes. As I said the other day, that was meant to have been how Ragnar Lothbrok died. That is not where the story ended. Once his sons found out, they went to England, found the king who murdered their father and killed him," Hela said.

"And?"

"He was killed in pretty much the same fashion as we see here. His ribcage was hacked opened from the back and his lungs pulled through the gaping hole that was created. Usually, this is done when the victim is still alive, but I will have to determine if that happened in this case."

Glancing at McBride, Hela thought that she could see a slight change in his expression. She wasn't sure what he was thinking. She was good at telling what was going through someone's mind, but Stephen McBride was different. She struggled to read him much of the time. He was a hardened detective who had seen more than his fair share when it came to the worst of humanity. She had always presumed that he was doing nothing more than keeping his emotions under close raps, but there was a niggling feeling, at the back of her mind, that something wasn't as it should be.

"I'd better go and check on Mulligan. He seems to be taking his time," McBride commented. "Maybe, he doesn't want to come in and say hello."

Nodding, Hela turned her attention back to the corpse. The cause of death was obvious, but that did not mean she didn't have her work cut out for her.

Walking to her car, Hela understood why many of those who worked in the hospital hated the long journey to the staff car park. It never bothered her, even in the dark of night. She never felt threatened, but that did not mean that she was not aware of her surroundings. Her car was a short distance ahead, and she began to rummage in her bag for the keys.

At the same time, she got a nagging feeling that someone was close at hand and following her. Placing her other hand in the pocket of her long coat, she could feel the cool metallic canister of her pepper spray. She got to her car, but before she could get inside, a heavy hand grabbed her shoulder, forcing her forward against the body of the car.

"I hope that you're enjoying my presents," her attacker hissed. "I hope you appreciate all of the effort I'm going to."

He was standing behind her, stopping her from going anywhere. Hela threw one of her elbows back and made contact with her attacker's torso, forcing him back as he gasped for air. That was enough to give her all of the space she needed. Spinning around, she took aim and sprayed the contents of her pepper spray into his masked face. With a cry, he staggered away.

"Are you sure that you're all right?" Mulligan asked. "You have had one hell of a fright. We certainly wouldn't blame you for taking a few days off."

As soon as the attacker had run off, she called the police. She had expected McBride, yet it was Mulligan who had rushed over.

She may have been a goddess, but her powers and abilities did not protect her from everything in the Nine Realms. There was only so much she could do when it came to the living. Once they were dead, that was another matter.

"No, I'm fine. I'll not let this bastard stop me," she hissed. "Are you here by yourself?"

"I called McBride when I heard about what

happened, but he wasn't answering his phone. No one's been able to get a hold of him either. Don't ask me why," Mulligan told her. "Did you get a look at the guy who attacked you?"

"I didn't see his face, but I know that it was him. I know he was our killer."

"How do you know? It could have been any nutter waiting for an opportunity to attack a woman out by herself."

"He referred to the two bodies that were brought into the morgue," she told him. "I know that neither of these deaths have been mentioned in the press. No-one involved in this has talked. So, the only ones who know are us and the killer," Hela stated.

"Are you worried he'll come after you again? You want someone to stay with you?"

"No, I'll be fine. You have other things to be dealing with. You don't need to babysit me. I shouldn't have been stupid enough to walk into a carpark, by myself after dark," Hela told him.

"You've given your statement, so you don't need to stay any longer. Why don't you head home?"

With a weak smile, Hela got into her car. Closing and locking the doors, she started the engine and drove home. Pulling up outside the building where she lived, Hela studied the street. It was quiet, not a soul visible. Once inside her own apartment, with the door locked behind her, Hela relaxed. Someone was taking the power of life and death into their own hands. That was a power they were never meant to have and she was not willing to stand by and do nothing.

The sound of a phone ringing forced Hela to wake up quickly. It was early in the morning and it was still dark. Forcing herself to sit up, she answered the phone.

For someone to call her at that time, it had to be something important and she didn't need to be told what the phone call would be about.

"Yes."

"Hela, it's McBride. I'm sorry I wasn't able to help last night. There was something of a family incident that I had to deal with. Get down to the mortuary, ASAP. That sick bastard isn't stopping."

"I'm on my way."

It took her only a few minutes to get herself ready. She was soon out of the flat and in her car. The roads were quiet, allowing her to get to the mortuary quicker than usual. Striding through the front door of the lab building, she headed down the stairs, only to find McBride pacing along the corridor that led to the mortuary.

"Is it really that bad?" Hela questioned.

"That's the understatement of the century," he replied. "It appears that this poor bastard had his stomach ripped open and his intestines nailed to a tree. He ended up with his guts wrapped around the tree itself."

McBride walked away, heading towards the viewing gallery, allowing Hela to ready herself. Once she was fully kitted out, she walked over to the examination table where the corpse had been placed. Looking at what was left of him, it was clear that McBride's description hadn't missed the mark. Whoever he was, he had been subjected to another ancient form of execution. He would have been forced to walk around the tree, tying himself to it by his guts. Then he would have been left like that, to die slowly and alone.

"Is this what I think it is?" McBride asked, from the viewing gallery.

She didn't pay attention to him at first - she had been

too absorbed with what she was doing. She had been shaken slightly the night before, but she was refusing to allow that to stop her from doing what she needed. No-one had ever gotten that close to her, with the intention of doing her harm. Not since she was a child and she was dragged from her mother's arms, only to be exiled to the world of the dead.

"What are your initial thoughts?" McBride asked.

Finally answering, Hela hissed. "I wish I had brought this all to an end last night."

"Leave that to us, just deal with what this piece of shit has decided to send up this time."

"Where's your partner? Is he in the toilet?" Hela asked.

"He phoned in sick this morning. He sounded rough," McBride replied. "Why'd you ask?"

"I just wanted to thank him for helping me last night. I hope he's feeling better soon."

"I'll pass the message on," McBride told her. "I'll leave you to it then. You have a lot to deal with and so do I. I'll speak to you soon."

McBride turned and marched out of the viewing gallery, leaving Hela to her work. There was something he hadn't told her. There was more to this than ancient execution methods. Had she been sought out by the killer? Or was she reading too much into it? How much did he know about her? Had he chosen these methods out of a sick fascination with history, or was there really a message behind it all?

Now that she had time to think about it, there had been something familiar about the man she had seen the night before. She was sure that she knew his voice, but it was clear that he had tried to disguise it. She hadn't been able to put her finger on it, but her thoughts on what had happened were beginning to clear.

Once the autopsy had been carried out, Hela quietly left the mortuary. There was someone she had to find, before anyone else ended up on her table.

Hela hated to see someone die before their time. As she walked through the streets that surrounded the hospital, the city appeared devoid of all life. She slipped into the nearby park. Evening was already beginning to fall. The park was dark and silent, making it the perfect place for what she had in mind. No-one would see what was going to happen and that was the way that she wanted it.

People had always been warned about the dangers of setting foot within any of the city's parks after dark. That did not stop her. She could smell him. It was the familiar smell of someone who was meant to be upholding and protecting the law, but who had decided to take it into his own hands. The air was filled with the metallic scent of blood. Another victim had met his end.

Her eyesight was sharper than any mortals, especially in the dark. This allowed her to see a figure, crouching in the shadows, partially hidden by the park's shrubbery. The killer. He was hard at work, unaware he had been discovered. Hela moved towards him. He didn't notice her presence until she was standing over him. Reacting quickly, he grabbed at her, hoping to knock her off her feet. Grappling with him, Hela got her first glimpse of his face, confirming her suspicions.

Allowing herself to fall when he renewed his attack, Hela felt herself hit the ground hard. She could hear him laughing, as she pretended to be hurt. He was taking his time, thinking he had already won. He knew that she had seen his face, and recognised him, but was certain that her death would stop her from telling what she knew.

"I wondered if you would figure it out," he laughed. "Mind you, I did try to make it difficult. Those bastards deserved it, but I wanted to enjoy the game."

Getting to her feet, she looked McBride square in the face. "You give yourself too much credit."

As he moved towards her, Hela backed up against one of the trees, but there was no fear in her eyes.

"Really?" he scoffed. "What makes you think that I care what you think?"

Hela could see the blade in his hand, still covered with fresh blood. He lifted the knife to her throat. Even in the dark, Hela could see the momentary look of disappointment. He had wanted to see her react, or to hear her scream. Instead, she continued to hold his gaze, defying him. His disappointment was replaced by anger as he began to press the blade against her skin.

Hela laughed, infuriating him further. She could feel the tingling of energy in her hands. Before he had the chance to cause any damage, she lifted her hands to his face, allowing the energy to flow through her. He tried to talk, but he only managed to babble incoherently. His muscles relaxed, forcing him to lose control of his body.

Allowing him to fall to the ground, Hela watched McBride as he fought for breath. She could see the fear in his eyes as he struggled to understand what was happening. It slowly dawned on him, that there was nothing he could do about what was happening. Hela crouched down next to him.

"How does it feel? Did you ever think you would feel the terror your victims had to face in their last moments?" she questioned, tilting her head to one side.

He couldn't speak, leaving it as a one sided conversation.

"There's something I never told you. It's easier if I show you."

Hela drew herself up to her full height. The scales dropped from McBride's eyes, allowing him to see her for who she really was, showing her in all of her glory. The power that radiated out of her was enough to push McBride over the edge. She watched as his life slipped away. Hiding herself behind the mask that Midgard had come to know, Hela walked over to what was left of McBride's last victim.

It was Mulligan. There was nothing that could bring him back now, but she needed to know. Placing her hands on his head, she focused. The sound of a rattling gasp told her that it was time to ask her questions.

"Why did McBride attack you?"

"I found out what he was doing," Mulligan hissed. "I was going to tell our superiors and he needed to silence me."

"Why did he resort to murder? He had to have his reasons," Hela continued.

"He thought that criminals weren't being properly punished. He'd become disillusioned with how things were. He was taking matters into his own hands," Mulligan told her.

"He's been stopped."

"I'm dead, aren't I?" Mulligan whispered.

"Yes. It's your time to go."

She could feel Mulligan slip away. He would find peace. McBride, on the other hand, would find his place in the darkest reaches off Helheim.

Walking back to the laboratory building, she took her mobile out of the pocket of her coat. Punching in the number, she left an anonymous tipoff that something had taken place in the park near the hospital.

Hela sat in the hospital's café. She was eating by herself, not being one for spending time with others, unless she had to. Everyone in the labs had heard about what had happened in the early hours. All were struggling to come to terms with the knowledge that McBride had been behind the recent murders and that he was said to have committed suicide, after killing one of his colleagues. It wasn't just those who had known him. Even those who didn't know him could not understand how or why he carried out such terrible acts.

Someone came to a stop next to the table Hela was sitting at, breaking her train of thought. "How are you holding up?"

Looking up from her food, Hela found one of the lab assistants smiling at her. She smiled back, it was the only thing that she could do. Taking a moment, she thought about what she wanted to say.

"I'm holding up. As with everyone else, I'm shocked by what has happened," Hela answered. "It just reminds us that we should always expect the unexpected and never take things for granted."

The young woman gave a shy smile, and made an excuse before going on her way. Turning her attention back to her lunch, Hela allowed her mind to wander, until another presence pulled her back. Looking up, Loki stood next to her table, looking down at her. It was clear that the others already knew.

"Father. What can I do for you?"

"Am I not allowed to visit my daughter?" he asked, sitting down at the table.

"You only come when you want something," she

answered with a slight frown.

He laughed. She watched him closely. He was dressed in faded jeans, a T-shirt featuring the logo of some long forgotten rock band, was topped off by a tattered leather jacket. As always, he could not keep still.

"To be honest, I thought the All-Father would have shown up," Hela continued.

"Well, he's kind of busy at the moment. If I'm not mistaken, he's dealing with something in Iceland. Something that he wasn't even willing to tell me about," Loki told her. "So, did you manage to sort out what happened here?"

"Yes."

"Is that all you're going to say on the matter?"

"Well, the man is now dead. He's gone to the grave with what he knew," Hela told him, sharply.

Nodding, he got up. After one last look, he walked towards the exit of the hospital. Watching him go, Hela wondered when they would see each other again.

She wasn't the sort for sentiment, as she had become used to her own company. But the others were still out there. That was enough to stop her from feeling completely alone. Soon, her father was out of sight. Getting up, she made her way back to the mortuary and to the work that was waiting for her.

Yggdrasil

Deep, deep, run the roots of this tree,
deep into three worlds.
High, high grow its branches,
winding through many heavens.

Upon its bulk rest all the worlds.

Upon this tree hung Odin, all-father,
for nine long days and nights.
Half-blind, pierced with his own spear,
sacrificed to himself.

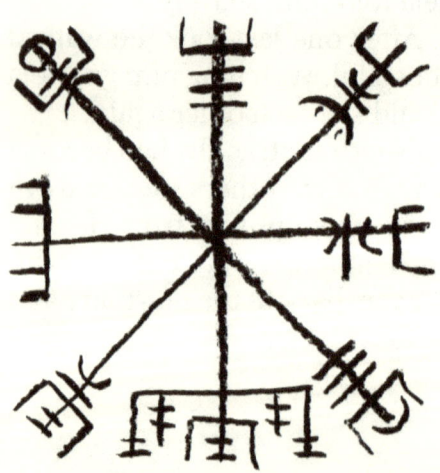

Closing Time

Beneath a wide grey sky, within a wide grey land, stood a grey tower. Nine-sided, it rose straight and smooth, and in each of its sides was a door. A wooden stair circled it, spiraling to a narrow platform at its crown.

Up that stair a figure toiled. It had run up the steps at first, then jogged. Now, more than halfway up its ascent, it panted for breath and clutched hard at the stone, for want of a railing. Inconvenient at the best of times, the climb became outright impossible when the master did not wish to be disturbed.

At last, the little figure reached the platform and flattened itself against the stone's curving face just long enough to catch its breath. At the top, the tower boasted ranks of glittering windows and yet another latched and bolted door, a weighty construction of oak and iron. Not the sort of door to encourage visitors, if indeed the tower, the stair, or the vast unchanging moor had done so.

The little man——not so little, when seen in his proper perspective——lifted a hand to knock and the door swung silently inward.

Within the tower room, wildfire leapt on the wide hearth and the snowy pelts of bears softened the chilly stone floor. Shelves lined the room, heaped with books, minerals, bones and other assorted bric-a-brac, and beyond the deeply notched windows hung a black sky peppered with white stars. The man glanced behind reflexively, and grey sky, grey moor swam in the corner of his eye before he looked back into the room.

A low bed, untidy with furs, books and fine woolen blankets, stood near the fire. Facing the door stood a desk, a massive affair of black wood, the visible corners supported by tiny, fiercely carven figures; a snarling wolf, a coiled serpent. A man sat there, poring over a massive book, his chin supported in one hand, while discolored pages rustled beneath the thoughtful caress of the other. The messenger tried to breathe a little more gently in that studious quiet.

"Yes?" said the man without looking up. His breath crackled in the cold air.

" –" said the messenger and pounded his chest with a fist, hacking. "My lord," he said on the second try. "My lord. The ship . . ."

Bored fingers lifted a page by its extreme corner, let it drop. "Yes?"

"It's ready."

The fingers stilled. Poison-green eyes lifted, startled and startling. It was not the sort of attention a man craved, and the messenger straightened up a fraction.

"What?"

"The ship, my lord, it's ready. It's finished." The man sat up straight and curled his hands around the edges of the book, blinking. He seemed disconcerted.

"What do you mean, finished? ALL finished? Seaworthy?"

"Yes, lord."

The man opened and shut his mouth. The messenger fidgeted anxiously.

"The quarter rudder's been fastened to the wart?" the man said at last.

"Yes, my lord."

"The osiers firmly anchored?"

"Yes, my lord."

"The topside planks; do they overlap the plank above and below by three fingers exactly?"

"My lord, yes."

"And the rivets. A man's length apart where the planks lie straight and a long stride where they turn?"

"Exactly so, my lord."

"Sea chests - ? The sail? The oars?"

"Yes – yes – yes, my lord."

The man at the desk brooded for a moment. "The figurehead is carved and detailed down to the least, smallest scale?" he ventured finally, but without much hope.

"The ship is finished, my lord, down to the most insignificant and unimportant detail." The messenger spread calloused hands wide and his voice grew hushed as he said once more, "Naglfar is ready."

Loki Laufeyjarson heaved the book shut and fell back in his chair, rubbing his forehead with the heels of his hands. "Well, shit," he said.

He clattered quickly down the stairs, shrugging into his cloak of wolf-skins. The messenger followed. Down the inside of the tower, past shelves of foodstuffs, jewellery, books, silks, down and down, through a veritable dragon's hoard of things both necessary and strange.

When they came to the bottom of the stairs––in mere moments, the messenger noted resentfully––Loki went straight to the south-south-west side and unlatched the door, a massive slab of ancient oak several inches thick and reinforced with iron, but hung and balanced with dwarfish precision so that it swung lightly under his hand.

An arctic blast shrieked at them and they shivered, looking out onto a teeming world of white light and cold shadow; tall, slow shapes turned at the opening of the door, eyes showing red in the fine haze of snow whipped up by the wind. Some stopped their work and approached; most turned back to their labor. An air of tension and barely restrained violence hung about the place; the feeling, unmistakable to anyone who has known battle.

Loki frowned at the unseasonable cold and huddled a little deeper into his furs, but the messenger threw up a hand to shield his eyes and shrank back, ice forming in his beard.

"Remain," Loki snapped impatiently, and set off toward the harbor and the shipyard, his long legs eating up the ground. Jötnar fell in beside him as he went, moving with the deceptively ponderous speed of an avalanche.

"You've heard then," one said to him, eschewing formality, and he nodded. The giant waved widely around them. "You see how it is. The Fimbulwinter is upon us, and all things come to their end. We were about to send for you, if you did not come."

"I'm here now," Loki said shortly, saving his breath for walking.

The air grew ever more bitter and hard to breathe as they approached the shipyard. Loki fancied he could see the skeletal shape of his ship even from so far away. He had not been often to see her of late; with the work lingering so long, he had come to think that perhaps it would never be finished.

And yet, here they were.

"Well, you've really screwed the pooch," said a voice like a tenor bell, in tones of scathing disgust.

Loki's head snapped to the side involuntarily, then he hunched his shoulders and kept on walking, but the speaker stood away from the wind-whittled stone he'd been huddled beneath and followed. The giants looked askance, many turning to keep him in sight as he passed; he was very clearly Not From Around Here, as evidenced by the fuming heat that baked off his skin, not to mention the half-visible wings that shimmered behind him like an angry mirage.

"Can't you do something? Sabotage it somehow?"

Loki grabbed him by the front of his tailored suit and dragged him out of the beaten path and into deep snow in several floundering strides, abandoning his escort.

"*Don't* say things like that around here," he hissed, letting go with a push so that the other staggered back a step, scowling and straightening his jacket with angry flicks of his hands. They were filthy, Loki noted with distaste.

"What are you doing here, anyway? Surely your Infernal Majesty is too busy for idle calls."

"Idle calls!" Lucifer lunged so far into his personal space that Loki nearly stepped back himself, stabbing with a jagged-nailed forefinger. "Do you realize what's happening?! It's the End Times! Seals are breaking, trumpets are sounding, the lake of fire has risen three – no, FOUR POINT EIGHT feet in the last ten minutes! My demons are running mad! And do you know what TRIGGERED it? Your bloody boat! Your bloody fingernail boat!"

A high, angry color mounted in Loki's cheeks and he scowled. Being shouted at always reminded him of Asgard, and thinking of Asgard always got his blood pressure up.

"Don't be ridiculous," he snapped. "Naglfar has nothing to do with your cosmology."

"Not just mine!" Lucifer howled, throwing up his hands. "Not just mine! The sun came up in the west this morning! The dead are rising, and yazatas are running around melting mountains! The Temple has been restored! Nation is rising against nation and kingdom against kingdom! I don't even KNOW how many frigging trumpets I heard on the way over here. There goes another one! And not to mention numerous supernatural beings on white horses. I'm pretty sure I spotted at least three suns in the sky, though good luck decimating the earth before the floods, landslides, wars, famine and pestilence do the job! And what started it?! YOUR," poke, "BLOODY," poke, "FINGERNAIL," poke, "SHIP!"

A taunting phrase hovered on Loki's lips as he considered saying, "you know, you're beautiful when you're angry." It was true enough, even in his Fall, Lucifer's face bore the ruins of an otherworldly beauty – but for once, discretion triumphed over impulse.

"Why should the corpse ship be the spur?" he asked, reasonably. "Possibly one of those other things . . ."

Lucifer shook his head sharply, shoving his hands into his pockets, the pilot light behind his eyes dying down a little.

"No," he said impatiently, pacing, "No, believe it or not, your ridiculous boat is the ONLY quantifiable measure of the end times. The persecution of the righteous, the degeneration of society, descent into total corruption, that's been going on for two thousand years and more, depending on who you ask. Every passing generation thinks it can't get any worse; and then, behold! it does! When is enough enough? Who knows? It's always somebody's personal end of the world, but that doesn't make it official."

He stamped his feet in the cold, rubbing his hands together. "No, the only objective, concrete measure is your RIDICULOUS boat, made from dead men's toe nails. Loki's corpse ship! The one that had mankind burying their dead with nails cut to the quick for centuries, lest they hasten the end times."

He shook his head. "Degeneration of society, well, I don't know, that's a judgment call, but the fingernail boat? It's built!" He flung out dramatic arms. "It's finished! Time for Ragnarok! Not that I give a tinker's curse about that, but you've set off ALL the end of the world scenarios!"

It was hard to credit, but then this was shaping up to be an unusual day. "This makes no sense," Loki fretted, scratching at his wrists; an old habit, from the dark centuries chained to a rock. "Ragnarok isn't relevant anymore, not to the mortal realm – the old religions died long ago. Not a single living creature still believes in us!"

"Oh, well then, I'll just tell everyone to pack it up," Lucifer said sarcastically. "Did you hear that?" he bellowed, lifting his head to the churning sky and making a funnel of his hands. "It's all a mistake! Go home! The Apocalypse is canceled!"

His voice rang across Jotunheim and in the silence that followed, angry cries and murmurs began to rise. Loki looked around. The bustling hordes, as mindlessly active as an ant-nest stirred with a stick, paused and turned, staring in their direction. They were looking forward to the bloody battle with the gods, and obviously disliked the joke.

At this point, destruction seemed a matter of when, not if, but Loki still didn't care to be torn apart right this minute.

"Will you get out of here?" he hissed, giving Lucifer another shove. "I have duties! Things that must be done!" Lucifer cocked his haggard head and didn't seem to be listening, at least not to anything anyone else could hear. Then he shook himself.

"You're not the only one. The ninth circle of Hell just melted," he said morosely. A final jab of that foul fingernail. "YOU may be looking forward to your pyrrhic victory, dying on someone's sword, drinking the blood of your enemies, yada yada, but all I've got to look forward to is the outer darkness and the worm that dieth not. DO SOMETHING. FIX IT," he said, in a voice that made even Loki shiver.

Then those charred and half invisible wings snapped open with a sound like the clap of mighty hands, and the Lightbringer disappeared with a boom.

Somewhere, very faint and far away, a mocking trumpet blew.

A ship made of dead men's nails is not a lovely sight. Her lines were graceful and dangerous, but every inch glimmered with an opalescent sheen, like marsh-light.

The broad dark shapes of the shipbuilders swarmed over her, checking and rechecking, for she had been thousands of years in the building and they seemed drunk with the accomplishment, unwilling to finally relinquish it, only moving aside as the trickster came through the crowd.

Loki ran his eyes over the flare of the belly, made of millions – billions? – of nails bound tightly together by strong glues and stronger spells. They shone every shade of white and yellow; he passed a hand over the nearest plank as though admiringly, scrabbling furtively and fruitlessly with his own nails, succeeding only in making a strange musical thrum. Lovely. They had the makings of a washboard band.

He stood back to gaze up at the sturdy mast and then at the snarling, intricately scaled figurehead. The neck curved downward, but in threat not submission, and the staring eyes were touched with ruby. It looked vaguely like an albino serpent, hissing and pulling back its head to strike. Loki found it disturbing; he had no great fondness for snakes, in spite of his progeny.

The giants had not bothered with a dry dock, or an apparatus for getting her into the water; there had been no need. When the time came for Naglfar to be on her way, the sea would come to her.

Taking hold of the gunwale, Loki hoisted himself easily to the leprous deck and felt it shiver beneath his feet like the flank of a restive steed. Ironically, the corpse ship felt nearly alive, eager to move. He paced between the ranked rower's benches, scaled for giants, then turned to gaze toward the shoreline, one hand clasped familiarly around the sea serpent's neck. The ocean was rising; seething water already lapped at the furthest giants' boots.

Surely it was too late to stop this now, even if he wanted to. And yet . . .

The crowd around the ship shifted and murmured, gazing up at him with red eyes, and fierce faces. His feelings might be mixed, but theirs were not, and who knew if damaging the ship could actually halt the onset of Ragnarok. Still, Loki curled his fingers furtively over the sea serpent's lower jaw and gave it an abrupt downward jerk, using all his considerable strength. It gave slightly, but did not come even close to snapping. A nearby giant put out a frost-black hand.

"Careful, little god," it rumbled. "You'll break her." Loki looked around as a murmur of laughter ran through the crowd, flushing under their amused, slightly contemptuous eyes.

"Oh, we wouldn't want that," he muttered, and dropped lightly over the side, back to the frozen sand.

He fished a smartphone out of his pocket as he hurried back up the snowy slope to the door. Through it, the cool grey of the tower's stone could be glimpsed. He thumbed in his security code and hit 'call.' Very few people had his number, but those that did could be relied upon to answer.

Indeed, someone answered on the first ring.

"Daddy," said a cool, deep voice. "I'm really busy."

"I know," he said, picking up his pace a little. "So you've heard about the ship." A low, melodious laugh sounded in his ear.

"Daddy, of *course* I've heard. I'm readying your crew." Delight made her voice run quickly, in a way he had never heard. Despite his hurry, he slowed a little, pressing the phone to his ear.

"So," he said, "You're pleased then. That this is the end of all things."

"Of course I am!" A pause, and then her voice grew closer, lower. He could picture her half turning on her throne to shield the phone from whoever else might be there, holding it tighter as if that might bring him near to her. "Aren't you?"

"I . . . don't know." He stopped walking. "It's the end of all things, Hel," he said morosely, waving his free hand in a vague figure eight. "Not just a change, the *end*. Who knows what we'll be after, or even if we *will* be?" The messenger gesticulated at him from the tower and he started walking again. "Better a king in hell than a—"

"Oh," she interrupted immediately. "Oh, you've been talking to that old serpent, the Devil."

Loki shut up, startled.

"You shouldn't listen to him. Of course *he's* worried, he's to be cast into the pit. But we're nothing like him! *We* are and have always been a part of the natural order; without us, the worlds would have collapsed and rotted under their own fecundity millennia ago. This is the end foretold, a swift, fiery purge, and who better to usher it in? Chaos, piloting a ship of death, with all the elements raging behind."

That damn ship, Loki thought, slitting his eyes against the flying snow.

"And after that," Hel went on quietly, "a new and

beautiful garden."

"We're not included in that part," Loki objected bitterly.

She didn't laugh, but he could hear her smile in her voice. "We will be, nonetheless. Energy cannot be destroyed, daddy, it continues on in new forms. Perhaps," she went on lightly, "I'll be a butterfly, on a flower. In the sun."

He snorted. "When you were once a queen?"

"I will be a very queenly butterfly," she said reprovingly, still with that thread of happiness running through her voice. He could just make out the faint urgent moaning of her servants. "Daddy, I have *got* to go."

"Right, of course. I'm sorry. Listen – have you heard from anyone else?"

"Oh, the girls have been calling nonstop. Kali, the Morrigan, Ereshkigal, Izanami, Melinoe, Proserpina... We're going to try to meet up for a drink, since there probably won't be time after." She hesitated. He had reached the door and the messenger waved both hands in a bid for his attention, making frantic faces and mouthing something Loki did not trouble to interpret. He turned his back, looked out across the wind-scoured wasteland of Jotunheim, listening to the silence on the other end of the phone.

"Daddy," Hel said at last, and her voice was that of a queen. "I love you. Die well."

It startled a laugh out of him, and his first genuine smile in quite some time. Centuries, possibly. "I will," he said, and ended the call just as a hand fell heavily on his shoulder. He spun around, more startled than angry; very few ever laid hands on Loki. In fact, the last had been . . .

"Loki," Odin said, familiar in worn cloak and

battered hat, and far, far too close for comfort. In the tower behind him, the messenger had effaced himself utterly. Loki shrugged free and stepped back a couple of wary paces, which unfortunately left him outside in knee-deep snow, and Odin in possession of the tower. That rankled.

"Old god," he said by way of greeting. "I've got a lot going on at the moment."

"What I have to say won't take long," Odin replied mildly and stepped away from the door, leaving Loki room to enter. He hesitated, but the wind rose to a particularly savage shriek just then and in any case, they'd be facing each other on a battlefield soon enough. He stepped quickly inside, glancing at the door to Asgard only to find it still securely locked and double-bolted. He raised an eyebrow as he swung the door to Jotunheim closed.

"I have been a wanderer all my long life," Odin said in answer to the look, smiling slightly. "Do you really think there is a road I do not know? Even the roads to this hidden place." He tapped the flagstones gently with his staff. "I have let you be these past centuries as a courtesy."

Loki shrugged out of his sodden cloak and tossed it aside, irritably wringing ice water out of his hair. How like Odin to play the indulgent king, even now.

"Then why are you here?" he asked resentfully. "What do you have to say that couldn't wait, oh, a couple of hours?"

Odin's eye narrowed but he kept control of himself. He'd always been hard to get a rise out of, unlike almost everyone else Loki had ever known. "I want you to do something for me," he said.

Loki's mouth fell open. He blinked. "What?" he asked finally, because he really, really had to know, if only for the pleasure of refusing and then throwing Odin out of the tower so he could go strap his armor on and get ready for his glorious death.

"I want you to sabotage Naglfar."

For the second time in the last several minutes, a startled laugh escaped Loki. "Are you serious?" he sputtered. "YOU? You, of all people?" He kicked the cloak out of his way, pacing nervously. The tower, so silent for so long, had begun to fill with a vague indeterminate sound; a murmur like the sea, or a football crowd, or a schoolyard, or possibly all three, and it made the back of his neck creep.

"Ragnarok cannot come," the Allfather said quite reasonably. "Not yet. It is not yet time."

"It IS time," Loki objected distractedly. The doors; the sound was coming from behind the doors. It was the sound of the end of the worlds. "Ragnarok IS here, and therefore it IS time."

"The time is here because the ship is ready," Odin replied. "It is time, because the ship is ready. If the ship is not ready, then Ragnarok does not come."

Loki hesitated. It sounded like the logic of a madman, and he had heard something very similar not too long ago. "Have you been talking to Satan?" he asked finally.

A fleeting look of disgust tightened the bearded mouth. "No," Odin said with finality, "though that scalded reprobate has the right of it. It is the ship that has brought on the end of things. And it is you that can delay it - not stop it, since all things must end, but delay it for a time."

How, was on the tip of Loki's tongue to say, but instead he said, incredulously, "Why?" Because of all the character flaws that might be laid at Odin's door, cowardice would never make the list.

And Odin hesitated. "A promise," he said at last. "That this world would not end so long as any still prayed to me."

Loki snorted.

"Lovely as that is," he said, "Much as I'd love to help you play the great benefactor, and happy as I am that *you* still have a few scabby worshippers squirreled away somewhere - why in the Nine Realms would I want to help you? Why would I sabotage my own ship? Which has been a complete pain in the ass to build, let me tell you. I mean, you try building a ship out of toenails sometime."

"Are you so eager to see the end of the realms?" Odin asked, watching him keenly. "When there is still so much to see? When you stand to lose as much as the rest of us?"

"Really?" Loki's bitter gesture took in the cold stone walls, the silent height of the tower above them. He had built it, and felt justly proud of it, but it remained a far cry from the glory of Asgard. "I think you overestimate what some of us have to lose, old god."

Odin sighed and put his cloak aside, reaching for something, and Loki backed away.

"Because it will be the greatest trick you have ever played, then," he said, and held out his hand. "A trick that only Loki could play. I know that must tempt you." And Loki stared at Mjolnir hanging from the strong fist by her leather strap. "Thor is at this moment tearing Asgard apart, looking for her," he added with a flicker of humor.

"You are giving me Mjolnir?" Loki asked finally, a smile trying to fight its way onto his face despite the distant screams he could hear behind one of the doors. He restrained it with difficulty, resenting the answering glint in Odin's eye, the look that said the old god knew he had him. The short handle spun into Odin's hard palm with a slap and he held the hammer out toward Loki, reversed.

"I am lending you Mjolnir," he corrected. "It requires an uncommon weapon to damage a fated ship like Naglfar."

"And you trust me to give it back," Loki said, sidling closer, reaching out. Odin pulled his hand back, warningly. "Trust you, Loki? Never. But you may trust that if it is NOT returned, then we will come and take it."

Loki's lips skinned back from his teeth and they grinned at each other, the trickster and the gallows god, in complete understanding. Then Loki dropped his hand to a pocket, held it out again with a coin braced between thumb and forefinger, turning it to show both sides.

"Call it," he said, and Odin's heavy brows raised.

"You would leave the fate of the worlds to chance?" he asked. Loki laughed, his heart suddenly light.

"Call it," he said again, and snapped the coin skyward. "Tails," Odin said, just before it slapped back into his palm.

They both regarded it for a quiet instant.

"I don't know how I'm going to make it up to Hel," Loki sighed, and held out his other hand for Mjolnir.

Odin left swiftly after that, through a neat little door he conjured up out of the shadows beneath the stairs. Loki scowled - the cheek! - and resolved to seal up that particular rat-hole as soon as he got back. Assuming he did, that is.

"Your wife sends word to ask when you will be home," the messenger said urgently, materializing out of nowhere in the habitual way of servants, adding delicately, "she complains of having no company but the snake and the bowl. She says she should have listened to her mother. She says . . ."

"Yes?" Loki tossed over his shoulder, taking the stairs three at a time. Armor, sword. Odin had offered no advice, saying only that he trusted to Loki's ingenuity. He always had, that was true, saying only, *do this*, and relying on Loki to find a way. Mjolnir or no Mjolnir, his best weapon was and always would be his wits.

He grinned fiercely, running lightly up the stairs. He suddenly realized, it really didn't matter. Either he would be in time, or he would not. Everything would find a way to its appointed end eventually, despite the best efforts of gods and men. And that was as it should be.

Only, hopefully, not just yet. As Odin said, there remained so much still to see.

Time had run very short; he could hear a nearly nonstop din of trumpets behind the tasteful fiberglass door that led to Midgard. Ice crept beneath the frost-rimed portal to Niflheim and a din like competing smithies roared behind the doors to Asgard and Nidavellir. If that was not bad enough, the heat-shielded door to Muspelheim was smoking, and beginning to buckle. In the sky outside the tower, thousands of ravens were calling as they circled.

The messenger coughed apologetically, several steps below him now. "She says," he shouted above the chaos, "she says you promised to be home before Ragnarok!"

Loki threw his head back and laughed. "Tell Sigyn," he chuckled, climbing faster now, "not to wait up."

He stared out at the chaos forming outside his tower and sighed. Time to save the world.

Contributors

MJ Kobernus is the editor of the Northlore anthologies. He also wrote *Odin's Saga* and *The Gospel of Odin*. He is an Anglo/American novelist and short story writer. He lives under a bridge in a small town in rural Norway. He is also the author of the Guardian series. He writes Metaphysical Fantasy, likes vintage motorcycles, sailing, guitars and The Beatles. MJ has been published in a number of anthologies, magazines, and e-zines, is the founder and Editor in Chief of Nordland Publishing, the creator of the Northlore Series and father of three beautiful girls. Find out more about him at mjkobernus.com.

Loic Lendemaine wrote *The Saga of Egill Olafson*. Loic was born near Paris. He has always been fascinated by History. After graduating in International Business, he began to work with people from all around the world, travelling and discovering new cultures and new places. Influenced by Arthurian legends, Norse myths and fantasy writers, he is the author of several short stories, mostly published in French.

Franklin Babrove wrote *The Mountain-Farer*. He received his MA in literature from Florida Atlantic University in 2013. His poetry has previously appeared in The Black Magnolias Literary Magazine and The Hartskill Review.

David W. Landrum wrote *Váli* and *Freya's Graces*. He has published speculative fiction in Silver Blade, Non-Binary Review, Modern Day Fairy Tales, Nebula Rift, After Happily Ever After, and many other journals and anthologies. His latest novella, *Sinfonia: The First Notes on the Lute,* is available from Amazon

Jo Mason wrote *I am of Jötunheim, Creator Deceiver Destroyer, Sapling* and *Trickster's Grace.* She exists online mainly as Corvicula1979, which should tell you her age. She's Torontonian born and bred. She wrote a lot of poetry as a teenager (who didn't?) but very little as an adult until the writing bug bit her again in early 2014, and now writes fanfiction as well as poetry. For most of 2014, Loki decided to be her muse.

John Reinhart wrote *Dark Period, Balder, Loki and Thor's Exclamations.* He is an arsonist by trade. He lives on an urban farmlette in Colorado with his wife and children. He has two chapbooks currently available: "encircled," from Prolific Press, and "Horrific Punctuation" from Tiger's Eye Press. More of his poetry and links are at patreon.com/johnreinhart. You can also connect with him at: facebook.com/JohnReinhartPoet.

Kelly Evans wrote *Burnt Einar* and *How 'Bout Them Apples.* She lives in Toronto, Canada with her husband Max and two rescue cats (Bear and Wolf). Her short stories have been published in numerous magazines and E-zines as well as a horror anthology. When not writing Kelly enjoys reading history books, silversmithing, playing the oboe and medieval recorder, and watching really bad horror and old sci-fi movies. She is currently working on the second book in her Anglo-Saxon series, set in the years prior to the Norman invasion.

Odin Asagrim wrote *The Song of Spells.* Best known as the Wise One and the Lord of the Aesir, Odin's sayings, The Hávamál are still used today by those who follow the old ways. His secret writings, described in the story *The Gospel of Odin*, have yet to be discovered.

Steve Klepetar wrote *On the Tree* and *Valkyrie*. His work has appeared widely. His poems have been nominated for the Pushcart Prize and Best of the Net. Recent collections include *My Son Writes a Report on the Warsaw Ghetto* and *The Li Bo Poems*, both from Flutter Press, and *Family Reunion*, forthcoming from Big Table Publishing.

David Grigg wrote *Hungry is the Wolf* and *Yggdrasil*. He is a retired software developer in Melbourne, Australia. David had several short stories published during the 1970s and 1980s. In 1976 he also had two short fantasy novels published. These were *Halfway House*, and its sequel, *Shadows*. During this period, David was deeply involved in the science fiction community, publishing fanzines and helping organize SF conventions, eventually becoming Chairman of the 43rd World SF Convention in 1985. Since retiring, he has returned to fiction. Collections of his stories are available for purchase on his website at: http://rightword.com.au/books.

Andrew James Murray wrote *Into The Storm* and *Saga*. He is a poet and writer from Manchester, England. His work has been published in various anthologies and publications, including The Best Of Manchester Poets. In 2015, Nordland published a collection of his poetry entitled Heading North. He can be found writing about anything and nothing over at cityjackdaw.wordpress.com

Paul Kater wrote *All that Glitters*. He was born in the Netherlands in 1960. He quickly developed a feel for books and languages but somehow ended up in the IT business. Books and languages never ceased to fascinate him, so since 2003, he's been actively writing. Paul currently lives in Cuijk, in the Netherlands, with his books, two cats and the many characters he's developed in the past years, who claim that *he* is a figment of their imagination.

Claire Casey wrote *Past Bound* and *Death Amongst Us*. She is an archaeologist from Scotland. She has worked on a variety of sites in Scotland, England and Ireland, including a Neolithic settlement in the Orkney Isles. A Viking re-enactor, she loves all things Scandinavian. As well as publishing her own work, Claire has also published a collection of songs and poems by Robert Tannahill, called The Weaver Poet. She has also published a collection of poems by Alexander Wilson, called Lines Written on a Summer Evening.

Margrete Vik Gagama wrote *Old Gold's Last Stand*. She is a mother and wife, a geologist, a feminist and a writer. She comes from the mountainous part of Trøndelag and loves chocolate and the colour green. Margrete is previously published in a handful of anthologies. Check out her writer blog at https://mvgagama.wordpress.com/

Damon Chua wrote *They're Coming*. His short stories have been published in the US, Canada, Malaysia and Singapore. They were included in "Twenty-Two New Asian Short Stories" (Sliverfish Books 2016) and Singapore Noir (Akashic Books

2014). A published playwright and poet, he is a recipient of grants from the National Endowment for the Arts, Dramatists Guild Fund and UNESCO.

Robyn Merckx wrote *Closing Time*. She lives in the sticks of New Jersey where she manages her company's CRM and sales reporting. In her leisure time she likes gardening and reading, and occasionally writes for pleasure. She finds Northern mythology to be "cold, spacious, severe, pale, and remote," and as CS Lewis once said; it is her favorite of all the world's many cosmologies.

NORDLAND PUBLISHING
Follow the North Road.

http://nordlandpublishing.com
www.facebook.com/nordlandpublishing
http://nordlandpublishing.tumblr.com/

www.ingramcontent.com/pod-product-compliance
Lightning Source LLC
Chambersburg PA
CBHW052042240626
47153CB00006B/2194